I0829801

ISBN 979-8-9879290-6-3
© Copyright Brandi Hudson, 2025
All rights reserved.

No part of this publication may be reproduced, stored in any form whatsoever, or transmitted in any form or by any means without prior written consent from Brandi Hudson.

Written by Brandi Hudson

Cover Design by Debarim Publishing, LLC

Published by
Debarim Publishing, LLC
807 W Broadway
Spiro, OK 74959
www.debarimpublishing.com

# Acknowledgements

The original idea for this story came about while exploring River Circle Farm in Franklin, TN, and its close proximity to Cheekwood. Special thanks to Christian Currey and Kathryn Currey for inspiring a wonderful setting for these characters.

Books aren't written in a vacuum, and I owe tremendous gratitude to wonderful editors: Gail Delaney, Sarah Williams, Julie Patterson, and Stephanie Weber. The readers reap the benefit of your insight and input.

To my friends and family too numerous to list here: thank you for entertaining countless conversations about these characters and their lives as if they were in our own circle; each of you helped them be successful in their endeavors.

# Fulfilled

## in their

# Time

*One*

Bright, glorious rays of late March sun-kissed Marnie Foster's fair skin as she sat near a tall spruce tree upon a beige and brown-striped afghan. She ran her slender fingers over the newly greening Kentucky bluegrass as she brought a Brie-topped Honeycrisp apple slice to her mouth. Juicy and sweet, she savored the flavor and let her eyes wander through her surroundings.

She watched a small man-made waterfall rush over large limestone rocks into an Olympic-sized water haven for turtles, frogs, and a few fish. From the forest edge, she spied three robins flitting from the hibernating trees across the pond toward the Cheekwood Estate, the botanical gardens' home in Nashville, Tennessee.

Rivaling the treetops, the gray-brick mansion stood proud on the hillside, surrounded by hedges, walking paths, and a cobblestone drive. The floor-to-ceiling windows on the east side of the mansion reflected the sun with laser-like precision onto the shy tulips bedded three feet from the windows.

Marnie sipped water from a blue metallic bottle. Every breath was a welcome reminder that spring was no longer a vague and distant correspondent but a returning estate holder for the next three months. She inhaled the fragrance of moist earth; the combination of dirt, grass, and the heavenly aroma of daffodils caused a smile to crease her youthful face.

Marnie closed her eyes, basking in the warmth of a perfect spring day. She wore a gray sweater dress with black leggings paired nicely with black and red striped flats. She'd pulled her long, blonde hair into a ponytail to showcase silver earrings that matched a silver bracelet. The cherry on top of her ensemble was a black, yellow, and red stone necklace. The temperature and her attire allowed her to enjoy the sunshine without needing a scarf or coat.

The winter had been one for the books. Three inches of ice fell in January, followed by two February snowstorms. Marnie had been homebound for a good portion of the winter. This blossoming warmth of the day was paradise to Nashvillians.

Though not crowded, Cheekwood had many visitors. Marnie saw mothers pushing strollers, elderly couples walking along, and the ever-present and steady stream of entire families of tourists, ready to see and explore all the gardens had to offer.

"How's the event planning, Couz?" Drew, Marnie's dark-haired cousin, plopped down on the afghan next to her, wearing jeans and a navy button-down shirt. He picked up and munched on some of the baby carrots Marnie had packed for lunch.

"Overwhelming at times." Marnie looked down at her smartphone, checking to see if she had any new emails or texts.

"Did they hint that you'd be helping out in a much bigger role next year? I mean, they've loved all of your ideas. Didn't you give the Swan Ball a theme this year? What was it, Wild West?"

Marnie proffered a quizzical look. "Drew, do you listen to anything I say?"

He placed another baby carrot in his mouth.

"The Victorian Era. That's the theme," Marnie corrected.

"I was close," Drew said.

Close also described their relationship. Marnie and Drew were the same age, twenty-five, first cousins, and were more like siblings. Close also covered their living arrangements. Marnie stayed in a rustic guest cabin on Drew's parents' family farm, not ten minutes from Cheekwood.

Her aunt and uncle welcomed their niece for as long as she wanted, which, she hoped, would not be much longer as she vied for a job promotion. Then, she would have enough for a down payment on her home.

"So, is Simone going to bring you on full-time or what? Nobody plans an event like you. They are constantly Tweeting and Instagraming pictures you've taken."

"You know I run those accounts, right? I always post the pictures I take."

"Well, Simone always shares them."

Simone was Marnie's somewhat eccentric boss. She agreed that Marnie could intern for the Swan Ball event, hinting that she had the potential to join her prestigious event-planning company. Jasmine Rose Events, Inc. was at the top of the list for fashion shows, galas, swanky soirées, charity events, and corporate gatherings.

Employment there meant travel, unlimited budgets, and enough prestige to open any doors Marnie wanted.

"She said she'd let me know after the ball, which means everything has to be perfect." Marnie brushed her hands along her dress. "What are you doing here today? I didn't think the lab ever let you out in daylight."

Drew grabbed an apple slice from Marnie's beeswax wrap and took a bite. "I'm picking up a document to do some radiocarbon dating on it." Drew flashed a piece of paper covered in a thick plastic casing. "The museum procured a certificate of authenticity for some sculpture, and they need me to check out the timing. Routine stuff in the life of a scientist."

Forensics, to be exact. Drew worked downtown in a lab, concentrating on document and art authentication. He may have been the newest and youngest hire, but he was precise, thorough, and efficient. "Did you know that, at this time of year, in 1836, James Marsh published his findings on how to detect arsenic?" He beamed. "I read that today in my forensic toxicology magazine."

"Is that a line you use on girls?"

"Whoa. No, but do you think it'd work?" Drew's eyes brimmed with hope.

Marnie rolled hers, "no." She glanced at her phone. "Nice. Simone needs me to check the swampy area by the reflecting pool to see if we can fit more tables down there."

"I literally just saw her outside on the veranda when I picked this document up. It's like ten steps. She can't just check it herself?"

"Nope. She wants me to go spend the next two hours over there to see if I 'detect anything odious or assaulting upon the senses.'" Marnie stood and shook her dress to remove stray pieces of nature.

Drew stood, too, and helped clean up the picnic. "Are you eating at the farm tonight?"

"Yeah, after I finish up here." She collected the afghan, folded it, and put it into a large canvas bag along with her picnic items.

"OK, I'm headed back to the lab. See ya!" Drew walked toward the parking lot across from the visitor's center.

"Bye!" Marnie threw her things over her shoulders and trekked toward the reflecting pool.

* * * * *

As Marnie situated herself on a flat rock near the reflecting pool, she listened to the season's first crickets' debut. To her back was a partially hollowed-out granite wall that resembled a small cave. It was as though the builders intended to enlarge it but abandoned the project. Perhaps it had weakened the road above, so they had left a gutted piece of earth behind. It was bricked around the entryway, creating an arch that provided an aesthetically pleasing entrance to the man-made cave. If C.S. Lewis had written about this space, it would have been a gateway into another world. The floor of the cave was pebbly and opened to a swamp-like section that could have been the beginning of a moat in medieval times. Presently, it was a mosquito's honeymoon suite. Marnie tried to picture a table and chairs on the grass, moving them around, trying to center on the best placement.

The reflecting pool could be seen from Marnie's perch, but not easily. On either side of the pool rested two cream-colored sculptures of what appeared to be toga-clad women who Marnie guessed were supposed to be Greek in nature. She never understood using statues as decor in a garden or a home, and she didn't see the reason for having busts in the cave behind her either. If anything, her imagination anticipated the headless, handless, legless busts moving robotically and coming toward her.

That thought sort of scared her, and she made a mental note to limit her intake of crime shows and podcasts. She watched a frog with a bright green streak on its back slowly emerge from the mini-swamp to rest on a rock, and she was pleased to see several dragonflies land on the water. It was a delicate and mesmerizing dance to see them glide along the water, gently balance atop the still surface, and speed away to the next location.

Periodically, Marnie received texts from Simone needing updates. Marnie had few. The location seemed a little too far out for the likes of her when the music, dancing, and dinner would be beyond the veranda, behind the house on the lush, green lawn.

After forty-five minutes of soaking in the atmosphere, uncovering a bed of newly hatched ticks, and needing a social media break, she stood to stretch. She tucked her phone in her pocket and walked over to the reflecting pool, lined with polished and smooth cream-colored marble stones.

Snap! Marnie turned in the direction of the noise, like the sound of a twig breaking under the weight of a foot. She heard the noise near her belongings, and her first thought was to reach for her purse. The purse she had left behind with the picnic items sitting by the rock, partially hidden by blue spruce branches and needles. She chastised herself for not at least grabbing her purse, hearing the voice of reason in her head lecturing her about identity theft.

She thought she would see tourists, but she was entirely alone in this section. She looked around the tall hedges surrounding the reflecting pool and strained to hear any voices, but no one walked out carrying on a conversation.

Marnie looked over at the small cave, praying the statues were not twisting and jerking their way toward her. They remained as still as they always had been. Buzz, buzz, buzz. Marnie grabbed her chest. Her phone vibrated. She inhaled sharply and slowly exhaled.

Simone needed her opinion on where to place some art.

"Marnie, get it together!" She scolded herself for letting her imagination run wild. She walked back to gather her things, and just as she did, she glanced at the hollowed-out cave once more. She squinted in the bright sunlight.

A piece of paper was peeking out from between two bricks in the brick archway. Marnie looked to her left and right; no one was around. She carefully maneuvered her way to the archway and gently pulled the paper out. Crisp, off-white, folded neatly. Marnie unfolded it and saw inked penmanship.

She read: *I am staying with my relatives at present, and I have noticed you on the grounds, yet the servants and my family members cannot place you. Your estate must be near ours, but my daily walks to our neighbors have proved fruitless. No one knows who you are. My aunt jests you are a gypsy living on our land, and my young cousins believe you to be an angel. The servants whisper you are an apparition, but I do not believe in such things. My own theory is that you might be common, and I want to let you know I do not care about societal status. I am looking for conversation and friendship, but I will respect your wishes not to grant me an introduction and audience with you.*

*I apologize for my forwardness. I should like to make your acquaintance. I will write again soon.*

"Unsigned? What a letdown." Marnie glanced around again to see if anyone would come forward to claim the note. The vocabulary was not contemporary. Estate, common, apparition. Marnie did not know anyone who spoke like that. Her imagination began playing storylines before her eyes.

She saw a male suitor from the pages of history penning a note filled with unrequited love for a pretty peasant girl who never received the note because she was married off before she found the love letter. She wondered if it was a note from a married man to a potential mistress. As thoughts and tales swam in her head, Simone text her again.

Marnie tucked the note into her bag and planned to show it to Drew. He would enjoy unlocking the mystery just as much as Marnie.

For now, she had an appointment to keep with her boss.

* * * * *

Marnie found Simone standing on a wooded path, speaking to a group of men wearing white T-shirts with a picture of a flexing man on the back of the shirt. Simone wore a black pantsuit and a bright orange blouse, which complimented her newly colored auburn short hairstyle. She kept having the men move a large metal sculpture a few feet to the left, then to the right, and so on.

Marnie stood before her and waited until she had Simone's full attention. The sculpture was shaped like a lotus and had been painted black. Marnie was not a fan of modern art.

"How was the ambiance of the reflecting pool?" Simone asked behind dark sunglasses.

"I didn't notice any bugs; it was quiet; you can easily get ten to fifteen people there, but I would use a platform to put the tables on because the ground is slightly uneven, and we don't need any turned ankles." Marnie awaited Simone's remarks.

Simone appeared to be lost in thought. "Good work. No, move it back five feet." She spoke to the men. "Marnie, where would you put this piece?"

*Well, I wouldn't put it anywhere because I don't see the purpose or the point.* But she didn't say that. "I think you should contrast it with something lighter. It's lost against the dark forest background."

"You are absolutely right. OK, boys, take it up by the fountain."

The men grunted as they obviously strained to pick up the metal sculpture and carry it toward the light gray fountain with swan statues in the middle of it.

"Marnie," Simone pulled out her phone. "I'm sending you a list of local tailors who've offered to put on a fashion show for us. They will showcase various period pieces they can create for Swan Ball attendees, and I've scheduled an event in two weeks for them to do that right here at Cheekwood. I want you to procure ten food trucks for the night instead of catering and ask the tailors what their preferences are for food. As you get a confirmation for each vendor, send the info along to me." Simone never looked up from her phone.

"Certainly. I understand."

"Excellent. Before you leave today, provide me with a lavatory status, men's and women's."

Marnie had no idea what Simone wanted. How much soap comes out with each pump from the dispenser? How thick is the toilet paper? Is there graffiti on the doors? She was uncertain about the status, but asking for an explanation could jeopardize her future with Jasmine Rose.

"Not a problem. I'll send you a report this evening."

"Lovely. I've got a thousand things to do. I'll see you later." Simone tucked her phone away and briskly walked toward the mansion.

Marnie went indoors to start her bathroom inspections, passing a painted timeline on the walls of the Cheekwood home, which featured the founding family: the Millers.

Smart railroad investments by the matriarch of the Miller Family, Helena, in the early 1800s birthed excessive wealth and enough money to invest in South American rubber, thus creating sustainable, continued wealth for all successive generations. The Millers were often quick to invest in innovative designs and machinery. Throughout history, they were the voices for reform. Being staunch abolitionists who endorsed and implemented a living wage for their workers, Helena's son, Richard, freed and then employed hundreds of Amazonian slaves in the rubber industry. If there ever was a poster family for the now-popular social responsibility, this family's business practices made them just that.

Marnie eyed the various significant business decisions on the timeline, which included their involvement in the steam engine, locomotive, telephone, electricity, and rifle. The painted images and words ran the length of the sixty-foot wall. She had read about financial backing from other key businessmen of the day and how the Millers provided money to invent novelties such as tanks and even computers—both of which, depending on how one looked at it, were essentially members of the same category: weapons.

A side door opened, and Marnie watched men carry in various brown paper-covered items. She guessed these were the portraits of the Miller family the museum would be displaying for the next several months. They usually put the Millers on display about this time. Marnie had her favorite Miller painting hung in one of the furthest galleries upstairs. It was Richard Miller holding two of his young children on his lap, reading to them while all three of them sat snuggled together by a fireplace. Marnie imagined how they posed together. Did he read them a fairytale, and they were enthralled? Did he use the time to teach them a Bible story? Whatever it was, Marnie loved the look of wonder on the blonde, curly-haired boy's eyes as he pointed to the page Richard had turned to in the book. She loved the painting so much because it reminded her of her own childhood.

Nathan and Anna Foster, Marnie's parents, had recently decided to move to Costa Rica and start a faith-based orphanage. Marnie had the option to move but felt her life was in Nashville at present. Startup costs and a lack of full-time staff kept her parents busy, so they did not have time to return to the US for visits, but Marnie made it a priority to visit them in Costa Rica as often as she could.

Nathan's brother, Caleb, and his wife, Ginny, gladly became surrogate parents to their niece and enjoyed her presence on the farm.

Being independent was important to Marnie. She offered to pay rent to her aunt and uncle, but they wouldn't hear of it. She thought they wanted her to save her money so she could afford plane tickets to and from Costa Rica for the holidays, and she did want to save for that, but she also wanted to buy the old plantation home on the Old Natchez Trace about ten minutes from her present location. She dreamed of opening her home as a retreat center and hosting all sorts of events for her community.

The capital that it would take could only happen with a hefty job promotion and probably a few more years' worth of work before she would have a down payment on such a lavish location. The renovations and possible additions an older home like that would need were another matter altogether. She had only spied the old house from the road. The live oaks in the front yard hid much of the house, so Marnie was left to create the layout, which she often did in her mind, occasionally with sketches of how she would redesign it.

She appreciated the privacy the greenery afforded and intended to stay tucked and secluded in her sanctuary. A sanctuary that would be comprised of numerous gardens splashed with pizazz of color and fragrance. Edible gardens accompanied by companion flowers, she could see the hummingbirds and butterflies already gathering nearby to sample the nectar-rich lilies and irises. She felt the sun filtering down, dappling her face and arms from the cool shade where her bare feet touched manicured grass, all to a steady hum of the spring and summer insect orchestra. They needed no tuning, no practice. They made the soundtrack of paradise, directed by the Great Composer, in flawless, perfect rhythm. Marnie dared to breathe in the air she knew would be heavy with heavenly scents when a pungent odor smacked her from her reverie and back to the job at hand.

Presently, Marnie found herself standing before the men's bathroom door and gave a heavy sigh with a dejected look before knocking.

*Two*

Aunt Ginny served Uncle Caleb, Marnie, and Drew homemade peach ice cream as they sat on the screened-in back porch. Aunt Ginny had long ago given up on dyeing her hair, and surprisingly, the gray and white made her look lovely and youthful, even if it could be so. She had tossed her hair up in a loose bun and wore the standard flower-patterned apron Marnie had grown accustomed to seeing when she dined with her family.

Uncle Caleb had two priorities when it came to income: his horses and his organic cotton. He bred horses for pleasure riding but recently found a market in Hollywood and, with Aunt Ginny, began training horses to work on movie sets. They had five major motion pictures under their belts. The previous year, they signed on to train horses for a new show that would be released for streaming in another year. With some of that initial capital, Uncle Caleb invested in organic cotton, and a local manufacturing company made him an offer on the cotton for a crop-sharing deal.

Simplicity was Aunt Ginny's motto, but that didn't mean life was boring at all. The couple traveled frequently to the sets and kept tabs on every animal they sold with extensive contracts designed to protect each steward they entrusted to the buyers.

Tonight, Uncle Caleb relaxed in a pair of worn overalls, the stereotypical farmer. His hair was a darker brown than Drew's but graying more each year.

"So, what kind of notes did you take about the men's bathroom? I mean, they're pretty straightforward." Drew laughed a little.

Marnie had shared the highlights of her day at dinner.

"For starters, there's always way more soap in there than in the women's. Trust me, I checked four sets of bathrooms today. I'm not saying I'm drawing any conclusions, but..."

Aunt Ginny joined Uncle Caleb on the two-seater swing with her ice cream.

"Now, bein' in the trenches is just part of it." Uncle Caleb began with his wisdom.

"Hey, I'm just aiming to get above janitorial duty at some point." Marnie placed a spoonful of soft ice cream into her mouth, letting the flavor linger. No store-bought or chain could compete with this homemade deliciousness.

"Did I ever tell you about the time your dad and I cleaned fish for a summer and sold 'em by the roadside?"

"Yes, Uncle Caleb, I remember. I'm not complaining. I'm just hopeful I'll get out of the trenches and onto other jobs. I don't know if encountering toilets, swamps, and ticks on a daily basis is how I viewed this position."

Two horses moved in silhouette beyond the porch, a red-orange fire of a sunset burning behind them. "That reminds me," she reached into her purse and pulled out the letter she'd found earlier. "Drew, can you run some tests on this to see if it's authentic?" She handed him the paper. "I think it's a historical letter or something."

Drew studied it for three seconds by the lamp Aunt Ginny had turned on. "Fake."

"There is no possible way you could know it's fake by glancing at it."

"This paper is brand new, so it looks like a knock-off of late nineteenth-century stationary. I'll grant you it's a really good fake, though."

"But look at the language and the penmanship. This looks like a lot of the letters hanging in the gallery that are framed from the nineteenth century."

"Where'd you find it?" He took a closer look.

"Tucked between some bricks in the archway that leads to that little cave by the reflecting pool. It's not a high-trafficked spot, so couldn't the note have been hidden there, and maybe through erosion worked its way out, and I found it today?"

Drew removed his spoon from his mouth. "Fake."

"Well, I thought we had an old-fashioned mystery on our hands or something."

"Tell you what, I'll humor you. We just got some new equipment for dating documents, and I'll run some practice tests on it."

"Really?"

"Yeah, so if you won't believe me, you'll believe the machine."

"Thanks." Marnie sat back.

"No problem."

The four of them sat in peaceful silence for a few minutes. The only sound was the creaking of the swing as Marnie's aunt and uncle slowly swayed to and fro.

She couldn't think of anything sweeter than the two of them. They were so giving and loving and were the ultimate compliments to each other. Marnie didn't have illusions of how hard a good marriage was to attain, but in moments like this, her aunt and uncle made it look so easy.

Was she seeing before her what every woman wanted? Resting next to the man you did life with, created life with, and made life so wonderful. Marnie knew their commitment to Yehovah and constant devotion to servanthood were the foundations of their successful marriage.

She'd seen her uncle do every household chore at one point, and she'd seen her aunt help him with every outdoor chore. While she didn't know every tender moment, she knew the man they'd raised. Drew would make a fine husband one day, and she looked forward to seeing her aunt and uncle become grandparents and seeing the fruits of their labors perpetually prosper.

Marnie yawned. "Thanks for dinner. I think I'm going to head over to the cabin and get some sleep. I'll see you all tomorrow." She stood and kissed her aunt and uncle goodnight. She loved that Aunt Ginny consistently smelled like jasmine, and her uncle smelled like sandalwood.

"Sleep well." Aunt Ginny said.

"Goodnight," said Uncle Caleb.

Drew yawned and gave her a parting wave.

Marnie stepped through the porch door into the full evening air. The sun had dipped below the tree line, and all that remained of the fiery sunset was a soft glow from the embers of the rays slipping below the horizon.

It was chilly yet fresh and welcoming, as if the twilight offered endless pledges of renewal and rebirth. After all, twilight is the beginning of a day in Scripture.

Marnie listened to the frog frenzy of songs, proclamations, and promise play from the Harpeth River as she leisurely walked to the cabin.

* * * * *

"I am so borrowing that adorable dress!" Marnie's best friend, Briscney, walked up as Marnie sat with her laptop open while writing in a notebook at one of the stone tables just outside the gift shop at Cheekwood. It was a pleasant seventy degrees.

Marnie wore a mesh-sleeved A-line yellow dress with black leggings and boots. A denim jacket hung over the back of her black wrought-iron chair.

"Briscney! Hi! I'm so glad you could meet me for lunch!" Marnie stood and hugged her friend, who was wearing a lavender sweater and blue jeans with black flats. She had beautiful heliotrope-colored earrings with a matching bracelet. "And your hair! It looks so good. I haven't seen your natural color in years!"

Briscney hugged Marnie back, beautiful and tight curls held together half up in a clip. "My days of hair relaxers are over. Did you see the most recent lawsuits?"

"I saw some headlines, and I think your look is perfect. I'm amazed you could get away and fit me in today."

"I live like five minutes away and what kind of a friend would I be if I passed up an opportunity to hang out with you?"

"You'd be the 'I-just-got-married-a-year-ago-and-have-a-baby-on-the-way-still-decorating
-my-home' kind of friend, and I would completely understand." Marnie smiled. "Sit down and let's catch up."

Briscney was in her second trimester, but there were no outward signs of it yet. "So, tell me how the Swan Ball is going." Briscney unpacked the soup and sandwiches she'd stopped to get for their lunch date. "I got you the roasted red pepper soup."

"It looks scrumptious. Thank you."

"Swan Ball, what's the latest? I follow Jasmine Rose on Instagram, and you guys have some costume event coming up?"

"Yes. I've been able to line up all of the tailors on Simone's list that she wants to host here for a costume display, and I've gotten a list of all of their favorite food trucks, so today, I'm arranging for the trucks to be here. Then I had this idea of hiring musicians, too, and Simone loved it, so at some point, I've got to get the musicians booked for that night. But right now, I welcome the break." Marnie closed the laptop. "Catch me up on you." She opened the lid of the plastic container holding the soup and inhaled. "Mmm."

"Well, I have a guy making us some awesome metal gates for the driveway. They're lined with bars and have handmade Fleur-de-lis throughout. Jeremy thinks the added layer of security is a good idea. I think having them be aesthetically pleasing is a good idea." Jeremy was Briscney's attorney-husband.

"I'll have to drive by and check it out." Marnie ate a bite of her sandwich.

"And, the big news is he became a partner at his firm, so we are thrilled."

"Congratulations!"

Briscney met Jeremy at Princeton, where they attended undergrad; they were engaged at graduation, married soon after, and Jeremy started at Vanderbilt for law school. For the past three years, they'd been in an apartment in Nashville, but with a huge signing bonus at Lion, Loudin, and Lewis, PLLC, they put a down payment on an estate off of Chickering Road in Nashville, one of the most affluent areas Nashville offered.

Briscney was tasked with decorating the 8,000-square-foot home.

Jeremy was tasked with handling the estate planning for Nashville's numerous music industry professionals.

"Thanks, it's quite the promotion. He sent me pictures of the office. It overlooks the Cumberland. And they gave us Tennessee Performing Arts Center and Titans season tickets."

"Wow. That's a really nice package." Marnie was impressed.

"I just wish I saw more of him. He swears these eighty-hour work weeks will stop when the baby comes because the firm values family, but I have my doubts. I love the new house and all; I don't want to sound ungrateful, but I feel like we spent more time together in the old, cramped apartment." She rubbed her abdomen pensively.

"I really hope his hours cut back, too," Marnie sympathized. She thought back to Uncle Caleb and Aunt Ginny. They were their own bosses; they decided when the workday began when it ended, and they did it together. Marnie imagined it could be lonely in that big house off Chickering. On the other hand, what did Briscney expect? Jeremy always said his aim was to be a partner, but it had come with a cost.

Marnie stole a moment to think about her own path. Was she like Jeremy? Always chasing the next big promotion? Or could she learn to be content like her aunt and uncle? Weren't they delightfully happy together? What did she really want?

"Well, I did bring some paint samples for the baby's room. I have colors picked for a boy or a girl. Wanna see?" Briscney brought Marnie back to the conversation.

"Absolutely."

They went over all shades of blues, pinks, whites, off-whites, light browns, and grays. Briscney was undecided about whether she wanted a theme room or just color on the walls. She also showed Marnie some Pinterest ideas.

Marnie had a fun time and hated to see the lunch end. Why couldn't they just spend the entire day together like they did as teenagers? They'd met at a camp south of Nashville during a family camp week and had been inseparable the rest of high school. Why was life so demanding and pressing at this stage, and did it have to be? Couldn't they take the day to sit on a picnic blanket, listen to the radio, laugh, and talk about all of their hopes and dreams? In a flash, childhood was over, and the precious moments untouched by time faded. Marnie knew she couldn't go back, but could she order her life in such a way that she maintained those pleasant pockets of time brush-stroked with tranquility, carefreeness, and ease?

Briscney stood with a sigh, "I hate to run, but I also need to get my car inspected today. I'll swing by again soon and check on you. Don't let Simone work you too hard."

"I won't. Thanks for coming."

With Briscney's departure, Marnie returned to the food truck booking and kept Simone abreast of the progress during the day.

Simone popped by Marnie's "office" of the day in the late afternoon.

"Marnie, I've had an epiphany," Simone announced. She wore a silvery silk dress with hot pink and black leopard print leggings.

"I'd love to hear it."

"Carnations." Simone declared.

Marnie had no idea what this meant. "Carnations?" She looked around; maybe they were in a sea of carnations, and she wasn't catching on. No, they were near beds of pansies.

"Carnations." Simone walked around the table and stood before Marnie. "You will place a different colored carnation as a boutonnière on the men and women who have the top costumes, and those tailors will be the ones we recommend in our newsletter. I'm looking for authentic and true-to-the-time period pieces."

Marnie nodded. Where Simone saw brilliance in the plan, Marnie saw busy work. *So now I'm going to chase down people all night and fight safety pins to satisfy this whim?* There were already twenty confirmed tailors coming from Nashville alone, and Marnie guessed another thirty from the surrounding area would attend.

"Don't you find it inspiring? It just came to me when I was having tea earlier."

*Tea? You have time to sit and have tea? Is my smile too cynical-looking right now or am I passing it off like I'm not utterly jealous?*

"Or, here's an idea. I could also take pictures of the couples and send them to you with my notes and rankings." Marnie offered, hoping Simone would agree.

"But where's the creativity in that?"

"I'd use a fun filter."

Simone tossed her head back and laughed. "Oh, Marnie, you are a humorous one. Go ahead and order two dozen different colored carnations for our event. You can forward me the confirmation info when you've got it." And just as she darted in, she darted away.

Marnie sighed as she looked up florists on her computer. While she didn't share Simone's vision, she would put in the necessary time to climb the ranks.

* * * * *

Marnie stepped out onto the mansion's stone-paved veranda at the end of her work day and stared at the grounds and forests before her. Was there a more verdant lawn in all of Nashville? Her eyes looked up and down.

Before long, the light green petite leaves would enlarge, darken, and fill all of the blank spaces she counted at present. She relaxed against one of the rock columns and watched people below by the reflecting pool. Squirrels flashed up and down tree trunks, chasing one another. She saw children chasing one another by the pond and people taking pictures. It was a wonderful place to work for the time being.

This peaceful point allowed her mind to relax, to ponder, to collect her ideas, and see what new visions emerged. She thought about being promoted to work with Simone full-time and played out the various ways she would accept a position. She fast-forwarded into opening her own event planning company, and buying her dream home; she always saw her parents there with her. Did she want the 8,000-square-foot home like Briscney? Marnie was content in her tiny cabin as it was. What was the end goal? More money, greater position? She kept coming back to the image of family and recalled how good it felt to be with Drew and her aunt and uncle. That's where her heart's desire was if she looked deep enough. People. Family. That was her passion.

As she turned to walk down the outside stone steps, her eyes caught a glimpse of something white.

"No way." Tucked in the rock wall across from where she'd been sitting was a piece of paper, much like the one she'd previously found.

Marnie looked around. Again, she was entirely alone. She cautiously approached the rock wall where the note appeared to be gently and recently placed between a small crack in the rocks, for surely someone would've seen it otherwise.

She glanced over each shoulder before carefully pulling the paper out. It was the same kind of paper as before. Marnie toyed with opening it. Maybe someone was toying with her, making up a mystery and distracting her from her duties. But that didn't make any sense. She knew of no one who would be remotely interested in playing a practical joke on her.

She walked over to the wrought iron bench six feet away from a door leading into the mansion and sat down. She stared at the unopened note, wondering what was written on it. She could put the note back and just go home. This was probably a prank someone was playing, and she was undoubtedly falling for it. She cooked up ideas that the notes were historical. Drew said it was a fake.

Marnie tapped the folded note against her knee. She couldn't resist. She opened it.

*A name. I must know your name. Could we meet in a fortnight? I am called away on business until then. I shall introduce myself the very next moment I see you. I wanted to speak with you days ago. You were by the carriage house, but I could not find the words. Words do not usually escape me so easily.*

*The note I left for you is gone, so I believe you've received my communication. I still have no clue as to your identity.*

*I am not often shy when it comes to introductions. I admit it was easier to practice my sketching than to properly greet you. If you are here when I return, I will make your acquaintance. ~An Admirer*

Marnie looked at the sketch included on the note. "Finally, a clue." The author skillfully drew a woman sitting on a rock bench with her hair partially pulled up. She was reading, and Marnie could see her horse-shaped earrings, earrings that looked similar to the ones Marnie was wearing days ago when Simone had her sit by the carriage house to see how it would work for another table placement. "Oh my gosh." The image was Marnie!

She reread the note and pored over the drawing. How could she remain objective?

Is my hair really that long? Do I sit like that? Do I cross my right leg over my left ever? Was I wearing a bracelet?

Again, she looked around, befuddled. Not only was she alone, but it was closing time. The sunlight had disappeared. The outside lights came on by the veranda; she saw headlights and taillights on the road below her. "Great."

Marnie prayed hers was not the lone car in one of the back parking areas, the woodsy, off-the-beaten path, would-anyone-hear-me-if-I-screamed lot.

Marnie hurriedly folded the note and put it in her purse. She rapidly walked to her white Kia Niro, carrying her keys in weapon mode in one hand and holding a can of Mace in the other.

Upon safe entry into the car, she locked the doors and headed straight to the farm.

## *Three*

Once she entered the main house at the farm, Marnie exhaled deeply. Aunt Ginny had kept the lights on both outside and inside. The light gray walls and light wood floors made the living room cheery and welcoming.

"Drew, is that you?"

Marnie heard Aunt Ginny call from the kitchen.

"No, it's me."

Aunt Ginny came out of the kitchen, "I'm making dinner and am taking some to your uncle. Juniper is in labor, so we're probably going to spend the night down there." She turned and went back to the kitchen. Juniper was a four-year-old Rocky Mountain horse having her first foal.

Marnie followed Aunt Ginny to the kitchen.

Aunt Ginny packed a picnic basket, which rested on the kitchen's marble-topped island. "I've got the rest of the chicken in the oven, along with some veggies and mashed potatoes. Please let Drew know where we are."

Marnie nodded. "Aunt Ginny, can I stay here tonight?"

Aunt Ginny looked at Marnie. "Of course. Are you alright? You look a little pale." Aunt Ginny touched Marnie's forehead, full of care with her furrowed brow as she put on her metaphorical doctor hat.

"I parked in the back lot, and it was dark. I just got myself worked up, I think."

"Well, I hope you're not still watching any of those scary shows." Aunt Ginny always expressed her concern when Marnie and Drew watched crime shows or listened to crime podcasts. She could embrace a good mystery but shied away from too much exposure to crime as entertainment. It had recently rubbed off on both Marnie and Drew as they dialed back their viewing and took to reading classical novels more than streaming.

"No, it's not that. I just should've left before dark tonight. My imagination played tricks on me." Marnie hung her purse on the black chair by the counter.

Aunt Ginny took her apron off. "Well, the guest room is made up, and if you need anything, just get Drew to handle it. I'm headed off now." Aunt Ginny kissed Marnie's cheek. "If you need us, just call, OK?"

"I will. Thanks."

Aunt Ginny left.

Marnie got her plate ready and sat at the island.

Drew came in about ten minutes later.

"Your parents are at the barn waiting for the foal. Dinner's in the oven."

"Great, I'm famished." Drew put his bags down on the floor and grabbed a plate. He piled it high with potatoes, chose a leg and a thigh, and put his peas on top of his potatoes. "How was the work day?" Drew began eating.

"Entertaining more of Simone's impulses." Marnie moved what remained of her potatoes around with her fork.

"What now?" Drew got up and got a glass out of the cabinet, filling it with water from the refrigerator.

"Pinning carnations on certain models attending this costume party so we know which tailors to recommend in our newsletter."

"Why can't you just take pictures?"

"Don't." Marnie shook her head and wagged her finger.

Drew drank half of his water.

"What about you? Any results on the note I gave you?" Marnie asked.

"Yeah." Drew shoveled in mashed potatoes.

"And?" Marnie asked with raised eyebrows.

"Fake." He said with a mouthful of food. He held up a finger, indicating he needed a moment. He finished his water. "Fake with anomalies I can't account for."

"Such as?"

"The paper, the ink, those are authentic to the nineteenth century. What I can't account for is why neither show the process of age. Everything ages when it's exposed to air. Just think about your notebooks from even a year ago, they show age. There's no possible way paper from that long ago would look so fresh. It's like whoever wrote on the paper kept it sealed in an airtight container for a couple of hundred years."

"How do you know the paper isn't fake?" Marnie took a bite.

"Right about 1840, this style of paper made its debut. Stationary-sized paper, which was smaller than the typical nine by twelve inches, gained some traction." Drew went over to his bag and took the note out. "High-end paper made from then till 1890 has a little embossed imprint usually with the year it was made." Drew held the letter up to the light. "There, on the upper left corner. It's the manufacturer's name. See it?"

Marnie looked up. "Yeah." She could make out the year: 1847 and a name: Jessup & Moore Paper Company.

"That's a real company. Well, it was in Delaware and it was around in the 1840s. That's not all. The ink used was made of iron, too. Today's black ink is made from particles of carbon black. So, whoever did this has pristine writing tools from the nineteenth century. Which is possible, but I don't get it."

"Present tense, Drew. Is doing this."

"Huh?"

"Look at this." Marnie pulled out the second note. "They not only have the tools from that era, but they don't write like our contemporaries."

"Where'd you find this anyway?"

"I was by the reflecting pool, and in that small cave, it was just there, tucked in between the rocks as if someone had recently placed it there."

Drew studied it over. "Um, that girl looks an awful lot like you."

"Yeah, I know."

"You don't think she is you, do you?"

"I don't know. I'm a little freaked out, so you and I are going to go get some stuff from the cabin and I'm staying here tonight. And can you test this note for fingerprints?"

"I'll see what I can do. Do you want me to get the authorities involved?"

"No, I don't want that."

"You know, if we were in a movie right now, it would be best to get the authorities involved. Or an episode of *Forensic Files*. She was an up-and-coming event planner with Jasmine Rose." Drew was acting as though he was narrating a show. "But a secret admirer had events of his own in mind."

"Stop it!" Marnie shoved his shoulder.

"Well, you're already scared. I'm trying to get you to see that we should let the police know."

"I'm sure it's nothing. I won't ever stay at Cheekwood again while it's dark. Now finish up so we can get over to the cabin."

* * * * *

"What was that?" Drew stopped walking and whispered as they approached the cabin. The siding was wood, and while it was two stories, it only had six hundred square feet inside a bathroom and bedroom upstairs and a tiny kitchen, living room, and laundry room downstairs.

"Drew, I told you to stop it!" Marnie gave her foot a stamp to emphasize she found no humor in his teasing.

"I'm just messin' with you. There's nothing to be afraid of out here." They were half a mile from the main house, surrounded by woods and the quietness of the country.

"Just wait while I get some things together." Marnie entered the cabin and went upstairs. She gathered an outfit for the next day: plum pants, a black and white shirt, a black jacket, and silver flats. She placed her toiletries and makeup into a bag, found some reading material, tossed a T-shirt and sweats into her duffel, and headed downstairs.

"Drew?" Marnie poked her head outside. She saw the picnic table on the brick patio, the large maple trees, but no Drew. He was nowhere to be found.

"I have Mace, and I will spray you if you scare me."

Drew poked his head out from behind a tree. "Relax, Marnie," he held his hands up, gesturing he was not going to cause her any harm.

"No, you cut it out. I'm already a little on edge."

Drew sighed, "Let's get your mind off things and drive by the barn and check out the new colt."

"He came?"

"Yeah, Mom just texted." Drew held up a picture of him.

"OK." They loaded up in Marnie's car and drove over to the barn.

* * * * *

"Here he is." Aunt Ginny introduced Marnie and Drew to Juniper's new little boy; he was still wet and very dark in color. The stall floor was covered in a deep layer of pine shavings for bedding.

"He's gorgeous," Marnie said.

Juniper ate grain from a purple feeder hung on the slats of the stall while Aunt Ginny used a towel on the little guy who sat with his legs tucked under him. They were in one of the sixteen stalls Uncle Caleb had in the barn. Other horses near Juniper paced and whinnied, anxious to see the new colt.

"Did he try to stand yet?" Drew asked.

"Not yet. He will." Aunt Ginny assured him.

Uncle Caleb entered the stall carrying a bucket of water. Juniper went right to it and drank.

"Does he have a name?" Marnie asked.

"Lev." Aunt Ginny said.

"Hebrew for heart. I agree, he's going to be so sweet." Uncle Caleb said, giving the colt a rub on his forehead.

Lev licked Aunt Ginny's hand.

"I think we'll leave them for a bit and check on them later." Aunt Ginny said.

Uncle Caleb helped her stand.

"Awesome. I was hoping to have more people for tonight's feature." Drew said.

"What feature?" Marnie asked.

"*Back to the Future* marathon. Who's in?"

"You know some of us have jobs, right, and have to get up early? It's already after eight o'clock."

"Marnie, have you ever heard of coffee?" Drew shook his head. "Mom, Dad, you in?"

"Drew, I'll watch a little bit, but I need to wash off before anything. I'll need to wake up in a couple of hours so I can come check the horses if I fall asleep." Aunt Ginny said with a yawn.

"Good enough for me. Marnie?"

"Like I have a choice. I'm still a little wired. I can't go to sleep right now."

"Sweet. Mom, you ride back with Marnie. I'll help Dad. Oh, and maybe you two pretty ladies could pop some popcorn or bake cookies or something? I don't know. I just had an idea that a little somethin'-somethin' would be good

18

for the movie." He grinned, showing both rows of teeth.

Marnie gave Drew the side-eye. "Altruism is dead. Come on, Aunt Ginny."

Ten minutes into the movie Aunt Ginny was out. She was snuggled up against Uncle Caleb, and he stroked her head while he watched the movie.

Marnie had magazines in her lap, planning on working through the film, but she let her thoughts run away again. Where was Jeremy tonight? Was he home with Briscney? Were they watching a movie together while she cuddled up next to him, and he rubbed her back or her feet, whatever might be a little achy from pregnancy?

Marnie watched Drew. He had seen the film a dozen or more times, but he acted like this was his first time. She watched Uncle Caleb; he and Drew laughed at the same parts of the film. The apple certainly didn't fall very far from that tree, but in this case, it was good.

Marnie flipped through a few pages of the decorating magazine, acting like she was interested in the staged kitchens and bedrooms on the pages, but she wasn't.

She was more interested in knowing where those notes came from. Had someone been watching her while she was working? Was it possible she had a secret admirer?

Boyfriends weren't really Marnie's thing. Dates were offered, and many were turned down. Her parents instilled in her the concept of choosing a mate who was spiritually linked to her. Though she lived in the Bible Belt, most of the church-going folks weren't following Scripture. They were following man-made religions and rules, and as soon as Marnie got into a theological discussion with a date, which was bound to happen at the beginning of the evening, it turned sour from there.

She held her own in Hebrew apologetics, showing the truth about biblical translations and hijacked holidays. Teachable spirits were rare, so Marnie politely declined more and more dates until she wasn't receiving as many offers as before.

She partly enjoyed the break from the pursuits, but in these moments with her family, she wondered if she'd ever meet someone like the men in her family. Men who weren't intimidated by a woman's intelligence. Men who faithfully served their wives and never demanded a thing. For when a man loves his wife the way the Bible instructs, he will never want for respect. She will treasure, adore, and admire him, and together, they will fulfill the purposes of marriage.

*That's what I want. I want a kind, loving man who understands the truth, receives the truth, and promotes it. But where are those men? I mean, look at Drew, he's still coming into his own. I guess we're still just too young.*

Uncle Caleb and Aunt Ginny married in their mid-30s; her parents were in their early 30s when they married. Perhaps Marnie was destined to wait, which was fine with her. She had many items to knock off her Bucket List with or without a mate.

"Great, Scott!" Christopher Lloyd's character said in the movie.

Marnie turned her attention back to the film.

"Honey, go on to bed. Drew and I will go check the horses in a bit." Uncle Caleb said to Aunt Ginny.

"Are you sure?" She yawned.

"Yeah, you've had a big day. I'll be done in a couple of hours."

"OK. Goodnight, Everyone." Aunt Ginny left the couch and went to the master suite, located just down the hall from the living room where they watched the movie.

*Four*

The days seemed to race along over the next couple of weeks. Temperatures steadily increased, more flowers blossomed, Daylight Saving Time occurred, and Marnie remained a constant visitor at the main farmhouse. She enjoyed evenings with the family. From movies to board games to Aunt Ginny helping her remember how to use a sewing machine, Marnie didn't dwell on her parents' absence as much when she was spending time with this side of her family.

The Victorian fashion show day arrived without issue. Marnie found no more mystery notes, heard no eerie noises at Cheekwood, and felt at ease as she prepared for the evening. Simone requested simple attire for the event, so Marnie chose a black maxi dress with a full skirt and semi-sheer tulle, which looked very similar to Victorian dresses in design. Low-heeled black shoes accompanied the dress, and she kept her jewelry minimal, with only three gold bracelets. She wore her hair in a slight bouffant up-do with curly tendrils near her face.

All of the food trucks arrived, and all confirmed fashion designers appeared. Marnie organized them in the way that Simone requested. The models were to walk on the sidewalk near the tulip beds closest to the visitor center, then follow a path lined by tea lights to another sidewalk that led to the mansion, which provided the best lighting for people to select the designer they wanted for their costumes. The halls of the mansion were brimming with hors d'oeuvres and music for the guests to enjoy while the models paraded about in their Victorian costumes.

The costumes were varied. Some designers took a creative approach with color, while others blended the era with other eras–such as steampunk, 60s through 80s paired with Victorian attire. Marnie felt that too many liberties were taken with fashion. She appreciated the costumes that stayed true to the era.

She had her carnations in a small black wicker basket and pinned them as she could, apologetically fastening them to the models in runway mode. Only twice did she stick herself with the sharp end of the safety pins, but she never broke the skin, so it was a win in Marnie's book.

Close to eight o'clock, Marnie took a much-needed break pausing just off the beaten path on an old stone bench by the pond underneath a large oak tree. Simone text her, congratulating her on a job well done, and informed her she could head home when she wanted.

Marnie breathed in the fragrant night air. She saw the season's first fireflies flicker above the water as their light reflected on the still surface.

Near her, children played with glowing sticks, as did some of the Victorian-clad models.

"Good Evening." A Victorian-dressed man approached Marnie. "You look enchanting tonight. Are you enjoying the party?"

"If you call this a party."

"I do not, but my aunt does."

"Yeah, well, I call it work." Marnie studied the man's attire. He wore a matching brown cutaway coat and trousers. His shirt featured a high straight collar with a thin cravat. The coat buttons were large, possibly made of ivory. He wore trousers tucked into high boots and looked every bit from the Victorian Era, at least from the pictures Marnie had researched.

She looked at his face. His clean-shaven, handsome face was framed by wavy dark hair that covered his ears and stopped around his collar line. She blushed as she realized she'd been staring at him without speaking for a good ten seconds. She didn't consciously notice he'd also been staring at her for the same amount of time, speechless.

"Your name, good sir?" Marnie broke the silence, slipping into a character she thought seemed appropriate.

"Arodi Bellamy at your service, miss?" He bowed slightly.

"Marnie Foster," she said.

"It is a pleasure to make your acquaintance. Are you enjoying yourself this evening? Can I get you a drink?"

"No, thank you. I'm not thirsty. I just had some water."

"All of the entertainment is in the mansion; you could be missing out on some excitement. I believe my aunt is going to sing soon."

Marnie couldn't remember who they'd hired for the night for music, but she'd heard various singers already. "Actually, it's nice to relax out here."

He nodded. "May I join you?"

"Sure."

Arodi sat next to her on the bench.

A small child raced down the green slope across the pond and fell. A woman rushed to her, scooped her up, and moments later sent the child on her way again.

"So, Mr. Bellamy, what's your story?"

"I am spending time with my family and choosing a career path."

"Oh, do you sing, too? This is the place for music."

"You mean sing for a career?" He laughed.

Marnie thought he sounded surprised that she suggested someone in Music City would want to sing for a living. "Yeah, that's what a lot of people come to Nashville for."

"Fascinating. No, I'm visiting from New York and am looking to open a factory here. The growth potential in Nashville is huge."

"Some would argue we're already at capacity." *Just ask any commuter on any weekday.* With an interstate system that desperately needed updating, it wasn't uncommon to have commuters stuck in traffic over an hour on a normal day.

They shared a smile.

"Could I interest you in a stroll?" Arodi asked.

"Why not?" Marnie stood, and Arodi offered his arm. "Ha, you sure know how to play the part." She latched her arm to his, and they walked through the grounds. Marnie breathed in the fresh night air as they walked, looking forward to warmer nights and more outdoor activities.

"Tell me how you fit into all of this," Arodi said. They paused on a bridge where water peacefully, almost silently, flowed under them. Solar lights glowed on either side of the small creek.

"All of what?"

"Tonight. This gathering."

"Oh, that. I'm helping with the Swan Ball, and tonight is just a smaller presentation for the patrons."

"Of course! I would imagine it will take a large staff to host such an event."

"You don't know the half of it."

A group of people walked past the pair toward the pond.

"Does that mean you will be working here on the grounds for some time to come then? The Swan Ball isn't until June."

"Yeah, I'm here almost every day."

"Wonderful." Arodi cleared his throat. "Would it be alright if we met up on occasion? My family has been the extent of my social interactions, and I do not have many other acquaintances here."

The way he spoke was odd to Marnie, but she figured it was part of the role. "You mean meet up here? At Cheekwood?" *Wait? Is he asking me out? Or just asking to be friends? This guy-girl relating stuff is killer.* Yet, she was flattered and intrigued.

"Yes, I am conducting most of my affairs from here. My family spends ample amounts of time on the grounds. But if you prefer another location, I can be accommodating."

"No, here's fine. I practically live here." Marnie had multiple changes of clothes in her car, including an emergency overnight bag if she needed to stay at Briscney's; she tried to be prepared in a moment's notice.

They walked from the bridge arm in arm toward the mansion. The night air was a little chilly, yet filled with the fragrance of new beginnings.

They stood before the front door of the well-lit mansion. Marnie saw a valet jog off after a nicely dressed couple handed him keys.

Marnie heard the piano playing from inside.

"Would you like to hear the performance? My aunt has requested my presence at half past eight. I would offer to extend our visit after her performance, but we must retire to be fresh for family portraits tomorrow."

Marnie looked inside the mansion. Finely dressed people moved in and out, and laughter came from the doorway. It was tempting, but she was exhausted. "I'd better go, Mr. Bellamy."

"My friends call me Arodi, Miss Foster."

"Well, mine call me Marnie. So, I'll just see you around then, OK?"

"Naturally."

Marnie still had two yellow carnations left. She had been holding them as they walked.

"Oh, here," she said as she pinned one to his lapel. "You are by far the best dressed. Where is your female counterpart? I'd love to see her dress."

"I can assure you, I attended alone."

Was it just Marnie, or did his eyes twinkle when he said those words? And why did it suddenly feel unseasonably warm?

"Then that makes my job simple. I have this one as an extra."

"I would not want this last flower to go to waste. Allow me," Arodi reached for the extra carnation, slowly taking it from Marnie's hand. He brought it up to her face and delicately tucked it behind Marnie's ear, careful not to disturb her hair.

She was suddenly internally singing *I Could've Danced All Night* from *My Fair Lady* even though they hadn't danced and even though she wasn't sure she could even move her legs at the moment.

"It's lovely. You are lovely." He smiled at her as though he was drinking in the scene before him.

Marnie felt her internal body heat race to her cheeks.

"Shall I send for your carriage?" He placed a hand on her elbow.

The heat overflowed from her face and flooded her core and extremities. *Focus, Marnie. Focus!* "No, valet was only for the patrons, not the staff. I've got some things to finish up, and I'll just fetch my own carriage in a bit. But, thanks for the offer." She nervously raced through her words.

Arodi checked his pocket watch.

It was an impressive piece of costume jewelry, golden in color with a matching chain.

"It's time for me to go. Adieu, Marnie. The conversation and company were delightful." He bowed.

Marnie curtsied. It just seemed to fit the moment. "Well, it's been fun playing these roles for the night. I'll see you around." Marnie felt as if she were floating as she walked to her car, smiling the entire way.

* * * * *

"Arodi! Come on!" Ari, Arodi's look-alike brother, called from the doorway of the mansion. Lanterns burned and atop the fence; horse-drawn carriages aligned the pathway.

Arodi turned in the direction of the mansion. "Ari, did you see her? I told you she was real! She just left to finish some affairs. Did you see her?"

Ari peered in the same direction as Arodi. Ari was slightly taller. "There's no one there. Aunt Belinda will not begin without us present. Come, let's get inside."

"Look, she gave me this." Arodi pointed to the carnation on his lapel. "It must be some sort of custom or tradition in her family. I think it's splendid."

"Look," Ari pointed to his pocket watch. "We are being rude."

"I am not imagining things. We spent part of the evening together. You'll see. She's agreed to meet me here. She's helping with the Ball."

"Oh, so you've been writing letters to a commoner? A woman who must work for a living? This will sit well with the family. Let's go." Ari pulled on Arodi's arm.

Arodi gazed into the woods seconds longer before going inside.

Belinda Miller's performance was about to begin.

* * * * *

Marnie entered the farmhouse aglow.

"How was the event?" Aunt Ginny looked up from sewing a pair of jeans, her wire-rimmed glasses resting on her nose.

"It was enjoyable, thank you. I had a good time."

Uncle Caleb was dozing in a chair.

Classical music played from a computer on the living room table.

"Your hair held up well. And that carnation was an inspired addition."

Marnie reached her hand to the carnation and smiled. "Yes, it was a lovely incorporation." Marnie yawned. "I'm really tired; I think I'll head up and go to bed."

"Sweet dreams."

"Thanks." Marnie climbed—or rather glided—upstairs to her room. She looked at herself in the mirror, turning her head to see the carnation. The carnation that was placed there by a gentleman. A stranger, but a gentle stranger. A handsome, gentle stranger.

Marnie changed into pajamas and washed her face, but she couldn't remove the carnation just yet. She admired its placement in the mirror a little while longer before lifting it away from her hair and resting it on her nightstand.

She got under the covers and checked her phone. *Why didn't he ask for my number? Would I have given it to him? What kind of business is he into? A factory in Nashville? Why wouldn't he just go somewhere else? I can't imagine how much real estate would cost to build a factory in Nashville.* Marnie shifted on her left side and looked at the carnation. She remembered his hand touching hers. *His hands weren't callused, so he mustn't do any manual labor.* She recalled his fingers touching her ear as he placed the flower. *If I'd have stayed, what would we be doing now? Going out for ice cream? An impromptu date?* Marnie knew better. She wasn't one to consort with strangers. But Arodi didn't seem like a stranger. He seemed strangely familiar to her.

Marnie turned onto her back, trying to find a comfortable position. She flipped through her phone wondering who she could tell about her evening. She thought about texting Briscney but decided it was too late. She wondered where Drew was but didn't really want to text him. She scrolled through her phone, but none of her female friends seemed like the right choice to share the moment with.

So she decided it would wait. Marnie looked over at the carnation. *I might never see him again. He could've just been playing a role like I was. Oh dear, I forgot to take his picture. I hope Simone saw him.* Thoughts of work re-energized Marnie, so she opened her computer, uploaded the pictures she took of the carnation-wearing models, and sent them to Simone.

## *Five*

The following morning, Marnie met Simone upstairs in the Cheekwood mansion. It was before operating hours, so they had the floor to themselves.

"I want you to go through the Miller Family galleries and choose some costume ideas for me. I'm looking for authenticity; I don't think the fashion designers understood the look that we were going for last night." Simone wore a double-puffed sleeved blouse with a black skirt and a slim belt around her waist.

Marnie wore a black mid-sleeved blouse, a mid-length high-waist skirt, and red slingback shoes.

"Just send me pictures. I'd like around five options. Thanks." Simone exited the first of four galleries that displayed the Miller family's portraits. Marnie's shoes click-clacked against the marble floors as she walked around the first room, her phone capturing each portrait. She'd narrow it down to her favorites after she'd studied.

Many of the portraits were not full-body images, but Marnie took pictures of the women's dresses: the Marys, Margarets, and Elizabeths. No one smiled. Every stare was serious, and Marnie wondered about the world these women had lived in. Did they have arranged marriages? Did they have choices of suitors? Was it an oppressive patriarchal society that dictated everything they did?

Marnie moved on to the Janes, an occasional Alice, and then Marnie stopped to look at the Williams, Jameses, Richards, and Arodi.

"Arodi?" Her voice echoed in the vast cavern of unfilled space as she stared at the portrait of a man who eerily resembled the same man she'd met the previous evening. Marnie had never met another human alive named Arodi.

She moved toward the painting to get a better look at the nameplate. "Arodi Bellamy, 1849." A coincidence? A relative with the same name, same hair, same eyes, same smile, and the same yellow carnation Marnie had given to a stranger a little more than twelve hours ago. "What on earth?" Marnie looked to her left and right. She was alone. Against the rules, she touched the painting to see if it was still wet, to see if she was being pranked. The painting was dry, and the artist's signature matched the other signatures on the surrounding paintings.

Internally, Marnie's stomach was doing back handsprings, front flips, and cartwheels. Her fingers felt frozen even though blood rushed through her veins. She found a bench to rest upon while she processed everything.

She felt light-headed. She sat staring, analyzing, thinking. *Is this a joke? Come on, someone come out with cameras rolling saying you got me. Because you did. Big time.* Was Arodi the mystery admirer the whole time stuck in a Victorian fantasy world and had somehow involved Marnie in his twisted thoughts? She could hear a mixture of Drew's voice and a *Dateline* narrator in her head. *He played the role of dapper-Dan before the ladies of Nashville while hosting a myriad of delusions, fighting inner demons.* Marnie shook her head. She had to stop watching crime shows with Drew.

How long she sat there, she wasn't sure.

Simone text her requesting pictures.

Marnie sent her five random shots. Her eyes were blurry from staring so long and so hard at the painting. Everything. Everything in that portrait was exactly how the man she'd met last night looked. The hair was the same length, the same deep brown shade, the eyes were the same milk chocolate brown, the smile with the left dimple; it was the same man. She half expected the portrait to speak at any moment.

Marnie now questioned if the previous night had been real. She knew her imagination often carried her away, but had it done that last night? *No, no, that didn't happen. He put a carnation in your hair. You didn't do that. He sat next to you on the bench, we passed by people. Someone saw him. Someone must know him.* Marnie played back the evening to see if she recalled running into anyone who saw them together so she could verify her memories. Who could she talk to who could shed some light on this mystery man? *His aunt! Of course, she sang at eight-thirty. Once I find out who she is, I can find out who he is!* Marnie metaphorically patted herself on the back.

She raced downstairs to the historian manning the desk tucked under the main staircase. "Hello, could you tell me who sang here last night at the event?"

The older woman with bright red hair looked around at the various stacks of paper on her desk. "Hmm, I don't think I have that list on paper, but we did post the schedule to the website. If you give me a moment, I'll pull it up." She had large rings on her fingers that seemed to slow her typing down.

"No, it's no trouble; I can do that on my own; thanks!" Marnie hurried out the front of the mansion doors where she'd parted with Arodi the night before. She glanced around to see if he would appear as he had the previous night: nothing.

Using her smartphone, Marnie pulled up the list of singers from the website. Three bands had played the previous night. She Googled each band member one by one from each of the bands, but she could never connect anyone with Arodi Bellamy. Besides, it was an all-male group who played from eight to ten. She was certain Arodi had said that his aunt was singing, and unless she was a twenty-year-old man with a beard lead-singing for the Stone Throwers, it couldn't have been her.

She walked to the parking lot, got into her car, locked the doors, and sat perplexed that she couldn't solve the mystery. She called Drew. "Are you busy?"

"I have a minute, what's up?"

"I met a guy last night at the designer costume event, and I think he's the one who placed those letters for me to find."

"Are you safe? Are you OK? Are you staring at a shrine filled with your pictures surrounded by burning candles?"

She imagined Drew hugging the phone closely because his tone got very low as he spoke. "Stop it! I'm safe; I'm in my locked car at Cheekwood."

"Did you check the backseat?"

"I'm fine." She said as she adjusted her rear-view mirror, just to be sure that she was alone. "I was upstairs in the mansion going through the galleries, and I saw this portrait that looked just like the man I met last night, down to the hairstyle and wearing the carnation I gave him last night."

"You gave a dude a flower?" Drew laughed.

"Never mind that. The year on the painting was 1849."

"Marnie, it's obvious he switched out the painting and is playing a really bizarre joke on you. I would ask someone to give you a list of employees, and we can start putting faces to names."

Somehow, it wasn't a comfort to Marnie. "I don't understand. So he pretended to be the real Arodi Bellamy last night? Why?"

"Why did people collect hundreds of beanie babies once upon a time? You'll drive yourself crazy trying to figure out a motive. It's nice to have, but it's not needed to draw conclusions. Whoever this guy is, his jokes aren't funny."

"Drew, he wasn't the least bit creepy at all." A butterfly landed on Marnie's windshield, and she flinched, realizing just how jittery she was.

"Yeah, psychos have been known to be charming. Do you not pay attention to any of the articles, books, or shows I talk about? That kind of stuff could prove to be life-saving someday."

"I'm just not usually so off in my judgment of character."

"Maybe the costume threw you off. Debonair gentlemen appear quite trustworthy."

"Maybe. I don't know. I'm going to head home. Can you run some tests on the painting to see if it's authentic?"

"No, but I believe we have some paperwork on previous tests run on a bunch of those paintings. I'll go down to the archives and see what I can dig up and try to find out what the real Arodi Bellamy looked like. Are you really OK?"

"I'm more befuddled than anything. The man I met last night could've easily escorted me to my car and harmed me, but I just didn't get that feeling from him."

"Just get home in one piece, and I'll see you later tonight."

"OK, bye." Marnie hung up and debated looking for Arodi on the grounds, but as she imagined the *Law and Order* doink doink sound, she decided it best to get to the farm.

* * * * *

That afternoon, Marnie helped Aunt Ginny make apple butter but couldn't stop looking at the clock, wishing Drew would come home early.

Aunt Ginny wrote on the label of the last jar they'd canned with a Sharpie marker, "This will be delicious," she said.

"Absolutely. This was such a fun afternoon. Thank you."

"You know, your uncle and I have really enjoyed you staying here lately. Do you want to move over here instead of staying in the cabin? I know you'd be giving up some peace and quiet, but you know we love you just like you were our daughter, and it's nothing to help you move your things over here. I just want you to feel safe and enjoy your time on the farm."

"I would like that very much. Thank you. Being here with you all makes me miss my parents less than I do at the cabin, for sure."

"That's Good. You can just let me know when you want to move everything over, and I'll come help."

"Oh, Drew and I can handle it."

The front door opened and closed. "Speaking of Drew," Marnie slid off her stool and went to the living room. "Tell me everything. What'd you find out? Do you have pictures? Gimme the details."

"Chillax." Drew hung his laptop bag on a peg by the door. "I went to the archives at lunch. The cute librarian and I belong to a mutual Facebook group for local history enthusiasts, so she let me see the Miller Family special collections. I had to wear gloves." Drew enthusiastically mimed putting on gloves.

"Did you find anything out or not?" Marnie had waited all day to hear the news; her patience was running thin.

Drew went straight for the kitchen.

Marnie followed closely at his heels.

Aunt Ginny was outside on the back porch watering plants.

"Here's what I found out." Drew looked in the fridge. "The real Arodi Bellamy was the nephew of Richard Miller, founder of Cheekwood. Richard's sister was Alice, who married Hutchison Bellamy and produced six offspring: Ari, Arodi, Noah, Tamar, Yitzak, and Sarah." Drew got out bread, cheese, meat, and condiments. "The Bellamy's were in the textile industry and had a large operation in New York first, then Franklin, Tennessee. Hutchison was way ahead of his time. He employed women, paying them triple what they could earn in other industries, and check this out: he matched them dollar for dollar if they elected to go to college, and seven out of ten women not only went to college but graduated." Drew started making a sandwich. "Do you have any idea how much of a statistical anomaly this guy was?" He took a bite of cheese

30

and spoke with his mouth full. "Anyway, his daughters…"

"Drew, what does this have to do with Arodi?"

Drew swallowed. "Nothing. I just find their history fascinating." Drew completed compiling his cheese and meat masterpiece.

"Did you find anything out about the original painting?"

"Yes, but don't you want to know more about the family tree?" Drew opened the fridge, replaced the condiments, and grabbed the milk.

"No, what does he look like?"

Drew poured a glass of milk. "Fine." He walked out of the kitchen and returned with a folder. "I give you the real Arodi Bellamy." He unceremoniously offered.

Marnie opened the file. "Oh, no, it can't be!" She shook her head.

"What?"

"It's the same guy. This is the same guy I met yesterday."

"Uh, no, that's Arodi Bellamy." Drew touched the printed picture with his pointer finger. "The librarian verified it, and she works with this stuff all the time, so she would know. Wait, do you think the guy you met had plastic surgery to look like Arodi Bellamy?"

Marnie squinted, "Are you sure we're related?"

"Life imitates art more often than you think." He took a big bite, gobbling almost half the sandwich.

"OK, Sherlock."

Aunt Ginny came in from the porch. "Drew, your dad is cooking eggplant parmesan. Why'd you make a sandwich?"

"Appetizer, Mom. I'll be hungry for dinner when it's ready." He said with a mouthful.

Aunt Ginny started getting dishes out.

Drew propelled Marnie back to the living room. "You'd better watch your back over there and tell Simone what's going on."

"And risk losing my promotion? That's not going to happen." Marnie crossed her arms.

"Well, then, what do you plan to do about this Arodi look-alike who's sending you letters and has now introduced himself?"

Marnie stared off toward the wall while the gears turned in her head. Her eyes widened. "I have the perfect confrontation plan." Marnie grinned.

"I know that look. It's the same look you gave me when you decided we should sneak backstage at a Trace Adkins concert to get his autograph."

"I give you Exhibit A," Marnie pointed to the framed picture of a teenaged Drew and Marnie with a smiling Trace Adkins in the middle of them, arms around both beaming kids, mouths full of braces. "Now, I think dinner will be ready soon, and then we'll discuss my plan."

## Six

"This won't work," Drew's voice spoke from Marnie's phone, which she held in her hand. She stood on the north side of the Cheekwood estate by a welcoming maple tree at the top of a green slope. The air was pleasant this early April morning with the faint hum of bees buzzing throughout the grounds. Automatic sprinklers kicked on in the various flower beds to give a refreshing drink to the thirsty foliage. The gardens were alive with activity. Patrons flocked to see over 150,000 tulips in full bloom. The whites, reds, yellows, oranges, and pinks stood row after row, bed after bed, and when the colors were mixed in any and all combinations, it was a kaleidoscope of brilliant, vibrant, and eye-catching wonder.

This was the backdrop for Marnie and Drew's morning at Cheekwood. She wore her hair down, the natural waves taking advantage of Nashville's humidity to express themselves fully. Her sundress was turquoise, adorned with cherry blossom appliqué throughout. She donned jewel-toned flats to complete her ensemble.

She held the phone up to her mouth. "It will work. Maintain position."

Marnie applied a little lip gloss and then looked to make sure Drew stayed mostly hidden at the bottom of the hill near the forest's edge. She'd suggested staying tucked behind the bamboo reeds, which provided maximum coverage, but Drew opted for concealing himself behind a sycamore.

"Ten-four," Drew said.

Marnie watched young children race up and down the slope near the pond, giggling and squealing. It was sweet to see how simplicity brought them tremendous joy. Did adults still find satisfaction in nature? While she didn't see any of them racing up and down the hills, she saw a few individuals taking pictures with macro camera lenses of the various flora and fauna Cheekwood offered. On one side of the water was an arrangement of foxgloves with lady's mantle directly in front, and pink petunias tucked alongside the lady's mantle. Marnie watched a teenage girl sit by the French lavender in close locale to the gorgeous flowers; she flipped her hair to the side then gave a smile for a lady clicking away with the camera. Marnie appreciated the joy of being outdoors and felt like those she observed also embraced it.

She thought about the carnation that hadn't left her bedside. Didn't it bring her a certain amount of joy? Or was it the memories tied to the reception of the carnation? Her cheeks felt flush with a rush of heat. *You are trying to catch a potentially dangerous man in a web of lies. Do not, do not think about the time you spent together.* Marnie continued her internal lecture.

She turned her attention away from the children and photography session to the older couple picnicking on cement benches by the pond. They conversed and stared at the world around them. A few times, the woman laughed after the man spoke. Marnie was just about to decide that adults still found joy in nature when she caught sight of the various men and women looking down at their phones as they walked on the pathways or sat on blankets. *Look up! Look around. You're missing the butterflies. And I can't believe you walked by that turtle. Um, your kid just fell down. And your other kid is like ten feet behind you. Oh, and there's an eagle's nest up there, but you're too busy to notice.* Marnie sighed.

She went back to staring at the pond and spied a familiar face near the water's edge. "Drew!" She spoke into her phone.

"Yeah?"

"He's coming!"

"Where?"

"Walking up from the pond! You got me?"

Arodi smiled as he approached.

"Yes, I'll make sure you're safe," Drew said.

Marnie ended the call.

"You look exquisite, Marnie," Arodi complimented as he walked up. His attire was more relaxed: linen-looking trousers and a white shirt with sleeves rolled up, with a dark brown vest fastened over the shirt. The ends of his hair on his neckline formed the tiniest ringlets from moisture. Had he been on a brisk walk already?

Marnie nearly forgot why she was there. *A picnic? Did I agree to meet him for a picnic? Or a stroll, another lovely stroll through the grounds?* She was sure she heard symphonic music playing while she tried to remember why she was there, but then she heard a loud record scratch in her head. *No, Marnie, remember you're here for the truth. No more games.* "Thank you. How did your portrait go?"

"I hope well. It will be finished in a month or so."

"You used my carnation in the sitting."

Arodi looked puzzled, "How did you know? Are you friends with the artist? Did you see me posing? I wish you would've called."

Marnie was stunned. *How can he just lie to my face? Dude, the painting is already hung in the museum. All we have to do is go look at it. How long are you going to keep this up? And call? I don't have your number!* His innocently aloof routine had come to an end. "What's your deal anyway?" Marnie was ready to expose the truth.

"I don't understand."

"The letters, the antiquated speech? The clothes," she pointed to his current attire, "the portrait in the museum, what are you trying to do? And why are you involving me? I'm just trying to get my job done, and I'm not looking for some weird Jane Austen fantasy role-play thing."

"I told you that I'm here to open a textile factory. You see, my father..."

"Oh, I know all about your father. Well, I know about the real Arodi Bellamy's father. I know nothing of your father." She used her finger to point at him as she spoke for emphasis

"I don't believe I understand. Have I offended you? I admit it was cowardly to write the

letters without signing my name, and you have my apologies. I should have started our conversation immediately with that expression."

"I don't understand you. Arodi, whatever your real name is, this isn't real." Marnie pulled out her phone.

"What an interesting device," he commented.

"Drew?"

"Where is he?" Drew asked.

"What?"

"Are you up there practicing what to say? You look ridiculous. Seriously, like three people have walked by and laughed at you already."

"What do you mean? He's right here." Marnie looked down toward Drew.

"What?"

"Just come up here." Marnie ended the call.

"What is that you're holding?" Arodi quizzically asked.

"Yeah, I'm not buying it."

Drew jogged up the hill.

"This is Arodi. See, he looks just like the real Arodi Bellamy." Marnie showcased Arodi moving her hands up and down like she was showing a studio audience a new product they could buy.

Drew's brow furrowed. "Uh, Marnie," Drew leaned in close to her ear, "There's no one here. It's just you and me," he whispered.

"That's not funny, Drew."

"I'm serious; it's just us."

Marnie looked at Arodi. Then back at Drew. Then, back at Arodi.

"Pardon me, Marnie, are you speaking to me?" Arodi asked.

"Arodi, can you see a man standing two feet in front of us?"

"No, Marnie."

Marnie looked at Drew, "Do you see a man to my right?"

"No, there's no one here. Are you feeling alright?" Drew asked.

She wasn't feeling alright. She was perplexed, confused, and beyond puzzled as to what was taking place. Her brain tried to analyze everything she knew: inductive reasoning, deductive reasoning, direct evidence, circumstantial evidence. She finally went with a theory. "OK," she nervously laughed. I can explain it now even though there's no such thing."

"Well?" Drew said.

Marnie whispered while pointing to Arodi, "he's a ghost."

"Drew is an apparition?" Arodi asked.

"No, not Drew, you!"

"Me?" Arodi pointed a finger at himself with raised eyebrows.

"He's a ghost? No, there's no such thing," Drew said.

Marnie let out a small sigh. "OK, I want you both to look at me and promise you're not in this together and playing out the most elaborate hoax ever." She looked back and forth between the men.

"Marnie, I'm not playing. There's no one here. Who do you think you are talking to?" Drew walked in circles. "See? No one is here."

"I am not tricking you," Arodi responded.

"Drew! Why is he appearing to me?" Marnie took a few steps away from Arodi.

"You really see someone standing there?" Drew pointed to the spot close to where Marnie had been standing.

"Yes."

Drew elbowed her, "Ask him what his unfinished business is." He moved his eyebrows up and down with a grin.

"That's a movie thing; it's not real. And he's not real." Marnie didn't find Drew amusing.

"Just ask him."

Marnie took a step toward Arodi. "What do you want?"

Arodi appeared to be thinking, so he didn't respond immediately. "My immediate family is in New York, and I am without friends here. I merely wanted to make your acquaintance, and even though my methods of communication are somewhat unorthodox, our evening together was better than I'd imagined. I'm looking for friendship."

He was so genuine, polite, and handsome when he was sincere. Marnie moved in closer and studied him. Nothing about him appeared ghostly or supernatural. He looked like a flesh and blood man. "May I?" She held her fingertips before his forehead.

"Certainly."

She touched his hair. She felt the heat of the sun upon his dark, wavy mane. She lightly touched his smooth, warm cheek and was close enough now to breathe in the traces of aftershave. His aftershave must've been extremely powerful because Marnie felt her knees give ever so much. She ran her hands over his vest and felt the silken fabric. It was real.

Marnie touched his forearm. Muscular. She then touched his hand. He opened his palm and extended his fingers while she examined the phalanges and traced the lines running along the inner surface of his hand. Not a trace of dirt beneath the nails. There wasn't any transparency to any part of him. He was as solid and sound as she and Drew. She looked into his eyes, eyes that looked back at her with nothing but kindness and maybe a touch of curiosity. "May I see your pocket watch?"

Arodi reached into his trouser pocket and produced it. He handed it to

Marnie.

"What the..." Drew flipped out. "Where did you get that? What just happened? The ghost gave you that?" Drew snatched it out of her hand and looked at it. He opened it, closed it, and studied it. "This is authentic. Not costume jewelry."

"I don't think he's a ghost," Marnie said.

Drew gave her the watch back.

She handed the pocket watch back to Arodi.

"I'm not a ghost, Marnie. I don't believe in those things."

"Here, take this." She then proceeded to hand him her phone. "Drew, watch what happens when I let go of the phone." She released it into Arodi's hand.

"Where did your phone go?" Drew excitedly asked like a three-year-old watching his first magic trick.

"I can see it, Drew. I can see Arodi holding it." Marnie tried to piece it together, but it wasn't coming together. It wasn't making any sort of logical sense. She explored another theory. "Arodi, what year is it?"

"1849."

"Drew, did the Bellamy's establish a textile factory around Nashville?"

"Yeah, around 1850, I think, maybe 1849."

So something added up; she wasn't sure what that something was, but it was something.

"Drew, he's not a ghost."

"OK? Then explain to me what's going on." Drew said.

"Arodi, what do you see around us?"

Arodi looked around the grounds. "To our left is the maple sapling my aunt and uncle planted over the grave of their beloved Newfoundland. To our right are the fields where I see my uncle riding, and the forest is just down the hill. We're digging a pond down there, too, since it's the lowest point and often collects water."

"What about people? Do you see any other people around?"

"No."

Marnie took back her phone from Arodi. "Drew, I am the last person who would ever draw this kind of conclusion, and I even hesitate to suggest or entertain it, but..."

"Oh my gosh," Drew appeared to be catching onto her train of thought.

"But it's the only thing that makes any sort of sense,"

"Say it, say it, say it!" Drew had his fists clenched together and teeth gritted.

Marnie sighed, "There's a hole in time."

"Yes!" Drew cheered and fist-pumped.

*Seven*

"But I don't understand what it means," Arodi said.

The trio sat upon French Louis XIV-style benches at a composite stone table that hadn't been moved since the 1840s. They were near an old well southeast of the house and tucked into a wooded area rarely trafficked, hidden by Green Mountain Boxwoods. The only clue to this secluded existence was the flagstaff stepping stones leading from the main mulched path to this grassy section. Sunlight filtered through the leaves, creating splotches and patches of light around them.

"Drew says it means that gravitational ripples in the fabric of space and time have some serious effects on Earth," Marnie explained, even though it made little sense to her. She wondered if all of this was just a dream. She could envision telling Briscney or her aunt and uncle about a hole in time and a man she met from the 19th century. Insisting upon the veracity of such tales could soon land her in front of white-robed professionals with clipboards. *Would you believe the story if you heard it? No.* It wasn't a story that could ever be told. In fact, it wasn't a story at all; it was an experience, and experiences can only be felt.

"It doesn't make sense to me," Arodi confessed, slightly shaking his head. "I don't see how it can be possible."

Drew scrolled on his phone.

"It's what Drew told me," Marnie offered.

"So you're from the future? And where is Drew from? And why can't I see him?" Arodi asked.

"Actually, no, Arodi. Drew and I are in our time and you are in yours. We aren't in 1849 with you."

"But your world looks just like mine. I guess not much has changed."

"No, you're not in my world. You can't see my world, and I can't see yours. No one from my time can see you except me, and it's probably the same for your time. I don't think your family can see me even though you can." Marnie sounded like she was doing an Abbott and Costello routine.

"Why?" Arodi asked the million-dollar question.

"I don't know. Drew's working on it right now." Marnie patted Arodi's hands, offering some level of comfort.

He seemed unnerved trying to grasp this new information because it was unnerving. The pages of countless fiction novels had borne fruit in Nashville, Tennessee, of all places, and now, in her time of all times, with Marnie Foster, of all people, receiving the cornucopia of its offerings, which consisted mostly of questions, bewildered looks, stumped expressions, disbelief, and a healthy dose of awe.

"I think I found it," Drew said, looking at his phone.

"Great, what is it?" Marnie asked. Her hands rested on top of Arodi's.

"OK, it looks like March 15th, both Washington State and Louisiana picked up the same gravitational wave signal, and that's the day Arodi first saw you, right?"

"We think so." She looked at Arodi and said, "Drew's explaining more to me. I'll tell you in a minute."

Arodi nodded.

"These two black holes converged, and that seemingly small ripple from their union spliced the years together, creating some sort of bridge through time," Drew proposed.

"But why and how? I don't get it. I need more info, Science Man." Marnie wanted answers.

"I don't know. I'm a forensic guy, not quantum physics; my guess is that it has something to do with frequencies. Like the two of you have some sort of attraction because of the frequencies you emit, and that's how you're able to see each other. Something in your makeup allows you two to connect."

"You lost me." *And there is no way I'm about to tell Arodi we are attracted to each other.* Marnie removed her hands from atop Arodi's.

"I lost myself." Drew stared at his phone, seemingly lost in thought. Then he looked up with wide eyes. "Do you have any idea what this means for the world of science?"

Marnie expected lightning to flash and thunder to sound from behind Drew at that moment, and she scanned his eyes to see if there was a crazy streak running through them. "We can't prove any of it." She instinctively felt protective of Arodi.

"No, you're right." Drew hung his head and rubbed his neck. "Wait," here came the eureka moment, "I've got some equipment. I'll be back in twenty minutes. Stay put, and don't let him leave." Drew raced off before she could object.

She watched as he rounded the side of the mansion and disappeared.

"Drew's gone, but he'll be back," Marnie said.

"What did he say? What is his understanding of this?"

"I don't know how to explain it. He thinks that somehow there's a bridge connecting us in time because of two black holes crashing together, and for reasons we don't understand, only you and I can see each other. It's not much of an explanation, but I'm sure he'll keep working on it."

Arodi nodded. "I've heard of black holes, but they are just a theory in my time. This is a most puzzling occurrence."

Marnie agreed. She wasn't sure what to say to Arodi. Having Drew there before helped avoid any awkward moments.

"Are we alone? Or are there others near us?" Arodi looked around their surroundings.

"There are some tourists over by the mansion, but they can't hear us. What about you?"

"I see my brother, but I don't think I could explain this to him right now. I don't even understand it." Arodi looked down at the table in front of him and sighed. "Tell me again why there are tourists here?"

"Oh, your uncle's mansion is an attraction in Nashville. All fifty-five acres."

"Fifty-five? His estate is five thousand acres." Arodi appeared surprised with a touch of offense.

"Well, there are fifty-five acres now dedicated to these botanical gardens in Nashville."

A mockingbird sang a medley overhead.

"Do I look like a tourist?"

Marnie laughed, "No, fashion has changed a lot."

"Then who did you think I was the night we met? My clothes didn't alarm you?"

"Well, in my time, a lot of women work for a living and it's my job to help prepare for the Swan Ball, so we asked some clothing designers to come here and showcase their work. I thought you were one of the models showing me the Victorian attire."

Arodi laughed. It was a warm and deep laugh.

"Who did you think I was?" Marnie asked.

"At first, I thought you were a neighbor living on another estate, and you did not want to speak to me without a chaperone present. Then my brother thought you were a commoner because I told him you were helping to plan the party. I wasn't sure who you were; I just knew I wanted to get to know you."

*Drew! Why did he have to go and use that word? Attraction. What did it mean anyway? Magnets were attracted to each other; moths to flames; bees to flowers; it's just natural.* Marnie looked at Arodi. *As natural as Arodi's chiseled jawline, amazingly shaped brows, and those breathtakingly dark latte puddles he has for eyes.* Marnie cleared her throat and sat erect on the bench. Imagination had once been a friend to her, assisting her with creative and decorative concepts that landed her this internship, but now it acted as a tempting foe, and she couldn't prevent it from running away with her. Or was she running along with it?

Arodi looked toward the mansion. "I'm trying to see it all. It sounds wonderful, except for the fifty-five-acre part. Can you tell me more about Nashville? What kind of a city is it, what does it become? And our nation? We are struggling at present with slavery, a vile institution. What happens, Marnie?"

*Slavery?* Marnie wanted to cry. In a few short years, Arodi's country would be ripped apart by the issue. What it would do to families living in Nashville wasn't a conversation she would ever be able to bring herself to have. From there, her thoughts quickly went to other events, more wars, economic, and natural disasters; it would be too much for him to handle. So, while Marnie was allowed to glimpse into the past, she had to limit Arodi's glimpse into the future.

"I don't think that's a wise thing to tell you all about that, Arodi. I've seen a lot of movies where it doesn't work out so well for the characters when you do that."

"Movies?"

Marnie winced, "and I've already said too much." Marnie wasn't skilled at censoring herself when it came to knowing how little or how much to share about modern times. "Why don't you tell me more about the 1840s? I learned some things in history class, but there's nothing like firsthand knowledge."

"Well, in 1849, I live in New York; do you know it?"

Marnie smiled, "Yeah, I've heard of it."

"I live there with my family, and we run textile factories. My uncle and father are men of impeccable character and strive to be fair and just with all of our employees. He's asked me to come here to find a location for a new factory."

"What do you do for fun in New York?"

"Theater, opera, minstrel shows, and I like watching this new sport, baseball. The New York Knickerbockers; they are swell to watch."

Marnie smiled. *If he thinks the Knickerbockers are something to write home about, wait'll he sees the Yankees. What? Are you going to take him to a game? He can't see your world.*

Arodi kept talking, "I like walking in all of the parks we have. Have you ever heard of the Croton Fountain?"

"No."

"It's an aqueduct bringing fresh water to New Yorkers, and the fountain has water fifty feet high. I love going to City Hall Park to sit by it. It would be nice to have a feature like that here at Cheekwood."

"It would be lovely here." Marnie clasped her teeth around the inside of her cheek. *Don't ask. Don't say it. Don't go there. You know better.* "What about religion?" Marnie never could shy away from controversial topics. *Why do you care? Why are you asking him? Is it for altruistic reasons or for reasons you refuse to admit?*

"I don't have an easy answer for that. My father has traveled extensively in Asia and Africa. After procuring a Hebrew Bible and learning the language, we wouldn't say we were orthodox in our belief system. Not that the pendulum swings to a paganist viewpoint. We just want to follow Scripture, experience the glory of Yehovah, and understand as much as we can of His character. Yehovah is the Hebrew rendering of God's Name."

Marnie felt goosebumps on both arms. "You know Hebrew?" *Did he just use the Creator's Name? Yehovah, this man knows You?* It astonished her.

"Yes, my father taught us all when we were little. I don't use it daily, but I can read most things. I suppose I could carry on a conversation if necessary."

Marnie was in shock. Statistically, what were her chances of meeting an intelligent, articulate man from 1849 who appeared to have a belief system close to her own? Her mind reeled with improbable calculations. She tried carefully not to trip on her words. "My family and I are also learning Hebrew. We probably aren't as fluent as you, but we don't subscribe to any man-made religious system."

"Fascinating. Then do you believe our meeting is by design?"

*Why? Why would He? Yehovah, why would You do this? Did You do this?* Marnie's head whirled with questions, but she smiled and said, "Well, doesn't everything happen for a reason?" *Oh my gosh, I can't believe that I just said the most cliché church-speak phrase.*

"I believe it does."

A robin landed on the table and cocked its head before flying off.

"And I do believe we will discover the meaning behind our meeting," Arodi said with an assuring smile.

* * * * *

"Where did all of this equipment come from, anyway?" Marnie held up a black electronic device with a screen on it. Green neon lights flashed and moved up and down on it, much like roller coasters.

The trio remained at the table at Cheekwood. Two hours had passed since Drew's return, and he had brought with him a large cardboard box full of gadgets and gizmos. He'd been running all sorts of "tests" since his return. Marnie doubted many of the apparatuses did anything besides make noise and light up.

"Be careful with that," Drew said, taking the piece from Marnie and gently laying it on the table.

"Do I get to see another device?" Arodi asked.

"Here," Marnie picked the piece back up and handed it to Arodi.

He began looking it over, focused, intently looking at the buttons that made no sense to him. Marnie thought it was adorable, watching his wonder-filled eyes study the equipment.

"Would you stop doing that? You're going to lose something in 1849, and you could change history altogether. He could take a piece and alter everything. Like he could sell it to our enemies or something." Drew lectured. "Can you get it back?" He partly pleaded.

"Sorry," Marnie said to Drew. "Arodi, do you mind if I take that back?" She held out her hands.

He handed her the instrument carefully.

She placed it on the table.

"I am most fascinated by the relaxed candor the English language has taken on. I understand your meaning but only from context, vocal inflection, and body language."

"Well, I'm afraid we're some of the best specimens, and much of the English language isn't well spoken by Americans," Marnie explained.

Arodi nodded. "I see. My aunt often discusses how our language is changing, but I don't see the way it's evolved as problematic. I enjoy your form of speech."

"Our main dialect as a culture is sarcasm, and I'm sure your aunt wouldn't enjoy that."

Drew held up a syringe. "Can you get me a blood sample?" He asked with a smile. Or was it a crazed leer?

"Absolutely not. I draw the line there."

Drew rolled his eyes. "C'mon, we could analyze his DNA and discover all kinds of information about nutrition and diseases of the time period."

Marnie looked at Arodi, sweetly sitting there while she carried on a conversation with Drew. He was so childlike, and Marnie could never take advantage of his innocence.

She looked at Drew and spoke lowly. "No. No pricking, poking, or probing. We don't know how long we'll even be connected, so we're operating under the Hippocratic Oath and will not do any harm. Besides, we'd look like fools if we shared what we know, which isn't much, mind you."

"Oh no, I've got surefire tests we could run. Verifiable proof." Drew pulled out another hand-held device, flipped a switch, and held it in front of where Marnie said Arodi was sitting. "Look, this shows atmospheric variances that appear to be humanoid in form."

Marnie looked at the screen. She didn't see what Drew saw. She saw colored lines in a blob shape. "I'm pretty sure only The National Enquirer would buy this story and maybe not even them." Marnie placed a hand on Drew's. "No mad scientist stuff, OK? I can't risk Simone finding out we believe we're communicating with a Miller family relative from 1849."

"Why not? She'd think it was cool and probably try to channel the whole clan."

Drew was probably right.

* * * * *

"Or she'd toss me out of the company. Tuck away your 'evidence' and don't run to the papers, blog about it, or share with anyone what's going on here."

"Can I interview him? Like, put some questions together for you to ask him?"

"I'll think about it."

The sun was barely visible from the thick tree line. Marnie looked up. "We should get going."

"Yeah, I'll just start packing up." Drew carefully put his gadgets away into the box.

"You must go?" Arodi asked, sounding saddened.

"Yeah, it's getting late, and Drew's gotta help me move some stuff tonight." Marnie had already packed up most of her things at the cabin and planned to move to the main house tonight.

Drew closed his cardboard box. "Tell Arodi 'bye' for me."

"OK, I'll meet you at the car."

Drew made his way toward the parking lot visible from their spot at the table.

"Car?" Arodi asked.

Marnie grimaced. It was like having a child and forgetting not to talk about adult things around little ears. Marnie and Drew were going to give away the future's mysteries before they realized it.

"Do they call carriages 'cars' in the future?" Arodi inquisitively asked. "It's like an abbreviated form of the word? Is that what you meant about the English language changing?"

"I'm sorry, Arodi, I don't know how much to share and not to share. Maybe we've said too much already. I'm sure those tests we ran today only created a deeper thirst to know more about our world, but I must ask you to respect that there are some things I don't think we should discuss." She stood and smoothed out her dress.

Arodi slowly nodded. "Can you tell me this? Are horses extinct?" Arodi stood as well.

Marnie laughed. "No, and I actually live on a horse farm not far from here." She took a few steps in the direction where she saw Drew head.

"Wonderful. Where is it?" Arodi followed suit, and they began walking toward the parking lot.

"Close."

"If you could supply the latitude and longitude, I could ride to the location and meet you at some point in time when you feel it appropriate. I understand if you want Drew or another attendant present."

Marnie tried not to smile. While Arodi's ideas on chaperoning were antiquated in her time, she appreciated the role virtue and protection of that virtue played. "Maybe," Marnie felt reluctant to tell him exactly where she lived. *He's still a stranger. Are you going to tell a stranger where you live?* "You see, Arodi," Marnie turned to face him, "we don't know what's going on with this rift in time. I think we both need to process everything, and I'm trying to balance a full-time job, too."

"Working for Simone, is that right?"

"Right."

"She's your mistress?"

"Well, we don't use that terminology, but yes, I work for her. She calls the shots. This ball is so important, and I think I need to spend my time focusing on it."

"The Swan Ball?"

"Yes."

"So, it becomes an annual affair," Arodi said.

"Oh, that's right. The first one was in 1849."

"It's a very formal event, the one my aunt is planning," he spoke with pride.

"I can assure you, it's still very formal." Marnie thought about all of the magazine write-ups and pictures she'd seen of previous balls. Gowns, glamor, and glitz, it was a night to revel in all indulgences when it came to hair, makeup, jewelry, and attire. It was hands-down one of the most prestigious engagements throughout Nashville's calendar year.

"Do you have a male companion accompanying you yet?" Arodi asked with a smile, one Marnie considered flirtatious.

"No, I'm not attending the ball as a guest. I'm working during the ball, so it's not the right time to have a date." Marnie ran a hand over her suddenly chilled arm.

"Would it be possible for me to speak with you during the evening if you have time?"

Was he making a date with her? Was this man from over a hundred years in the past making a date with Marnie? Was she entertaining the idea of accepting?

"I can't promise I'll have more than five minutes that night, but if you see me here, you can say 'hello.'"

Arodi grinned. "Thank you." He quickly looked toward the mansion as if he heard or saw something that captured his attention. "My brother is calling. I'm late for dinner. I should go."

"Sure." To Marnie, it was almost like Arodi were asking for permission to leave her. If she asked him to stay, would he? It wasn't a theory she decided to test.

He bowed his head and turned to go. He took a few steps, then he turned back. "Marnie, I do hope this bridge in time we're on lasts a little longer. I hope to see you again."

"Me, too."

"Please send my farewells to Drew. I should like to get to know him someday, too. Somehow." He said with a laugh.

"I will. Bye." Marnie gave a small wave as she watched Arodi walk toward the mansion and turn the corner into the shadows.

*Eight*

"I found some more info on Richard Miller's trips to the Amazon. He inspired a fiction novel. Wanna hear?" Drew asked while applying strong-smelling muscle cream after helping Marnie move "a few" things into the main house. He moved her entire wardrobe, a printer, an air purifier, and some heavy boxes full of items Marnie declared were "must-haves" in the main house.

At present, he had his laptop open and had been sharing all of the Bellamy family trivia he could find.

They ate popcorn while a Netflix documentary about sunken treasure played in the background.

Marnie wore comfortable cotton pajamas and had been able to unpack a fair portion of her belongings upstairs. "No, I don't. I don't want to know anymore, Drew. It's not safe. I could blab it to Arodi by accident, and then, as you said, I could change history. Leave me out of whatever you find. It's hard enough not telling him about the Civil War, Lincoln's assassination, and the other disasters that occurred during his lifetime."

"Hmm, lifetime. Do you want to know when he dies?" Drew started typing.

The thought was a dagger to Marnie's heart. Instantly, she felt her eyes tear up. Imagining Arodi dead wasn't possible, but she knew it would have happened historically. If Drew told her how, and if it was untimely, Marnie knew she'd try to stop it. She couldn't be trusted with such information. She waited for him to stop typing. "Did you find anything?" Curiosity was in cahoots with her imagination, and they both took her places she didn't need to go.

"No. It's hard because the Bellamy's are only relatives to the Millers. There's not a lot of information on the Internet, but I can check the archives."

"Don't tell me anything you find. I don't want to know, OK?"

"Got it." Drew started typing. "So, are you gonna tell Briscney?"

"What would I even tell her?" Marnie knew watching the documentary was pointless. Drew obviously wanted to talk.

"I don't know. Tell her you have a boyfriend from another century."

"He's not my boyfriend." She harmlessly elbowed Drew.

Drew grinned. "Look, even though I couldn't see him, I know you like him.

You stared at him, not in the objective observation way. I knew you weren't looking at the hedge, and your tone totally betrayed you. You like him," he teased.

Marnie was silent.

"What, no retort?"

"I don't even know him, so I can't respond to what doesn't make sense." She turned her attention back toward the documentary. *Drew, why do you have to say things like that? Like him? I don't know. What does that even mean? Why are you planting those thoughts in my head? Can't we just get to know each other and then make a determination? Oh yeah, like there's a future with a man from another century.* "No one would believe me anyway that I met a man from 1849. You didn't, and you were there to witness it. They'll just think the cell phone disappearing demonstration is a cheap parlor trick. So, no, I'm not saying a word to anyone."

"You could say it's a long-distance relationship." Drew chuckled to himself after he said it.

Marnie gave Drew the side-eye, which was becoming a signature response to Drew's attempts at humor: "Not funny."

* * * * *

Monday arrived, and Marnie awoke with renewed exuberance to go to work. Was it the promise of that potential promotion she faced with Jasmine Rose, or was it in hopes that she would see Arodi at Cheekwood? *Nonsense, I'm genuinely ready to go to my job. This is how I go to work on a Monday. This is normal.* Her heart sank a little when she saw the wilted carnation on her bedside, but she couldn't bring herself to toss it just yet.

Marnie selected navy pants, a matching long-sleeved navy shirt, and a navy and white duster over the top. She wore a pair of low navy heels. She accented the outfit with silver hoop earrings and a thin silver watch. She wore her hair fuller and down, using mousse to help keep it in its current coiffed state.

Makeup was still a simple affair; Marnie used a little eyeshadow, liner, and mascara and added a quick run of clear gloss over her lips. She attributed her clear complexion to proper hydration, non-chemical soaps, and using the right kind of essential oils on her skin.

"You certainly look the part of Jasmine Rose," Aunt Ginny mentioned as Marnie entered the kitchen.

"I'd say so. Very professional," Uncle Caleb added.

"Thanks." Marnie smiled and opened the fridge. She found a large mason jar filled with orange juice. It was the designated jar for freshly squeezed orange juice, and there was no substitute for it. Marnie pulled it out and filled a small glass.

"I've almost finished this omelet for your uncle, but he won't mind if I give it to you. Are you hungry?" Aunt Ginny offered. She took her apron off and began folding it up.

Marnie looked to her uncle for his blessing on taking his breakfast.

"Go ahead." He nodded. He adjusted his newspaper and returned to reading.

"Thank you." Marnie chose to stand at the kitchen island to eat.

"What's on tap today at Cheekwood?" Uncle Caleb asked.

"Simone wants me to plan out where to hang fairy lights. She made a map, so I have to scope out the locations and provide my recommendations."

"You should hang some on that back-wooded pathway, just off the yard, you know, by the large urn?" Aunt Ginny suggested. "It's perfect. It's secluded and private, but it would be so lovely lit up."

"I'll check it out. Great idea." Marnie finished her omelet and cleaned her breakfast items. "See you guys later!" She pecked her uncle and aunt on their cheeks and left.

Cheekwood was warmer this morning. Spring was making its presence known, shooing winter out the door. Marnie's breath no longer registered in the morning air. No longer did she have to cover her head and hands in the early hours to protect herself from the cold. She even cracked the window on her drive over to inhale that glorious, fresh morning air.

Marnie started her walk in the place Aunt Ginny suggested, down a few steps from the mansion's backyard surrounded by trees, oaks, hawthorns, and the hedges with the Woodland Trails path cutting through the sequestered nook. It was private, and Marnie saw a welcoming stone bench resting in a curve-shaped section of the space. Aunt Ginny was right. This was the perfect place to hang fairy lights. Marnie pulled out her phone and took pictures, then sat down on the bench as she made notes on where she thought the best places for fairy lights would be: in the surrounding hedges and a few around two of the oak trees' trunks and, if possible, wrapped around a few low-hanging branches, too.

"Good Morning," Arodi said, approaching, possibly wearing the same clothes he'd worn the last time Marnie had seen him. *I'm sure they don't have the wardrobe then like we do now, which I guess isn't a bad thing. You would save a ton of money.*

Arodi kept one hand behind his back as he stood before her.

Marnie smiled, pausing from her note-taking. "Hello."

"Was your weekend restful?" Arodi asked.

"It was, and yours?"

"Similar to yours. May I join you?" Arodi pointed to the bench she sat upon.

"You mean there's a bench in 1849 in this exact spot?" Marnie was surprised at how little some things had changed since then.

"Indeed."

"Sure, then." Marnie scooted over so Arodi could sit with her. "What's behind your back?" she playfully asked.

Arodi smiled. "I wasn't sure what was blooming now, but here's what we have in my time." He presented a gorgeous bouquet of tulips tied together with an olive ribbon.

"These are lovely. Thank you." Marnie accepted the flowers, and Arodi sat next to her. Just when she was missing the carnation he'd tenderly tucked behind her ear, he gave her a gorgeous bouquet of brilliant flowers. She admired the vibrant yellow and white tulips. Then she wondered if she was supposed to return the gesture with a gift. *I think I have a peppermint in the bottom of my purse.* What did Arodi expect? What was the social protocol for 1849? *Wait, did you only give flowers to your sweetheart? And by me accepting this gift, are we an item, or did we just get engaged?* Marnie now wasn't sure if she should keep the flowers. Did keeping them mean anything? She looked Arodi's way.

He didn't seem to expect anything in return. He just sat there with a small smile on his face.

She breathed a little easier.

"Are you working on something for the ball?"

"Yes." Marnie put her bouquet down next to her and put the cap on her pen. The note-taking could wait.

"Can you tell me about it?"

"I could, but then that might steal Mr. Edison's thunder, and we don't want that to happen, do we?"

"I don't believe I know Mr. Edison. Is he a friend of yours?"

"Let's put it this way. I can't tell you what I'm doing. It would give away too much of the future."

"I understand." Arodi looked around their setting. "This would be a lovely place for dancing. It's a very intimate space."

"Yes, my aunt recommended it." *Intimate? Why that word?* Marnie tried to ignore the goosebumps as they popped up on her arms as she pondered Arodi's word choice.

"Oh, is she here with you today?"

Marnie laughed. "No, she's at home. It's just me today."

"Is she with your parents? You haven't mentioned them. Are they living?"

"Yes, they are working with orphans and the local population in Costa Rica."

"Fascinating. And your aunt, is she married?"

"Yes, Aunt Ginny is married to Uncle Caleb, and Drew is their son."

"I understand." Arodi cleared his throat.

Marnie noticed he did that when he was risking rejection by asking her a question. It was adorable.

"I was thinking of taking a ride later. Would you care to join me? That is if you brought your horse. I see you are in pants, which must be common in your time, and I suppose it makes better sense for riding. I should like to see my sisters wearing pants; they often complain when riding horses in their dresses."

Marnie smiled at his train of thought. He worked with what information he had and deduced conclusions that made sense to him.

"Tell you what, Arodi," Marnie pulled out her phone and looked up the latitude and longitude of the farm. She took out a pen and a small scrap of paper. She wrote down the coordinates and handed Arodi the paper. "Can you read that, alright?"

"I can."

"That's where I live, so if you want, we can meet over there today around three o'clock. How does that sound?"

"Wonderful." He studied the paper.

"Great, I have a lot to get done before then, so you're welcome to stay, but I can't talk."

"Of course. I will leave you to your duties and join you this afternoon. Farewell." He bowed.

"Bye." Marnie returned to her project as Arodi walked away.

* * * * *

Arodi walked on the path toward the mansion with stars in his eyes. He couldn't hide his bigger-than-life smile. Moments in Marnie's presence carried him through the hours, sometimes days before he saw her again. She was kind and lovely and always smelled so good. Fresh. Clean. He'd spent a solid hour choosing the loveliest tulips from his aunt's garden. White and yellow together reminded him of Marnie. He wasn't sure of their meaning in her time, but he hoped they didn't convey the wrong message. His aim was friendship, always friendship.

He tripped as he walked up the stone steps from the walkway toward the backyard of the mansion where the family often had breakfast. Why did he trip? He was thinking of friendship in his head, but his heart was revealing something else, and the tug-of-war between the two was absolutely no match for his feet, so he lost his balance. Thankfully, he caught himself in time before scraping a knee and recovered swiftly. He continued his walk toward the mansion, having fully regained his ability to walk and think at the same time.

"Where do you keep disappearing to?" Ari asked, seated outside at a breakfast table adorned with matching porcelain dishes depicting scenes from the English countryside in blue paint. He wore a cutaway morning coat with light trousers and dark boots, suitably dressed for the day.

Arodi joined his brother, noticing an extra place setting had already been used. He guessed his aunt had already had breakfast.

"Aunt Belinda wondered where you were this morning," Ari said, nodding toward her chair. He sipped from his teacup. His utensils rested on his plate, so he had already eaten.

"I took a walk."

Fallon, the house servant, came outside wearing a brown dress, white bib apron, and cap. As Arodi sat down, she poured his tea from a porcelain pot and coffee from a silver one.

"Thank you, Fallon," Arodi said.

"You're welcome, sir." Her Irish accent remained untarnished by her time in America, much like the vibrant red hair that poked out from under her cap. She slightly bowed and moved inside.

Arodi carefully cracked the shell of his soft-boiled egg as it rested in its pressed-glass egg cup. He scooped out some of the yolk and took a bite. Then, he buttered and added jelly to toast from the breadbasket.

Fallon returned with a warm plate of salmon and potatoes.

"Thank you."

"Yes, sir." She quickly departed.

"I thought you and our darling aunt would enjoy the quietness together this morning. Besides, I am here for the summer while you're only staying another week or so. Don't you want to have all the time you can with our aunt?" Arodi added four lumps of sugar to his tea.

"Well, in our morning chat, our dear aunt let on that she's matchmaking for you." Ari smiled, "And by that look on your face, this is the first time you've heard about it."

"Who? When? There haven't been any female callers in my time here. To my knowledge, Our neighbors don't have any eligible young ladies." Arodi finished his egg.

"Oh yes, except your ghost woman," Ari teased. "How is she, by the way?"

"She's not a ghost."

"So, you have been seeing her, haven't you? That's where you've been. She's here, isn't she?"

Ari looked behind him at the hedge where Arodi came from. He turned back around to face Arodi. "Well, our dear aunt has no predilections for anyone except Nelly Taylor."

Arodi made a face.

Ari laughed. "She isn't that bad. It's not like I said you were being set up with Medusa." Ari referenced the Greek monster that had snakes for hair and could turn anyone to stone if they gazed upon her.

"Nelly is seventeen," Arodi said. He sipped his warm tea, letting it linger in his mouth before swallowing its sweetness. Simultaneously, he thought about Marnie. Why did he think of her when the idea of matchmaking arose? All he wanted was friendship, didn't he?

Arodi bit his tongue. It was becoming a pattern. His head would declare friendship was what he wanted, and then his heart would demand attention by messing with his motor skills and now his ability to chew. *I don't know her all that well, but yes, I suppose there could be some pleasant feelings of attraction for her.*

Was this the time to tell his brother the truth about Marnie? How would he even begin to describe the past few weeks to Ari in a way that would make sense and not find himself on bed-rest for the remainder of the summer? Arodi shook his head and rubbed his cheek. Now was not the time to share with his brother.

"And you're twenty-six. I fail to see the issue. She's at a fine age for marriage. Our parents were married young, and it turned out fine for them." Ari placed his napkin on the table.

"We are worlds apart. Hers is a plantation family. We're industry people who don't own slaves."

"Now, now, you know Nelly herself is an abolitionist. Why, I clipped the article from the paper in New York. She wrote a wonderful piece; it was very well written for someone so young. She has no control over her parents, and I've often heard her say that since she was little, she couldn't wait to move to New York. The Taylors are good people. It would be a good match."

"Then why don't you pair with her?" Arodi offered, pointing his salmon-covered fork in Ari's direction.

"And give up my bachelor life in New York?" Ari laughed. "Aunt Belinda is going to marry us off one at a time, starting with the oldest." Ari sat back in his white wrought iron chair.

"We're three years apart. You're just as much at the age to wed as I am."

Ari nodded.

"Are the Taylors in town? Or is she matchmaking from afar?" Arodi asked.

"Yes, I do believe their family has let an estate two farms over through the summer. They say it's not as hot here as in Atlanta. I'll take my New York summers anytime. I feel the humidity already choking me."

"Have you met with them?"

"No, Aunt Belinda received a correspondence and invited them over sometime."

"When?"

Ari pulled out his pocket watch. "Well, they will be here this afternoon in time for tea."

Arodi finished his tea. "This sounds more like a pairing for convenience's sake than anything. I'm sorry that I won't be able to join you all this afternoon."

"She's not going to let you miss tea today."

"I have a ride scheduled. It's not something I can change. Besides, how can I miss an engagement I was never invited to?" Arodi placed his napkin on the table.

"And just with whom would this ride be with, might I inquire?"

Arodi could never hide a thing from his brother. Ari could rival any archaeologist with his digging skills.

"I told you. There's a young lady I've met, and I've been keeping her company. We plan to meet at her family's estate today. Which reminds me," Arodi rang a bell.

Fallon appeared.

"Fallon, would you bring me the Tennessee atlas from the library?"

"Yes, sir." Fallon returned indoors.

"Atlas? How far is this place? Kentucky?"

"I am not sure, but I know it's close by."

As the brothers waited for Fallon to bring the atlas, they listened in comfortable silence to the birds' morning songs while the bugs played all around them.

Fallon returned carrying a leather-bound book. "Here you are, sir."

"Thank you."

Fallon began clearing the breakfast dishes.

Arodi opened the atlas and looked at his hand, confirming he'd recalled the numbers correctly. He had. "Here it is." He moved the book so Ari could see it.

"There's nothing over there. That's the farm next to ours. There's no estate over there. She's deceiving you." Ari was perpetually protective of his brother's interests.

How could Arodi explain to Ari that there would be a house in this location in the future and that their uncle's five thousand acres would be dwindled down to fifty-five?

"It's not worth missing your date for tea for, I'll tell you that," Ari said.

"If the Taylors are letting a place through the summer, there will be plenty of engagements and visits. Missing this one tea time will be without consequence."

"Not when you're playing the role of the bridegroom."

"I do not find your words humorous, Ari." Arodi turned the atlas back toward him, planning his route over Hill and Dale. Her estate was close to the Harpeth River and, according to Arodi's calculations, a little over six miles from his uncle's, as the crow flies. If he cantered his horse part of the way, he could make it to her estate in under an hour.

He was elated that she was so close, and yet, he wondered what her station in life was that she had to travel at least an hour to work every day. Perhaps carriages were much faster in her time. He hated to think she endured any form of hardship traveling to and from work. He thought of various ways he could help with her transportation, applying 1849 wisdom to the future. *If her horse isn't fast enough, I could offer her one of mine. I'll give her the fastest one I own. I could also gather a couple of hundred dollars for a horse if I'm not able to get one to her.* It was in Arodi's nature to fix, to cure, to find a way to make things better for someone.

"I wouldn't tell Aunt Belinda about your companion. She won't take kindly to her plans being thwarted."

"Why can't she leave well enough alone? I'll do just that when I am ready to find a wife. I will find her. I don't require any assistance from anyone in that arena."

"Arodi!" Aunt Belinda's musical voice carried on the air.

Arodi thought it was coming from near the place where they were digging a new pond.

"You'd better go," Ari suggested. "Try not to get lured into a trap while you're at it. I have my suspicions about your mystery woman."

"She's harmless."

Arodi grabbed two more slices of bread as he stood. His plan was to sneak around the back of the mansion, go downhill to the carriage house, saddle his horse, and get an early start on his journey.

He surreptitiously made his way, dodging the sound of his aunt's voice as she called for him on the grounds.

Ari would provide an excuse for him; he was a good brother.

## *Nine*

Arodi and Marnie sat under a poplar tree full of green leaves by the Harpeth River. It lazily flowed while the pair relaxed. Marnie had saddled up a horse and rode to the spot where she had told Arodi to meet her. The bay horse now stood tied to a tree, munching on leaves.

It was a storybook day that Emerson or Thoreau should've described or a day that should be captured in a Monet, Durand, or Cole painting. Foliage sprung forth from all facets of the forest. While green was the most prominent color, there were whites and blues, pinks and oranges accenting the forest with blossoms and buds. Insects flew, hummed, and buzzed, birds chirped and sang. Turtles basked in the warmth of the day from dead limbs resting on the bank, and a squirrel screeched from the treetops every now and then. Life surrounded the two while they spoke.

"Has Drew been able to ascertain why you and I can see one another?" Arodi had a stick in his hand and slowly ran it back and forth on the ground.

Marnie picked at the blades of grass surrounding the orange and white checkered blanket she sat upon. "He's doing as much research as he can, but so far, he hasn't been able to pin down any hard evidence."

Three bluebirds flitted by. Marnie watched as they raced skyward before disappearing into the branches of the trees across the bank from where they were.

"Have you decided to bring the company here to Nashville?" Marnie asked. *Obviously, I could just look it up for myself since it's not too hard to find information online about the Bellamy's.* She recalled Drew saying that the family brought a company to the region at some point, but she wasn't certain about the year.

"I am very favorable to the idea."

They shared a smile.

"My aunt is favorable to marry me off." Arodi cleared his throat as he spoke.

Marnie's heart raced. Raced, or it flung itself back and forth against her rib cage in a violent protest that Arodi could marry another? She noticed, but she played it cool. "Oh, to anyone you know?" She didn't think he sounded too keen on the idea, but she had to keep her emotions in check. *What if I just messed up his betrothal? No, no, no, I'm not going to look it up. I don't want to know.* She was lying to herself. Of course, she wanted to know. What good was having access to the riches of recorded history if she couldn't use the technology to find out about the things she was curious about concerning Arodi?

"She fancies a friend of the family. Nelly Taylor is visiting presently. I'm sure my aunt means for us to become better acquainted."

Marnie's horse chewed the bit loudly.

*Better acquainted? What does that mean? Like dating? Or like engaged? I need a book on relationships of the 1840s. No, I don't. Yes, I do.*

"Is your family also trying to find you a compatible suitor?" Arodi looked at her and stopped moving his stick.

Marnie smiled. Was he asking because he was just making conversation, or maybe he was asking because he was interested? "No, in my time, it's a decision each person makes, not their family."

"Do you fancy any suitors, then?"

"From my time?" Marnie asked.

"Yes."

"No." She wondered if he'd picked up on the flirty vibe she'd tried to pass off.

"What about from the year 1849?" Arodi asked with a smile.

He had indeed picked up on it, and he asked if she was interested in him. But how could she answer what she really thought when she didn't know? Besides, it wasn't right to pretend there was a future for the two of them anyway.

"Arodi, we don't know how long we'll be able to see one another."

"But we have time right now."

A monarch butterfly landed on Arodi's shoulder. Marnie didn't know if it was from her time or his. "Take this little fella, for instance. His life expectancy isn't comparable to ours, but that doesn't stop him from living in the time he has now. He's fully present where he's present."

"Well, he's just an insect. It's different for people."

"Marnie, I like spending time with you. Neither one of us is promised a tomorrow, but I enjoy your company."

"We hardly know each other."

"I'd like to continue to get to know you while knowing that it could end at any time." The butterfly flew away. "You're different from other people."

Marnie chuckled, "Well, I am the only person you know from the future, so that may have something to do with it."

"I don't think so. You're acutely observant, able to quickly process information, have an innate sense of justice, and embrace adventure with all of its unknowns. I haven't encountered many in my time with such a spirit."

"I hate to break it to you, but things haven't changed much; it's the same in my time. You're a breath of fresh air, refined, cultured, a gentleman."

"Could we continue to see one another?"

Marnie clasped the inside of her lip against her teeth as she thought. "Yes, I would like that." But how long could she resist her thoughts and feelings about this gentleman? Thoughts and dreams and hopes that could never be, and she was certain that he felt the same way about her.

Arodi pulled out his pocket watch.

It was the same one he had used the night they first met.

"I would love to stay, but it will take me some time to return home, and I must dress for a dinner tonight." He tucked his watch away. Arodi stood and offered hands to help Marnie up.

She accepted and stood.

He held her hands, and she didn't pull away. "When can I see you again?"

"I'll be at work tomorrow, so I'll see you then."

Arodi grinned with those beautifully straight, white top row of teeth showing. "Fantastic." He bowed his head slightly. "Until then." He released her hands.

Marnie waved as he departed, feeling ever so unsure of the multitude of emotions swirling inside. She wasn't sure what she wanted Arodi to be to her. A friend, certainly, but a love interest? Impossible. It wouldn't work, couldn't work.

How would that go over? Would she be the laughingstock all the way to a padded cell insisting she was in a relationship with a man from 1849? And what about Arodi? They'd lock him away, too.

*Eighteen forty-nine. Oh, Arodi.* He would bring a company to this location only to see a terrible battle in 1864 in Franklin, Tennessee. Marnie envisioned the Battle of Franklin playing out before her with Arodi innocently standing in the street as Union and Confederate soldiers encountered one another. Had a bullet found its way to Arodi? Had he left the area for safer ground? Had he tried to rescue dying men in their hour of extreme need, or had he risen to the occasion and volunteered to fight? What if soldiers burned his factory? What if he met financial ruin, and Marnie could stop it from happening? The endless possibilities manifested in dizzying fashion, both tormenting and tempting her. She could find out how he died. *Or dies. He's still alive right now, but in another time. Not your time.* This line of thinking was foolish and too torturous to continue.

She played out several heroic actions she could take by affecting the past from her time and hadn't noticed the descending sun or the chill in the evening air as she wandered around the farm.

Was Yehovah's plan to change history using Marnie?

Marnie felt a mosquito jab her, and with a slap, she realized she'd covered most of the farm, allowing her horse to graze. Now, she stood before the barn. The security light overhead attracted many bugs and illuminated the path before her.

Her horse snorted, telling Marnie it was past dinnertime. She led the mare in, unsaddled her, and gave her extra oats before placing her in a stall for the evening. On her walk back to the farmhouse, she noticed a missed call on her phone from Briscney.

"Hi, I saw you called," Marnie said.

"I'm flipping out a little."

"Are you OK? Is the baby OK?"

"The baby is fine. Jeremy called and said his firm is having a going away party for one of the partners. Can you guess where it is?"

"Mere Bulles?" Marnie chose an upscale restaurant in Brentwood, Tennessee.

"My house."

"What?"

"It gets better. The partner and her husband leave next week for a European tour, and the only evening they have available is Friday night. Marnie, this Friday night."

"What?" Marnie heard her. She just didn't know what to say.

"Jeremy said it would help his career if we hosted the party, leaving me with three days to prepare everything for Friday. I know Simone has you working a ton, but could you please help me plan this thing? It would mean the world to me."

Marnie would never refuse to help her best friend. "Sure, why don't you email me the number of people attending and any personal information on the partner, and I'll plan something. I'll send you some ideas tomorrow."

"You're a lifesaver. Thank you so much, Marnie."

"Anytime."

"I'm going to go soak in the tub and release some of this stress. I'll talk to you tomorrow."

"Bye." Marnie finished her walk to the farmhouse.

Aunt Ginny sat on the back porch, moving upon her metal glider. "Are you going to tell me about him?"

"Him?" Marnie wasn't sure she'd been able to hear Aunt Ginny over the pounding of her heart in her ears.

"I figure your frequent absences of late are due to the influence of a gentleman caller, though I can't guess why he's not made a debut here yet. Uncle Caleb doesn't bite that hard."

Marnie wished Aunt Ginny had seen Arodi on the farm earlier. Then, there would have been hope that their connection could continue.

Aunt Ginny moved silently to and fro.

"It's complicated, and I'm not sure it can work, but if it gets serious, we'll talk." It was the best Marnie could offer.

"If it's meant to be, it will." Aunt Ginny stood. "Supper's almost ready if you're interested." She walked inside.

Marnie stayed behind momentarily, peering into the darkness. *If she only knew.*

* * * * *

Marnie spent the evening poring over ideas for the party at Briscney's. She had to plan it for fifty people, which was no small undertaking. She received dietary needs, food allergies, personal preferences, and favorites of the partner. Marnie did some research on the partner to see if she had any interviews out there that would reveal more information to help her plan.

The temptation to look up Arodi Bellamy crept in like a slow-moving fog until it enveloped Marnie from her bed, where she sat with her laptop. Even taking a breath was difficult until she typed in his name in an Internet search.

"Twenty hits? Come on!" Marnie started clicking the sparse results only to read his name on a list of purported relations to the Miller family.

Drew walked by her bedroom doorway.

"Get in here!" She called.

"What's up? Did you see Arodi today?" Drew looked around her room. He whispered. "Is he in here right now?"

"Shh, close the door."

Drew did.

"Come here."

He walked over to her bedside.

"Look." Marnie turned her laptop to face Drew so he could see the Google hits.

Drew shook his head. "Why would you do this?"

"I had to know."

"No, you didn't. You wanted to know. Admit it, you want to change history. What happened to not wanting to know anything I found out? It's too tempting, isn't it?"

"Well, there's nothing here on him anyway, so it's not like I know anything to change. Why isn't there more?"

"He's one of a ka-jillion people who have walked on this earth and not achieved celebrity status. I'm sure the records kept on the Bellamys are not digitized, and you'd have to do some major digging to find out anything about them, which I don't recommend doing. What if you find out he's not who you think he is?"

"Like he's someone sinister? Not a chance."

"I'm just saying be careful. You can't un-know something once you know it. And you don't know what sharing information you learn could do to him or history itself."

"I don't tell him stuff, Drew. I don't try to poison him with details about our world."

"I didn't say you did. I just think you need to be careful. If I knew something negative was going to befall people I cared about, I would do anything to stop it, and he's going to bring a company here. That company is going to be in the crosshairs of a bloody battle. I don't know the history well enough to tell you what happens, and I'm not sure I want to."

"But maybe that's why we're in his life. Have you ever thought of that?"

"I have thought about it. It's pretty heady stuff, that's all." Momentarily, silence enveloped the two.

"Well, on a lighter note, why don't you go grab your computer and help me plan an event for Briscney?"

"Sure."

The two tossed ideas well into the evening before retiring.

## Ten

"Arodi, you're sitting here next to Nelly." Aunt Belinda said as Arodi escorted Nelly into the low-lit dining room where dinner was being served.

Nelly was plain. Her face wasn't memorable, but it wasn't offensive. Her dark hair was naturally curly, and she kept it pinned up very closely to her head. She resembled her English relatives with her fair skin and reserved manner. She wore a long off-white dress to dinner and thanked Arodi as he pulled out her chair for her.

Ari sat across from them with a constant grin on his face.

Arodi knew Ari found his aunt's matchmaking amusing. *Just wait, young man. Your day is coming.*

Richard Miller, Arodi's uncle, entered the dining room with Nelly's father, Winthrop, a heavy-set man, and her mother, Amelia, fancifully dressed and flaunting her wealth. They conversed about their latest trips to Europe while they entered.

"What is it we're having for dinner tonight, Fallon?" Richard asked as he sat down at the opposite end of the table from Belinda.

Arodi watched as Amelia's eyebrows raised. She appeared astonished that Richard would address a servant in the presence of the company.

"Vegetable soup, steak with potatoes and broccoli, and a cider cake for dessert, sir."

"That sounds wonderful."

"Fallon, you may serve the soup." Aunt Belinda said.

"Yes, madam." Fallon left the dining room.

Arodi watched Amelia make eye contact with Winthrop. *Why are they here? Slaveholders. Eating our food. My father would say something. He would object.* Arodi took a sip of water.

"Arodi is staying with us while he scouts out a place to build a textile factory." Aunt Belinda started. "It helps having him here. I don't miss my own children so much who are traveling with my parents to Africa for the summer."

"Is that where you keep disappearing to?" Winthrop said. "I've tried to meet you a few times but always seem to miss you. I would happily lend my expertise in scouting out the perfect place to build your factory."

"I'm seeking a cost-effective location."

"What's a few more dollars here and there to have the best place in town?" He laughed.

"When you pay your laborers, money is important."

Ari looked at Arodi, wide-eyed.

The entire room was speechless.

Arodi looked into Winthrop's eyes. *There's no possible way this man would ever want me to marry his daughter now.*

Fallon entered the dining room carrying a tray with bowls of soup. She began serving the silent party.

Winthrop averted his eyes from Arodi's glare.

"Father has recently started allowing our workers to hire themselves out as tradesmen." Nelly did her best to save the dinner and, quite possibly, the relations between the two families. Her words did not soften Arodi's countenance.

Fallon finished serving the soups and left the room.

"Workers? They aren't really workers, are they?" Arodi accurately observed.

"Well, the law says they are my property, and many fine men I know don't even hire their chattels out," Winthrop explained.

Arodi was furious. "I am not standing for this." He bolted upright.

Aunt Belinda was white. Uncle Richard was red.

"I'm not sitting here breaking bread with this man."

Ari had a look of utter amazement on his face.

"Mr. Taylor, I do not want your assistance in scouting a location for my company. I would much rather you scout your own heart and seek out grounds to build a place of compassion and righteousness for mankind regardless of a man's religious or ethnic background. My people were once also enslaved, and my heart goes out to all those living in oppressive environments. I refuse to dine with you upon my convictions. I also refuse to remain culturally polite and silent on an issue as pervasive as slavery. Now, if you'd like to converse on how to go about freeing and providing fairly for the men and women you legally, though certainly not ethically, own, I would be interested in assisting. Good evening," he turned to Nelly, "Miss Taylor." He bowed. Arodi walked out of the dining room with his head high.

He did not know if the evening was salvaged until Ari joined him in the kitchen, where he spoke with Fallon and the groomsman, Lorcan.

"What on earth was that?" Ari asked.

Arodi ate a bite of cider cake. "That was bold. I imagine now they'll be no more matchmaking with the Taylors."

"Not from Mr. and Mrs. Taylor, but Miss Taylor was clearly smitten. She watched you leave, and then, as she played the piano, she spoke of how much she admired your position and fervor."

"She'd never go against her father's wishes."

"I don't know if she'll have to. I watched Mr. Taylor sit, seemingly lost in thought over the words you spoke. And then I heard him ask Uncle Richard if you were serious in your offer to assist him."

"I can't believe it. No, he was just being polite."

Quick steps echoed down the hall leading to the dining room. All eyes looked towards the door leading into the kitchen.

Aunt Belinda entered.

Fallon and Lorcan surreptitiously disappeared, and Ari moved away from her line of sight.

"I do not support slavery, and if I went around judging everyone for their wrongs and refusing to have a connection, I'd be awfully lonely. The Taylors are imperfect people, just as your uncle and I are, and as are you. That was rude, embarrassing, and disrespectful. What do you have to say for yourself?" Her stare was plenty enough of a reprimand. Add to it both hands on her hips and the silence that now filled the entire room, and Arodi was at risk of being tossed out of the Millers' residence.

"I won't put up with pretenses."

"Pretenses? You brought up slavery, Arodi. You rudely began your discourse of your opinion in front of our guests. You picked a battle, not Mr. Taylor."

"If battles like these aren't picked between those who see slavery as an injustice and those who see it as a right, then I guarantee you, there will be a war over it. Men have time to make it right now before there's no turning back. I may be one of the few who sees the handwriting on the wall, but it is my duty to show others, to decipher what is surely to come."

Aunt Belinda softened. "There's no talking to you. You are your father made over. Nashville isn't New York."

"Are you sending me home?"

"Arodi, I would never ask you to leave. I would only ask you to pray before you speak and consider there is a time, place, and manner to convey your convictions." Aunt Belinda sighed. "I would also avoid your uncle for a few days. He's slower to forgive."

Arodi nodded.

"I'm retiring now. Goodnight." She exited the kitchen.

"That wasn't as bad as I thought," Arodi said.

"I told you, you got to Winthrop. He probably told them to go easy on you. That family isn't all that bad. Nelly's been working on them and why they may be a non-slaveholding family after tonight."

"One can only hope."

* * * * *

"Marnie, we've decided to create an enchanted forest carriage ride before dinner for our guests, so I want you to spend the day on the Woodland Trail deciding where we can place the various representatives from the different

62

charities that helped support Cheekwood. This idea came to me in a dream." Simone gave Marnie a colored map printed on glossy Cheekwood paper. "Just mark your placements here and decide the best placement for each of the charities on the list." She produced a document of several pages stapled together.

"Will do, Simone." Marnie held her package of papers and turned toward the trail.

"Keep up the great work. This is just the kind of hard work that leads to a promotion with us."

Marnie's eyes sparkled with those words. *So, she finds me valuable. An asset to the company.* "Thanks." As she made her way to the Woodland Trail, Marnie daydreamed about a future with Jasmine Rose, *an office overlooking the Cumberland. Standing reservations at all high-end restaurants. Clientèle consisting of royalty and top politicians.* Marnie redecorated Buckingham Palace and the White House and hosted dozens of events in both locations before she stepped in soft mud that covered the top of her boot. Humility wasn't yet a strength, but Marnie got the message. She ran her foot along some thick grass to get the mud off before starting on her present quest.

"Hello, there." Arodi quickened his steps as Marnie stood on the edge of the mansion's yard before a path that led down stone steps and into the woods. "Good morning," He bowed.

The bow. How antiquated it had become over time, but it made Marnie feel respected and even cherished.

Arodi approached in attire Marnie felt she must've previously seen—off-whites and browns that were simple. She wore a light blue sweater dress with gray tights, a black belt, and the now mud-free boots. The spring air felt warm on her arms.

"Hi," she said with a smile. "How was dinner last night?"

"Contrived." Arodi looked over his shoulder. "Shall we?" He gestured toward the woods.

"Is someone looking for you?" Marnie looked over his shoulder as if she would be able to discern who was hunting for him in 1849.

"Indeed."

Marnie and Arodi began their walk in the woods. "So, dinner, how was it?"

"My aunt is trying to salvage what she hopes will be a union between Nelly Taylor and myself."

The sunlight trickled through the treetops, splashed on the leaves, and rested gently on the forest floor in a few places.

"You don't sound convinced."

She's seventeen. She has a great family name, she is cultured, educated, refined, and in the South, but I'm not interested in marrying her."

Marnie wondered if Nelly came from a slaveholding family, but she couldn't go down that train of thought. She knew she'd start discussing the Civil War. That could alter everything.

"Well, why not just court her for a while?" Marnie teased.

Arodi shook his head. "That does not interest me."

She paused to make a note on the map she held. *Tennessee Children's Home should have this large sculpture for children to climb on if they bring them to the event.*

They picked up their pace again. For the most part, Arodi was quiet while she worked but presently asked, "When do women marry in your time?"

"Twenties, thirties, forties, fifties, there's not really a limit."

"What more can you tell me about life in your time?"

"Arodi, I can't tell you. I don't want to alter or change history."

The path wound to the left, the trees hugging tightly, narrowing the dirt pathway.

"Haven't you already?"

Marnie stopped at a collection of bronze sculptures and made some notes. "How?"

"Just by being here. By observation. It changes things."

Marnie shook her head. "You're way ahead of your time." *The observer effect.* She'd heard Drew speak about it before. Arodi espoused concepts and ideas that would be questioned in the future, Arodi's future.

"Can't you tell me something about what your life is like in your time? Anything?" He pleaded.

"Yeah, I have a huge party to plan for this Friday and not enough time to do this job and help out a friend."

"I will help." He offered with exuberance.

Marnie sighed, "Shouldn't you be scoping out a spot for your factory? Don't you have to work at all? I'm here every day, it seems like, trying to get this party planned, and you're always here." And he definitely was here, looking so adorable and wanting to spend time getting to know her better. *Here you are creating all sorts of marvelous distractions when I should be committed to finishing this task with the utmost excellence.*

Arodi stood ramrod before her. "I apologize. I shall leave you to your work. I was not aware my presence was so disruptive."

How was it possible her hand reflexively reached for his? She grabbed hold. She didn't consciously notice—or did she—but he grabbed back. "No, Arodi, I'm sorry. I'm a little stressed out, and 1849 probably isn't as fast-paced as it is now. It's none of my business how you run yours. Forgive me."

He looked down at their clasped hands. "Forgiven." His fingers gently caressed hers, setting her nerve endings aflame as they shot through every inch of her body. He treated his study of her hands like a scientist discovering a new species, poring over each pore and tracing over each line of her palm as if memorizing the look of her hands and the feel of them.

Marnie wasn't sure how long they stood gazing at one another, holding hands.

"I get it. It's a living mannequin piece. The bronze statues signify that over time, we become weathered when not moving, and this one was the embodiment of hope, but she, too, has fallen prey to the temptations of life and is herself becoming bronze." A woman's voice behind Marnie said.

Marnie realized she looked frozen in time to passersby.

"I disagree," a man's voice said, "It's the opposite. Nature is livening the statues and awakening their senses. She's the first, and the others will follow."

Marnie spun around.

The pair looked astonished.

"That's the beauty of art. It creates discussion. Now, if you'll excuse me," she quickly moved down the trail.

"What was all that?" Arodi asked, following after her.

"Patrons commenting on art."

Arodi paused and turned his head toward the mansion. "I apologize, Marnie, but my brother is calling. I should see what he needs. It sounds urgent."

"It's fine. I have a lot to get done today." Marnie hoped she was hiding the crestfallen look on her face as she looked downward. She pulled out a piece of paper. "If you want," she looked on her phone, then used a pen to write on the paper, "Meet me here at noon. This is the place where I'm planning the party." She handed him the scrap of paper with the latitude and longitude coordinates on it for Briscney's house. She didn't see any harm in enclosing a fragment of modern paper to him in 1849. Nothing had happened the first time she'd done it.

He took the paper from her and studied it. "I'll be there. Until then," he bowed.

"Bye." Marnie watched him disappear through the trees as she turned to focus on the map and her present duties.

Emerging from the forest that separated Marnie from his family, Arodi caught sight of Ari. Ari wore a military-style peaked hat and a brown cutaway coat, clearly dressed for riding. "Aunt Belinda will have your hide. You're supposed to be having tea right now. Were you visiting with your common friend?" Ari teased.

"It's an impossibility, Ari. I stand at this massive precipice, gazing below on lush, verdant, untainted realms and I wonder, how far, Ari? How far can I explore such a secreted, hallowed place?"

"Have you been reading Wordsworth again? You have the timbre of a poet this morning. Besides, all Aunt Belinda wants to discuss is Nelly Taylor, and you're expected to join them for tea at present." Ari pointed in the general direction of the mansion. "I would join you, but I've promised a fellow a hunt. We can discuss your betrothal later." Ari laughed, then walked toward the carriage house.

Arodi sighed. He stared back at the woods for a moment, thinking about the softness of her touch, the way she did not resist his study of her, and then the look. She felt it. She had to. There was a chemistry between them, an attraction. He had come to Nashville seeking a place for his father's business. He had come to spend some time with his family and explore this city on the cusp of the frontier he'd only read about in New York. He had not come to meet

Marnie, but now that he had, things changed for Arodi. He was in no hurry to return to New York, no hurry to choose a plot of land for the factory. Like the taste of the first bite of ripe peach, he wanted to savor each delicious moment in time that he spent with Marnie, coming not for her originally but planning to stay due to her influence.

Arodi smiled and then turned toward the mansion.

As he approached the outside wrought-iron table set for tea, he wondered if Nelly had come to smooth things over with the family after his outburst.

"My dear Arodi, you are impossible to track down. I nearly sent the hounds out to find you." Aunt Belinda mentioned as he strode up to the table. She was wearing a red and white striped dress with a matching hat bedecked with rubies around her neck. "Come, sit and have tea with us."

Nelly sweetly smiled as Arodi bowed before sitting. Plain. She was just as average by candlelight as by sunlight. Her purple dress did not convey the wealth of the Taylors, and Arodi knew it could not be easy growing up as an abolitionist in the Deep South. But that didn't change how emotionless he felt when their eyes met or when she smiled. If anything, he thought of Marnie the more he looked at Nelly. Marnie had the perfect-for-her-face nose with hazel eyes that reminded him of summers spent in the English countryside. Her lips were the color of the camellias he saw on a trip to Japan. Her hair was like the creamy butter on the table for the sweet delights elegantly placed before them. He daydreamed about what it would be like to sketch Marnie again and heard Aunt Belinda clear her throat.

"Arodi, I was just telling Nelly about our summer ball and was hoping to secure an escort for her." Aunt Belinda sipped some tea and looked at Arodi.

Bamboozled.

Yet, not to be outfoxed, he offered, "I have already offered my services to the staff for the evening. Knowing how you wanted the party to come together, I feel I must honor my word in this regard." Arodi hid a smirk.

Aunt Belinda fanned herself. "Oh my, it's getting warm. Nelly, would you be a darling and fetch my parasol, please? I believe it's in the library. Fallon can assist you if needed."

"Yes, Mrs. Miller." Nelly stood, curtsied, and walked inside.

Aunt Belinda spoke after the door closed behind Nelly. "What do you have against her? She's sweet, excellent breeding, talented, and well-traveled. She came over here to make sure matters between our two families were amicable."

"No, I'm sure her father sent her over as a peace offering."

"Arodi, I honestly don't know what to think of you."

He poured his tea from the teapot that was decorated with rosettes and friezes of palmettes in gold on an agate blue background into a matching teacup. "I'm not looking for a marriage of convenience."

"Here we go," Aunt Belinda rolled her eyes, "you're looking for romance, passion, to fall for the most beautiful girl in the land, perhaps, find that impossible dream? My dear boy, those are stories, fables, myths, tales. I used to read them to you as a child and thought that I had reinforced to you that they were simply fantasies. How do you know you and Nelly aren't compatible? There's much more wisdom in choosing a wife with her credentials."

"You married at twenty-five; I am just now twenty-six. I do not understand the rush you seem to be in to get me to settle. Nelly is a child, and what's more, I am not interested in her. I find her kind and knowledgeable, but nothing more." Arodi spread buttercream onto a scone.

"I just want you to find a trustworthy woman of virtue and grace. You're at a fine age to start your family line."

"So I am." Arodi bit into his scone and sipped some tea to help him swallow the bite. His was a world so different from Marnie's. If he wanted, he could spend the rest of his life in leisure, but what about women? Women did not have jobs or careers in his time. They could participate in politics and rallies, but for the most part, they were expected to be wives and mothers…but were they really content? Or were they acquiescing to a life they thought was the only option?

Boundaries, limitations, acceptance. Arodi pondered his own motives. A life with Marnie beyond what they had at present was not possible, but could he accept that? He sipped his tea again and heard the door open, seeing Nelly emerge from the house. What were her options in life? Was she looking for a well-suited husband? Did she hope for love over convenience?

Nelly handed Aunt Belinda the parasol.

"Thank you, dear." Aunt Belinda opened it to create instant shade.

Arodi stood and helped Nelly with her chair. He picked up another scone. "I apologize for my brevity this morning, but I've afternoon engagements that cannot wait." He bowed and walked toward the carriage house to get his horse ready to meet his impossible dream.

## *Eleven*

Marnie and Briscney sat outside on Briscney's patio, which was decorated with urns spilling with ivy, petunias, and geraniums. There were hanging pots of the fullest wisteria flowers and metal latticework where moonflowers climbed. It was almost like a secluded, secret garden in the back. The fragrance of honeysuckle was suspended in the air. Hyacinth hung thick around the edge of the porch where Briscney had placed it between tulips. Two large hydrangea trees blossomed as well.

A giant maple tree cast a shadow over the pair as they sipped their pomegranate-flavored tea and shared party ideas.

"So, if you can go get everything on this list, we can pull it off," Marnie handed Briscney a piece of paper. "The caterer will meet me here at one. I've got tables and chairs arriving just before then, so I can show them where to set up. The landscapers will come this afternoon, so we should be good to go if we have to deal with any emergencies tomorrow. I think we've got everything lined up swimmingly for Friday."

"Thank you so much. Do you want to stay for the party?" Briscney offered.

"I'll pass."

"I was just asking, partially because some of the men coming are single." Briscney smiled, showing her front and bottom teeth.

Was there some unwritten rule requiring friends and family to matchmake? Marnie began to appreciate how Arodi must feel dealing with his aunt. *Arodi. Isn't he the reason why you won't stay and mingle, the reason why you're not interested in meeting someone new?*

"I appreciate the offer, but right now, Jasmine Rose has all of my attention, and I need to stay completely focused. I wouldn't want to jeopardize my chances of a position with them, so I need to rest after this party so that I'm fresh for the next week."

"I get it. OK, let me run and get these things. I'll be back in a bit." Briscney stood up and stretched.

Marnie saw the slight outline of her rounded tummy in her white cotton shirt. It made her smile. She checked her phone as she heard Briscney drive away. She had missed Drew's call. "Hey, Drew, what's up?"

"Where are you? I took off early, but you're not at Cheekwood."

"At Briscney's. Why?"

"I want to run more tests."

"Drew, we can't let the testing get out of hand." If Marnie were being totally honest, she and Drew were not the best at checking and balancing each other. When, in all honesty, they both wanted to explore more about Arodi's past, run the tests, and ask questions.

"It's just for my personal collection."

"No DNA swabs and no needles."

"Done. Can I come over?"

"Fine."

* * * * *

"Wow, this place is awesome." Drew lugged his backpack to the table where Marnie sat. "It's like a South American paradise. She should totally have a giant waterfall for the pool."

"What's in there?" Marnie nodded at his backpack.

"Just science stuff. Is he here?" Drew looked around. "Or here?" He began feeling the air with his hands where there were empty seats.

"He's not here."

"So, what's goin' on with Briscney?" Drew began unpacking his equipment.

"We're working on that party for Friday, and she's out running some errands to get everything we need." Marnie drafted some notes as she spoke.

She sensed a presence, felt him before she looked up. "There he is." She knew that rush of joy that flooded her was on account of Arodi walking toward her.

"Good afternoon."

"Hi," Marnie said.

After a period of quiet, she could feel Drew's eyes on her.

"You guys stare in silence like this often?" He asked.

She ignored him. "Arodi, Drew wants to run some tests."

"Certainly, what shall we do?"

"Give him this." Drew gave Marnie his cell phone. "Show him how to push play."

Arodi sat on a stone he said was near Marnie and Drew, who sat at Briscney's table.

"Are you crazy? This is a cell phone. You're the one who said we shouldn't do the very things we're doing."

"He could be gone tomorrow. He doesn't know what I look like. Just show him how to do it. It's for science, OK?"

Marnie shook her head. "What is it anyway?"

"I recorded a simple introduction. That's all."

Marnie turned to Arodi. "I'm going to share a picture of Drew with you, but sometimes pictures in my time can include sound and movement. I won't answer any questions you have about the technology. I'm only doing this so Drew can say hello."

"I understand." Arodi nodded.

Marnie handed him the phone. "Push the triangle that's inside the circle."

Arodi did.

Drew's face appeared on the screen, and the video began playing.

"Arodi, I'm Drew, Marnie's cousin. I am a scientist by trade. Thank you for letting me run these tests. This is a great project to be a part of." The video stopped.

"Amazing," Arodi said as he held the phone and looked it over.

"OK, next test." Drew started typing on his computer. "Tell him to put the phone on the grass."

Marnie did, and Arodi sat it down.

"Did he do it?"

"Yes."

"I've been thinking, and I actually don't think it's a hole in time. I think it's some sort of gateway. I can't see my phone, so I'm assuming that my phone is in 1849."

Marnie asked. "So, why can't we pass through the gateway and into our respective years?"

"I don't know. Maybe you're like two sides of a bridge. Objects can go from one side to another, but you two can't cross because, then, there's no bridge?"

"Can humans cross or just objects that we pass to each other?"

"I'm not so sure I want to try sending living beings through the gateway, do you?"

"No, I was just wondering."

"Let's show him how to make a recording. I won't do a video, but at least let me record his voice."

* * * * *

"Hello, Drew. I'm Arodi Bellamy of New York. I live in 1849, and I am visiting Nashville, Tennessee. I'm a businessman by trade and enjoy being a part of your studies."

"It just gets cooler every time I listen to it," Drew said. He was like a young boy who had just received a new toy.

"OK, the landscaper is here, so I need to speak to him." Marnie turned toward Arodi, "I have some work to do, so just stay in this general area, and I'll be back when I can."

"Wait, give him this." Drew handed Marnie a piece of old-looking paper.

She didn't bother reading it. "Here," she handed it to Arodi.

Thus began the schoolboy note-passing using Marnie as a conduit. Back and forth, they ran notes over to her to give to each other while she attempted to speak and plan with the landscaper. She pressed forward through the

70

interruptions and multitasked the organizing of Briscney's estate to perfection. Meanwhile, she fielded texts from Simone, who asked her to pick up her dress from the tailors on Thursday.

Drew fervently typed away on his laptop.

Arodi fervently wrote on paper.

"This place looks surreal," Briscney said as she came out to the patio. "Marnie, I'm amazed."

The landscaper had erected and helped Marnie decorate a beautiful metal arbor added bushes trimmed in various animal shapes, and concocted a miniature stone waterfall with LED lights.

"Thanks, I had a vision and went with it."

"Hi, Drew." Briscney waved at Drew.

"Oh, hey." He smiled and then returned to his computer.

"He's in mad scientist mode," Marnie explained.

"Anything exciting he's working on?"

"Oh, you know, Drew. A butterfly flaps its wings, and he's looking for tsunamis." Marnie paused as she saw Arodi walking toward her with paper in his hands and a smile on his face. *How was it that when he came into her line of vision, everything else was in the periphery?* Her focus was laser-like on his features, from his self-assured saunter of a gait to the fullness of his physique. She couldn't help but feel that her senses were swept away when she perceived his presence.

"I've finished my entries for Drew. Here you are," he extended the papers toward Marnie.

She realized she couldn't explain the papers' sudden appearance to Briscney if she accepted them from Arodi.

"Not now, it'll look weird," Marnie tried to keep her voice low.

"So, you do think the baby bump makes the dress look awkward?" Briscney asked.

Marnie surmised while she was focused on what Arodi was saying that Briscney had been talking to her, too. She had only meant for Arodi, who now waited patiently holding the papers at his side, to hear her, not Briscney.

"No, I think a lime green dress will be flattering against your pregnancy glow." Marnie tried to recover.

"You're right."

Success!

"Briscney, I should go. Simone has a whole long list of errands I need to run for her. I'll be here Friday afternoon to make sure everything's put together."

Briscney embraced Marnie. "Thank you so much. Jeremy is going to love it, too. I know you're going to have your own company someday." Her phone made a noise. "Oh, Jeremy wants a to-go order from the country club, so I've got to run out again. Don't worry about locking up. I'll be back in half an hour. And Drew's welcome to stay even if you have to go."

"Thanks."

Briscney went back toward her car.

"Is the person you were speaking with gone?" Arodi asked, so very close to Marnie's ear, his warm breath felt like a soft breeze upon her ear lobe. If he slipped his arm around her, she knew that, in that moment, she wouldn't move. How much longer could she ignore her feelings? How much longer could she look into those eyes and not act upon possibilities?

"She's gone."

"These are for Drew." He handed her the papers.

"OK, let's head that way." They moved toward the patio. "Drew, we need to wrap it up."

"One more test."

"Well, Briscney is only gonna be gone about twenty minutes, and I'm exhausted. Have you even seen the work I've done today? No, you haven't because you've been busy using me as your note-passer. I need to go home, Drew. I've got a ton of errands to prioritize for tomorrow."

Drew held up his index finger but looked at his computer, and music began playing. "One more." He pushed a button on his computer. "Oh my gosh." Drew's face registered shock.

Marnie started at Drew, "What?"

"How did you do that?" Arodi asked.

Marnie looked from Drew to Arodi, trying to figure out what was happening.

"Are you talking to Drew?" Marnie asked.

"Marnie, I can see him." Arodi said, "And a mansion and boxes with wheels." Arodi stumbled forward. "Am I in your time?"

"I'm not sure," Drew said. "I think I just enlarged the bridge using frequencies."

"What do you mean, Drew? And can you fix it before Briscney gets home?" Marnie asked with a slight panic in her voice.

"I sort of used your genome, Marnie, and put it to music, then experimented with the types of frequencies I assigned to portions of your DNA, and well, whatever I did, it worked. I made your end of the bridge bigger so that I could see what you see, too. And whatever I did, it made Arodi's end larger, too, well, at least in our time."

"What if he can't get back home?"

"Is that so bad? It's not like you wouldn't take him in."

Marnie flashed a look at Drew.

Drew shrugged. "Well, it's true."

"Just have your meeting and then shut this down."

Drew walked up to Arodi. "Hi, Arodi. It's nice to meet you. Wow, you're very cool-looking."

They shook hands.

"Drew, it's a pleasure to meet you face-to-face. How did you do it?"

"It would take too long to tell you. Just enjoy it." Drew gave Arodi's upper arm a playful pat.

"You mentioned frequencies. Does this mean that Marnie and I have some sort of connection to each other, like a similar frequency?"

"Marnie, he's smart." Drew looked at her like he was about to ask if they could keep him like he was their new pet.

*Connection? What kind of connection? How could we possibly be connected scientifically?*

She listened as the two men spoke, playing out potential scientific ideas and theories. Was it fascinating? Absolutely. But the risks they were taking seemed only to get greater and greater. She glanced at her watch. "OK, fellas, it's time to wrap it up. Briscney could be home any time now."

"So, this may be our only encounter?" Arodi asked.

"Yeah, but we'll still communicate through Marnie."

"Very well. Goodbye, Drew."

"Bye."

They shook hands again. Drew went back to his computer and stopped the music.

"Arodi, are you back in 1849?" Marnie asked.

"I think so. I don't see Drew, and my horse is over there."

"Did he make it back?" Drew asked.

"Yes." She looked at her cousin, knowing he was slightly disheartened. Their conversation flew over her head when it came to science. Drew had just met an intellectual equal to him, and it was hard to part with his company. Their exaggerated science fair project had been shared fun for both men, albeit short-lived.

Drew closed his laptop. "Tell him bye for me. I'm gonna head home and analyze some data."

"Is he leaving?" Arodi asked. "Give him my regards."

Marnie did.

Drew slung his backpack over his shoulder. "I'll see you at the house."

"Bye."

"I suppose you will need to leave soon, " Arodi said. "I wish I could share this experience with Ari. I wish he could meet you both. My aunt, too. She would enjoy your company and probably stop trying to force me to spend so much time with Nelly."

"Why is that?" Marnie asked with a small grin.

"Women are observant creatures, and I wouldn't be able to hide anything from her."

Moments ago, Marnie would have sworn that she was feet away from Arodi. How on earth was she now mere inches away, facing him?

"Hide what?" Rule 15 of boy-girl relations: flirtatiously ask questions you know the answer to or hope you do.

His hand traced the outline of her face. Her pulse raced through her body.

His fingers tenderly ran through her hair. "Quite soft." He mentioned.

Emotions were flowing. It felt as though she was suspended in time, and she braced herself for what she hoped was coming. A moment of truth. A moment she'd seen in so many movies but believed it only existed there. Of course, weeks ago, she believed people from the past only existed in the historical records written about them, but it wasn't true. Arodi Bellamy, from 1849, stood before her, and she readied herself for what she knew would be coming. She lost herself in those eyes and felt certain the windows of their souls had their own form of communication. Time didn't exist. It was no longer a rift between them but a place of escape where they were tucked away from the unknowns of their connected timelines. She felt his fingers ever so gently apply pressure to her chin, tilting it upward. She knew what was coming, and she welcomed it.

"You're still here?" Briscney said. "Good, I've got extras. Why don't we eat together? Jeremy said he was going to be a while longer tonight anyway."

Marnie's back was to Briscney, and she scrunched her face together at the interrupted moment. "I'll be right there. I was just going to take some quick pictures of the landscape. Thanks!" She turned to wave at Briscney.

"OK, I'll get us something to drink and find a good show to watch." Briscney went inside.

Marnie looked back at Arodi.

"She came back?" He asked.

Marnie noticed the disappointment in his eyes and heard it in his voice.

"I didn't want that moment to end," he said.

"Why not?"

He pulled her in close, hands clasped around her waist. "Can't you guess?"

Instinctively, she moved her hands upwards, letting them explore his face and neck. She wanted nothing more than to remain with him, but the thought of how to explain herself to Briscney bore down on her. "She wants me to eat dinner with her."

"Do you want me to wait for you?"

She knew he'd do it. She knew if she said yes, he'd sit with his horse until she emerged from Briscney's. It could be several hours, and he would wait for her. He had no cell phone to keep him occupied, no book to read, and yet he would gladly pass the time waiting for her. She was beyond touched. Where were the men like Arodi Bellamy in her time? What man in the modern world would make this same offer? "It's getting late. You should probably ride home. I wouldn't want anything to happen to you."

"Why is that, Marnie?"

"I think you know."

Arodi smiled, and all Marnie could think about was those attractive-looking, how-do-they-feel-against-mine lips.

It was twilight. Marnie knew she had limited minutes before Briscney emerged, telling Marnie everything was ready. She also knew that she wouldn't go anywhere for hours if she kept entertaining this conversation with this man.

"I have to go." Marnie unclasped Arodi's hands from around her waist and held them in front of her. "I'll be back here Friday afternoon."

"I shall count the seconds."

*I cannot believe this is happening. I cannot believe I have to go. What if we never get a moment like this again? What if he is in a tragic accident tonight on the way home, and it's all my fault?* Fear snaked its way into her mind.

"Be careful on your ride home."

"It's only a couple of miles, and my horse knows the way."

"OK. Goodnight, Arodi." She wanted to tell him to call her when he got home so she knew he was safe, but Alexander Graham Bell was just two years old in Arodi's time.

"Goodnight." With obvious reluctance, he released her hands and moved away.

Marnie slowly made her way inside, closing the door, by gently leaning against it.

"OK, I've got strawberry lemonade, some great salads, and filet mignon. Plus, asparagus and some potato soup here." Briscney stood by an open kitchen window, fanning herself. "I'm just trying to cool off. Are you hungry?"

*Starving. Starving for more time with Arodi. Hungry for more of what I just experienced and more of what Arodi and I had shared.* "Yes, I'm ready to eat."

"Excellent, well, I'm ready to chat about one more thing: white orchids. Jeremy said the partner loves them. Can we get them? I think we should put centerpieces of them on each table."

"White orchids are a bit out of your budget. I think we'll scale it back and try another approach."

"Well, you're the boss. Now let's eat."

Marnie wasn't sure how she made it through the dinner and was able to have any sort of coherent conversation with Briscney. All she could focus on was that missed moment, which kept replaying over and over in her mind. All she had needed to do was lean in just a little, and he would've known what to do. Or was that too forward? Was that inappropriate in 1849? Was it inappropriate now?

Later, when she arrived home, she found Drew playing on the computer.

"What happened to you?" He asked.

"Briscney fed me." She sat down on the couch. "Where're your folks?"

"It's ten pm. Have you met my parents?"

"Right." They had probably gone to bed around 8:30 PM. "So, what was all that today? What did you do?"

"I'm not sure. I don't know if he was really with us or just seeing it like we see it. I am not even sure where we were. Maybe we were all on the bridge together and not really in either place."

"Is it stable?"

"No, I don't believe so. If the music had stopped, or if there was a glitch, a sunburst, or even another black hole converging, I don't know what would've happened. Being in there's a big risk, and you can't stay for too long. I did notice that when I got out, I was really thirsty, so I think that it may affect our vitals unless, of course, you're a part of the bridge like you two are. I just don't know. We should be careful."

"I agree."

"Good. I'm going to head to bed and look over Arodi's notes he gave me. It was a cool day. Thanks."

"You're welcome. Thank you for pursuing this, and congratulations on the new breakthroughs, even though we can't share them with anyone."

"Yeah."

Marnie spent some time reading Scripture to try to help her understand what was happening. She read about Paul proclaiming, while he was in Ephesians, that "to the Gentiles the endless riches of the Messiah and to bring to light the plan of the mystery—which for ages was hidden in God, who created all things." He was the One who would bring light and revelation to what was happening, and this gave Marnie a wonderful peace.

*Twelve*

How quickly Friday arrived.

Simone was pleased with her dress for the Swan Ball, and Briscney was equally excited and nervous about the party.

Marnie arrived at Briscney's wearing a knee-length V-neck, short-sleeved black cocktail dress with black flats. Her goal was to blend in while the guests arrived and then slip out and disappear as soon as the party started.

The large kitchen was abuzz with activity as the caterer set up for the night. The air was filled with the smells of roasted duck, garlic mashed potatoes, and warm bread.

Marnie was unable to fulfill Briscney's request for white orchids, so the centerpieces on the twelve tables set up in the back of the house held lighted vases with Betta fish and rocks. It was elegant, though the orchids floating in the slender vases would've been nicer. She let out a small sigh as she looked at the tables.

Briscney and Jeremy were upstairs getting ready, and the guests would arrive soon. Everything had fallen into place, and as Marnie surveyed everything, she was pleased with her efforts.

Marnie felt something soft run along her right clavicle from behind. It's not the first spot one would think of as a touch-point of romance, but it sent tingles flooding from head to toe for her. Things were about to get weird if she turned around, and it wasn't Arodi stroking her collarbone.

"Close your eyes," Arodi whispered. His warm breath created an intoxicating flood of feelings as he spoke.

Marnie did.

"Turn around."

She slowly turned in the direction of his voice.

"Place out your hands."

She did. She felt him place something in her hands.

"Open your eyes."

Marnie glanced down and beheld a stem of blooming white orchids.

"How did you know?"

Arodi grinned, "I might have heard a bit of your conversation from the other

77

evening."

"How did you do this?"

"Don't ask. I've brought plenty, and they are in a cart, so go ahead and start placing these on the tables."

Marnie added the orchids to each of the vases as quickly as possible. She couldn't wait to thank Arodi. "Will you meet me across the road in about ten minutes?"

"Certainly." Arodi strolled down the hill away from Briscney's house.

"Oh my goodness! How did you do this?" Briscney walked out of the veranda doors. She looked amazing in her lime green dress.

"Nothing's impossible when you have connections." Marnie smiled. She heard a car pull up. "Well, I parked across the road by the park, so I'll just head over there now."

"You know you can stay. I promise the guys who work with Jeremy are really sweet."

"I know. I just welcome a quiet, relaxing night alone. You understand, right?"

"Of course. Thank you so much for everything." Briscney embraced Marnie.

"You're welcome! You look lovely. Have a good time."

"I will, thanks!"

Marnie slipped away, looking for Arodi as she walked to her car. She saw him across the road from Briscney's mailbox, and her heart seemed to skip a beat.

"Are you sure you don't want to stay for the festivities?"

"Yes."

"Are you really looking to spend the evening alone?"

"No."

"Well, suppose I walk with you to your next destination."

"Suppose you do," Marnie said with a smile as she hooked her arm into his.

They walked along the road, Arodi leading his horse, which Marnie could see as long as he held the reins or had a hand on the horse. They made their way to the park, a park that didn't yet exist in Arodi's time. Marnie spied a large oak tree, one that must've stood tall even in Arodi's time. "Shall we sit?"

"I happened to have this," Arodi said as he produced a blanket. "Drew explained some of the science to me, so I think that you should be able to use it." Arodi laid out the blanket. "I also brought this." Arodi produced a picnic basket and pulled out a meal. "Cornish hens with spiced acorn squash and peach cobbler for dessert."

"That's amazing."

"I've had some assistance from Drew on how to plan this evening. It's very different in your time than mine, but I must say, this is better than any social gathering I've ever attended."

As Marnie and Arodi dined together under the oak tree, they were serenaded by the quiet whisper of the wind rustling leaves in the trees. The setting sun added a soft, pinkish glow to their picnic. Marnie felt that all her senses were heightened at being this close to Arodi. *Just keep focused on the food, not how handsome he looks.*

"Tell me more about your parents," Arodi began. "You mentioned they work with orphans in Costa Rica."

Marnie focused on the conversation and scolded herself for not knowing if Costa Rica had been founded in Arodi's time before she'd previously mentioned it. She made a mental note to brush up on her world history. "You've heard of it?"

"Yes, it's a relatively new country."

"They run a small orphanage and try to give the kids a sense of normalcy. My mom is really skilled at providing tools to help them navigate their emotions, and my dad is a source of validation, always reminding them that they matter and have a purpose."

"They sound like wonderful people. Have you been to visit them?"

"A few times, but it's hard with work and all. I am trying to maneuver through my current job and figure out my next steps."

"Did you always want to do what you're doing now?" His inquisitiveness added to his charm.

"Maybe in some capacity. I wanted to be a hostess of sorts, helping create places of leisure and relaxation with some entertainment thrown in."

"You sound like my aunt." He looked upward at the sky. "It is fascinating that we're both with our extended families at this time, isn't it?"

"Aunt Ginny and Uncle Caleb are like second parents to me. I used to spend part of my summers with them when Drew and I were kids, even though we lived like twenty minutes apart. I loved coming to their farm. My dad's parents, my grandparents, used to live there, too. It was this magical world where anything was possible. Drew and I would spend hours climbing on hay bales and making hay obstacle courses or hay forts. We fished and swam in the pond until dark. My grandparents told us the stories of their youth, and my grandpa used to take us on tractor rides. He passed away a few years ago."

"I'm sorry."

"We had a lot of fun on the farm. Like my mom, Aunt Ginny consistently prepared homemade dinners and desserts, so it always felt like home."

"It sounds most idyllic. I will say I don't recall a time my aunt was in the kitchen, but she always had a delicious spread for our dinners. I have been down here every other summer for as long as I can remember. I think winters in New York concern my parents, which is why my father wants a factory in Nashville. I soon suspect he will be scouting out an estate for the family."

Marnie wanted to look it up online. Did they move here? Would she see Arodi on a day-to-day basis beyond the summer? All the questions could drive her crazy.

As it grew darker and darker, Marnie wanted to have a little light and began searching in her purse for the LED flashlight.

Arodi seemed to read her mind. "I have a few candles." He removed a couple of candles with brass stands from the basket and lit them. The candlelight created an alluring contrast against the growing twilight.

Marnie glanced at Arodi through the soft glow and felt her heart skip a beat. Her eyes seemingly had a mind of their own as she found herself drinking in his masculine features: his square jawline, his expressive, dark chocolate-colored eyes, his refined Greek nose, and his perfectly shaped lips, lips that had almost kissed her. *Oh, why did I have to remember that?* Marnie glanced back down at her plate. *What did he say this was? Cornish hen? Focus, Marnie, on the food, not him.* Marnie forced herself to take a bite of food. What was wrong with her? It is not like she had never eaten a meal with a man, just not one as handsome and appealing as this man, and not one that she had almost kissed.

Somehow, Marnie managed to eat most of her meal and make small talk with Arodi. After dinner, the chill in the night air made Marnie shiver. "I should've brought a jacket," she said.

"Oh, that's right." Arodi stood and walked over to where he had left his horse. "Drew told me to pack an extra blanket." He brought it to her.

"Thanks." *Arodi, remember the other night when we were embracing and about to kiss?*

Silence was the dominant speaker at the moment.

Arodi cleared his throat and gently took hold of her hands, pulling her up to stand in front of him. He looked intently at her as he gazed deeply into her eyes.

Marnie felt her heart flutter. He was going to say something. He was going to ask her something. *Thud- thud, thud-thud, thud-thud.* Her heart pounded like a fast drum.

"I've given this more thought than I should care to admit. The questions, the uncertainties, the mystery that we find ourselves in; I could go crazy trying to analyze it all. The one thing I know for sure is that when I am with you, I feel everything will be alright. Every evening, I pray to get another day with you. Every morning, I ask for each minute to be just a little longer so that I can have more time with you. I believe I am falling in love with you. Every poem speaks of you, every story is a tale of us. I cannot go on without telling you how I feel. To move forward has many realms of unknowns and risks I'm not even yet aware of, but if I don't ask you to proceed, I fear I'm making the largest mistake of my life."

Marnie studied his face. "I know there's no going back. Drew constantly teases me about the feelings that I have for you, and while I certainly enjoy your friendship, I would be remiss to dismiss the ever-increasing feelings that I have for you. I have spent my entire adult life making sure that I guarded my heart against the wrong attentions and intentions. Meeting you is an impossibility in my head, but my heart says otherwise. I know that I only have a limited amount of time with you, and I don't want to spend it hinting at the possibilities. I want to know if what I'm feeling is real. Tomorrow, this could all end. This may be our last evening together, and I want you to know that I feel the same about you."

Arodi smiled as he cupped her face and leaned in. "If this is our last night, I want you to know that my heart will remember it for a lifetime." He came closer, and his magnetism drew her to him.

In unison, their lips met. Time stood still.

The aroma of gardenias danced around them as they kissed. They developed a rhythm to their discovery and expression of what they were feeling.

Arodi ran a thumb along her jawline sending a wave of tingles coursing through her.

She applied a little pressure to the back of his neck, encouraging his exploration of her lips' pure and pristine territory. Marnie felt her heart would explode with what she was feeling. *I have never felt like this. Is it normal to never want to stop kissing him?* Marnie reluctantly let their lips part as she looked up at him. "Arodi, virtuous women don't kiss men in 1849 like this, do they?"

Arodi ran a hand over his mouth and moved back, "No, they do not."

"So, am I not considered a virtuous woman by your culture's standards then?"

Arodi seemed to think over her words. "I don't know where you want this to lead, but I'm not here tonight because I want to stop pursuing you or stop learning more about you. I'm giving you my life and my heart. If you can say you're here for the same reasons, then that is virtue, honesty, and integrity."

"But where does it lead? How can we be together?"

"We're together right now, aren't we? Live for this moment, Marnie. We'll navigate these uncharted waters as they come, but for tonight, live in the moment with me." He ran a finger over her hand as he pulled her back into his arms.

He wrapped his arms tightly around her, kissing her along the top of her head, down to her neck, over to her cheek, and finally back to her lips.

*So this is what bliss feels like: truly being cherished.* Marnie reluctantly pulled her lips away from Arodi's with a sigh. "It will be different after tonight between us."

"In what way? You mean instead of me thinking about kissing you, I'll be able to show you without hesitation now?"

Marnie smiled. "No, I mean it only gets harder now. Desire will only grow stronger, and hearts will only grow closer."

Arodi snuck in another kiss. "So the uncharted water is coming, hmm?"

"We are literally in two different eras."

"You can ride the wave or jump ship."

"I'm not jumping ship, and I'm not going anywhere without you. I'm just pointing out what I think is going to happen so that I'm ready for it."

"Well then, Ms. Marnie Foster, brace yourself."

"Why?"

"A Nor'easter of kisses is headed your way." Arodi eased her back into his embrace, where his kisses consumed her.

She had no fears in this perfect moment, and he was an absolute gentleman in every sense of the word. He was tender, kind, respectful, and polite, never daring to violate the high morals she had hoped he held near to him.

As desire threatened to consume them, Arodi released her and leaned down to grab the extra blanket. He silently sat down and pulled her back into his embrace, with her back against his chest resting against him. He wrapped the blanket around both of them so they could enjoy each other's warmth quietly.

Secure in his arms, Marnie found sleep creeping in like the fog that now surrounded them. The candles' wax had melted substantially, so she knew their time together was coming to an end. *How can we make it work? In what world can we stay together for the entire night and wake up and face the morning together?* "It's getting very late."

"Indeed."

"You should go home."

"I am. This is my uncle's farm. There's a cabin beyond those trees; I will spend the night there."

Marnie was touched and suspected he had not mentioned the cabin to avoid temptation. "You refrained from taking me to the cabin, didn't you?"

"For now, yes." He entwined their fingers together. "Someday, the timing will be right, but we must move forward in a way that is pleasing to Yehovah. You are too precious of a gift to me to spoil things with an emotionally charged decision. I will treat you the way my father treated my mother and the way I want all gentlemen to treat my sisters and, someday, my daughters."

*I want those daughters, too. I want them with you. I know I shouldn't want these things, but I can't help it.* Marnie couldn't stop the tears from coming, though she tried. She was overwhelmed with emotion and this fairytale she was caught up in.

Arodi pulled her against him. "We will seek His wisdom and what His will is for us. Don't worry."

"I just don't understand how we can have a future together. I don't want to lose you, Arodi."

"You won't."

She wanted to believe his words. She clung to the faith and hope he had, for she had so little of it when it came to a future with him. She held fast to him until she could barely keep her eyes open.

It was only at Arodi's insistence that she head home that led her away from him.

* * * * *

Drew squeezed an orange on a manual juicer. "How was Briscney's? You stayed out quite late."

Marnie sat down next to Drew at the island, wearing a gray cotton robe over her pajamas. "Did you help him plan that evening?" She asked.

"He likes you. He wanted to do something special, so I may have given him a few ideas."

"I think I love him."

"Whoa. That's deep."

Marnie buried her head in her folded arms on the counter. "What am I going to do?"

Drew didn't respond.

Marnie sat up. "Can you figure out a way we can make a life in the gateway?"

"I told you, it's not stable. If the gate should close, I can't promise you that a part of you won't remain in 1849, and the rest of you in the here and now. You said I shouldn't go crazy, and I think now would be a good time to heed your own warning."

"It's a little late for that."

Drew began peeling another orange.

"Can we picnic today by the pond and you play the song so you can see Arodi?"

Drew sighed. "This is going to break your heart."

"I know, but not while I still have time with him." Marnie had tried to stifle every logical thought that told her there was literally no future for her and Arodi, but she made her choice to enjoy him while she had time with him. She wanted to spend all of the moments she could with him. She knew she risked a broken heart if she completely gave it to Arodi. Though she had avoided the romantic accouterments of love, Marnie knew that she could only love or not love; there would be no middle ground.

## *Thirteen*

"That's astonishing." Arodi had Drew's earbuds in. "They sound like they are right here singing the opera in front of me."

"Drew, you're corrupting him." Marnie removed the earbuds from Arodi's ears. She wore a purple and blue flannel shirt, jeans, and white tennis shoes. It was a warmer spring day, but she still needed the sleeves to protect her ears.

"Dude, you gave him a candy bar," Drew defended.

"You said you wanted to document Nashville's early history more accurately. This," she held up the earbuds, "is not the way to do it."

Drew's computer played the music he had previously created on a continuous loop as the three of them sat together by the pond at the back of the farm on a large quilt. Candies, sodas, and other snacks littered their blanket along with a few magazines, edited to make sure they didn't reveal any secrets about the future. Marnie had gone a little overboard with wanting to share her time with Arodi. But how does one assess and judge the actions of love?

"The future seems very close to the Utopian literature I've read through the years. Those authors had some astounding insight into your world." Arodi said as he laid back on the blanket.

Marnie and Drew shared a knowing look, which also meant they had to protect Arodi from the future. They could no longer simply show him the good if they weren't willing to share the bad as well.

"It's not a perfect place," Marnie said.

"You've said nothing of violence, war, disease, death. You both appear to me to be the pictures of health. Your parents are alive, you have fascinating careers, how can you say it's far from perfection?"

Marnie bowed her head. She couldn't disagree. If she wanted to defend her position, she would have to speak of nuclear war and modern-day slavery, which would lead to an explanation about what became of slavery from his time: World War I, World War II, constant fighting over religion, race, and politics. She let out a heavy sigh. "Arodi, we're giving you a very skewed idea of what life in the future is like, but there's more to the picture."

He nodded. "So, there really is nothing new under the sun, is there?"

"No, there's not," Drew said. "I think I'll shut down the music and go check my vitals."

Solemnity hung in the air.

Arodi extended his hand. "My entire group of New York friends would find you intriguing, Drew, as do I. I hope for another encounter on this bridge you've built."

Drew shook his hand. "Me, too." He proceeded to stop the music.

The sound stopped.

"Arodi, are you there?"

"Drew, I am, and I can still hear you, but I can't see you."

"Give it a second. It's just an echo. It won't last."

"Drew?" Arodi said.

Drew didn't respond.

"I don't think he can hear you," Marnie said. "Can you, Drew?"

"No."

She heard the disappointment in his voice and knew it would be hard for Drew, even more so for her, when it came to an end. Why did she persist along a path of certain perdition? "He can't, Arodi. It's stopped."

"I see."

Marnie watched Drew pack up the computer. "I'll get the picnic stuff when we're done."

"Cool. I'll go run some tests and tell you later about anything I have found." Drew took off toward the main house, disappearing in the ever-becoming thick foliage.

Arodi rubbed her shoulders. "Is he gone?"

Marnie closed her eyes, "yes." How wonderful it felt to have his hands relaxing those muscles she constantly used day in and day out working at her computer.

Eventually, Arodi gently pulled her down to recline on the blanket next to him. They held hands, staring up at the sky.

"Do you see clouds today?" Marnie softly asked.

"No, it's a perfect blue sky. You?"

"Just a few cirrus clouds, nothing is taking shape." The sun was warm on her skin, and she closed her eyes. "Have you found the spot for your factory yet?"

"Yes, there's some land outside of the downtown area of Franklin that I think will be the perfect place. The Harlin family owns thousands of acres there, and I think we can work with twenty or so. I always want to have enough room for more buildings and possible housing. One thing we've learned from being in New York is that you should not ask workers to commute for extended periods."

Arodi's wisdom and deep concern for his employees endeared her to him all the more, and she couldn't help but admire him.

"What else have you learned from being in New York?"

"Things about different cultures, people, celebrations, customs."

"Courtship?" Marnie smiled.

"Ah yes, courtship." Arodi propped himself on one elbow and turned toward Marnie.

"What kinds of things have you learned about courtship?"

"Well, for starters, since your chaperone, Drew, has disappeared, you are somewhat at my mercy, aren't you?"

Marnie nodded. "Helpless." She folded her arms behind her head.

Arodi moved closer. "And if I were to kiss you?"

"Defenseless."

He grinned and pressed his lips against hers.

She moved her arms so she could draw him in closer. His mane was soft, and her fingers disappeared into its darkness. She felt his hands move underneath her, cradling her neck, supporting her back, and drawing her closer to him.

His touch, embrace, and movements were tender toward her as they kissed. In between the sweet kiss exchanges, Arodi would tenderly stroke her arms or her head and talk to her. There was nothing out of place or awkward about their times together. It just fit.

* * * * *

Marnie and Arodi held hands as they stood inside the mansion early one morning before it was open to the public. Arodi was dressed in his double-breasted black vest with a gold chain across the lower middle, a white dress shirt underneath, and gray-striped pants touching the tops of his black ankle boots as he glanced at Marnie, who was dressed in a sleeveless salmon and white-striped dress with taupe flats.

"You look exquisite today." He complimented.

"Thank you."

The pair walked along the mansion's upper floor.

"So these rooms and this hall space are filled with family portraits, and no one stays in the bedrooms any longer?" Arodi asked. "My bedroom, right here, is empty except for the items on the wall?" He sounded like he didn't believe it was possible.

"Yes, it's what we call a gallery. It's open and bright, and there are more windows now."

"So the Persian rugs, the draperies, the furniture; all gone?" He looked clearly only seeing the room from his timeline. "I'm trying to imagine it."

"It's very different now." Marnie wanted to see Arodi's room the way he saw it. What books were next to his bed? Where did he keep his clothes, and what did they look like? Was his bed made up? She wanted to know the intimate details of his daily life. Where did he brush his teeth? Did he look in the mirror to comb his hair? Curiosity carried her along as they moved beyond his doorway.

They entered a large room filled with the Miller family portraits. "Whose room is this?" she asked.

"My young cousins share this room. Aunt Belinda had a set of twins about a decade ago, and they stay here. Presently, they are away for the summer exploring Africa with my grandparents."

"In my world, it's a room filled with paintings. Over here," Marnie said as she walked toward a portrait, "is your aunt wearing an amethyst necklace?" Belinda posed with a Newfoundland sitting next to a high, straight-backed chair with intricate details carved into the wood. The cream fabric covering the chair contrasted well with her emerald green dress. She looked as youthful as ever in the portrait, with her light brown hair pinned up and her lips a light shade of pink roses.

Marnie remembered reading about how arsenic was used to dye dresses green. "Arodi, don't let her wear that dress again."

"What dress?"

"Sorry," She forgot that he couldn't see the painting. "An emerald green dress. No woman in your family should wear that color. It's not safe."

"Interesting. My aunt has often expressed that she itches terribly after wearing it, so she hasn't touched it in years."

"Well, don't let her wear it again."

Arodi nodded and cleared his throat. "She also hasn't touched this in years," he said, pulling out the amethyst necklace his aunt wore in the portrait.

"It's beautiful." The unique necklace was elegant, with the amethyst trimmed in diamonds. "How did you get this?" Her fingers lightly grazed the smooth jewels.

"She insisted that if I escorted a lady to the Swan Ball, she should come wearing this." He held it before Marnie's twinkling eyes.

"It's breathtaking."

"Let's try it on for size."

Marnie turned and lifted her hair.

Arodi placed the necklace on her and peppered her neck with kisses as he positioned and clasped the jewelry.

His lips sent chills throughout Marnie's body. Quiver. Quake. Palpitation. Shake. There was no possible way this type of behavior was acceptable in his time. Marnie was sure he would be accused of cavorting around with a commoner, which most likely would have been her social status in 1849 and would not have brought a large inheritance to the table. Why did Arodi find her attractive? She was a dedicated employee striving for more, but was that what she really wanted? Marnie had a hard time focusing on anything other than those warm lips lingering on her neck.

Marnie stood in front of his aunt's portrait as he worked to put on the necklace. She stood in disbelief as she watched Belinda Miller's portrait transform. The amethyst necklace had been replaced by a ruby necklace, and the dress was now black.

"Hold on, Arodi, take it off."

Arodi removed the necklace.

Marnie watched the portrait as the ruby necklace faded back into the amethyst, but the black dress remained.

"I want to try something. Put it back on one more time."

Arodi followed the instructions.

The ruby necklace reemerged around Belinda Miller's neck.

"It's lovely, but I can't." Marnie took off the necklace and handed it back to Arodi. The painting returned to its original state except for the dress. Marnie realized she had altered the past with her knowledge of the future. She hoped that it hadn't caused any damage. "Drew warned me about changing the past."

"You've changed my life entirely. You have affected my past for the better."

"You can't know that."

Arodi tucked the necklace into his jacket pocket. He paused. "Can you hear it?"

"Hear what?"

"My aunt is playing the piano and singing. She has a heavenly voice." Arodi pulled Marnie into an impromptu dance in the upper levels of Cheekwood.

Marnie glanced around to make sure they were indeed alone. If the security guards monitored the cameras, she would give them a good laugh by seemingly dancing by herself.

Arodi led her in a waltz through the room. He was refreshing and playful, all the things Marnie could have ever hoped for in a relationship, except he wasn't really there with her, was he? They finished at the doorway. "I would ask that you wear one thing for me to the ball."

"Anything but the family jewels."

"Wait for me right here." He moved down the hall and around the corner.

Marnie stared outside through the window. The leaves had come in, blocking most of her view of the remaining gardens, but she could see tourists headed toward the mansion. She wondered if Arodi's household, as large as it was, held such great activity. It didn't sound like they were a slaveholding family, but perhaps there were servants. She thought Drew had mentioned something about it. Her musings stopped as she heard Arodi's footsteps approaching.

He held a brown paper parcel. "Open this." He handed it to her. He hadn't tied the parcel, so it was just brown paper wrapped around the object.

Marnie began unwrapping. "Oh my gosh." The paper fell away to reveal a gorgeous blue silk gown. Trimmed with black lace around the neckline and with short sleeves, it was as picturesque as the gowns worn by the women in the portraits before her. She held it up against her body to have an idea of how it would look. Would it make a swishing noise if she shifted left to right? Would it make a pleasing twirl if she spun in circles? Suddenly, she realized she would be the fairytale princess most every little girl envisions. She wanted to be the princess with her prince, who treasured her and adored her.

"You mentioned a fitting the other day, and I thought you should have the proper period gown for when you attend the ball," said Marnie's Prince

Charming.

She returned to reality. "It's beautiful! Thank you." She carefully folded the dress and tucked it back into the paper. As she kissed Arodi's cheek and embraced him, she breathed in the distinct traces of lavender and citrus.

"I'm pleased you like it." He gave her an equal squeeze and kissed her cheek. "Now, let us continue with the tour."

They continued through the rooms on the upper floors and out to the veranda, where they strolled through the large shrubberies behind the house. Arodi spoke of playing hide-and-seek games with his siblings on the grounds, hosting hunting competitions, enjoying the morning quietness, and watching the most spectacular sunsets. His world truly was a world of pleasurable pastimes.

Marnie struggled between scaling the ranks at Jasmine Rose and finding ways to spend more time with Arodi. After the Cheekwood job, where would she be? They could send her anywhere in Middle Tennessee. How would she get to spend time with Arodi, who couldn't get around as easily as she could? Striking the balance of living in the moment and staving off the hounds of modern times with their growls and howls of reality was proving to be very difficult.

## *Fourteen*

"I'm going to ask the librarian to go with me to the Swan Ball. You still have those tickets, right?" Drew asked as he joined Marnie on the enclosed back patio. While sitting on the porch swing, she was scrolling through event planning articles on her phone. She placed her phone down by her side when Drew came out.

She slowly moved along in the swing. "Does the lady have a name?"

"Bella."

"Beautiful."

"She sure is," Drew smiled.

"When are you going to ask her?"

"I just did." Drew held up his phone.

"You did not just text her!" Marnie moved forward.

"Even better. I sent her a singing telegram."

"In the library?"

"Yeah," Drew glowed, clearly proud of himself.

"I'm just gonna let you sit with that for a bit."

Drew appeared to be thinking. "Oh, right. She can't be on her cell phone at work, so she couldn't record it." He nodded along, oblivious to Marnie's train of thought of a quiet setting and a loud singing telegram not being perfect bedfellows.

"Yeah, Drew. That's what I meant." Marnie shook her head with a smile.

"Are you going with Arodi?"

"It's the 'going with' part that's the problem."

"Look, I've been up countless nights trying to figure out a way to close the bridge to get him here or you there, but it's beyond me. I don't think it's safe, but we could try some experimental tests if you want."

"Drew, I don't expect you to fix it. It is what it is."

"Marnie, the thing is, we've been so focused on the science aspect and us doing something about it that we've overlooked the Greatest Scientist of all. He's the One Who brought you two together, and He's the only One Who can give us the answers, but we gotta ask Him."

Drew was right. Marnie's thoughts had been so preoccupied with what she could do to stay with Arodi that she had forgotten that she should be earnestly petitioning Yehovah for answers.

"I'm not running any more tests. I just want to hang out with Arodi while it lasts."

While it lasts. It was another sad reminder that this couldn't last forever, or could it? Was there hope against hope? Tears pooled in Marnie's eyes as her heart began to weep.

Aunt Ginny came out to the porch. "Drew, there's angel food cake and freshly made whipped cream with strawberries to go with it."

Drew zipped off.

"Marnie, honey, what is it?"

Marnie looked up, and the tears started to fall.

"There, there." Aunt Ginny settled in next to her on the swing and opened her arm.

Marnie leaned in. "I don't know how to live in the moment, Aunt Ginny. I don't know how to stop making plans and thinking of the future. What is the future anyway? You can't change the past, or can you? I am just facing so many decisions that could be life-changing, and I feel so ill-equipped to make the right one."

"Shh," Aunt Ginny moved the hair away from Marnie's face and held her against her. The simple embrace began working its healing power instantaneously.

Marnie could feel the peace Aunt Ginny carried as she imparted truth and encouragement through her touch. Aunt Ginny was always able to calm Marnie's anxious heart. From the loss of pets on the farm to the loss of her grandfather, Aunt Ginny could soothe any woe. Marnie melted into her arms as she wept.

"Whatever decisions you face, work-related or heart-related, you know that all things should be placed before Him with prayer and petitions. And I'm not saying that to sound cliché. I know from experience that the hard choices come easier with thanksgiving. Do you remember my favorite horse, Bancroft?"

Marnie nodded. He was very special to Aunt Ginny, and there were so many pictures of them together. Bancroft was injured in a cattle drive and did not make it back home.

"Your uncle told me he was too old to make it on the drive. He wanted to leave Bancroft behind and use a younger horse, but I didn't want to listen. I knew Bancroft could handle it, and since the cattle drive was your uncle's gift to me, I wanted Bancroft on the ride." She stroked Marnie's head as they swung. "During a storm, Bancroft broke loose and ended up getting struck by lightning. By the time we reached him, he was barely alive. I wanted to try to save him, but your uncle said there was no way to do so. I was hurt and harbored misdirected anger at your uncle for the rest of the cattle drive. It was not fair what happened to Bancroft. I blamed your uncle for not demanding we leave Bancroft behind. I blamed him for the weather. I blamed him for choosing that particular spot to camp that night, and I blamed him for not trying to save

Bancroft when I begged him to do so. By the time we made it to Montana, I had let my anger and indignation become like a demon ruling over my actions. I had worked myself up so much that I saw no other choice than to leave your uncle."

"After we checked into a hotel room, your uncle went to get dinner. I had planned to write my goodbye note but felt led to open my Bible first. I turned to Genesis 37 and started reading about Joseph. It was not fair that he was sold into slavery by his brothers, nor was it fair that he was imprisoned for an unfair, untrue accusation. Joseph had been blameless and yet suffered because of the selfish actions of others. That was when I realized I had unfairly placed blame for Bancroft's accident on Caleb. It wasn't fair that Bancroft was struck by lightning, and it wasn't fair to Caleb that I blamed him and held on to my anger for so long that I was prepared to throw away our marriage. When I saw my selfishness and anger for the sins they truly were, it broke me. I pleaded for Yehovah to forgive me and not let me end my marriage. I realized how blessed I was and how selfish I had been. I prayed that Caleb would forgive me."

Marnie sat in silence. She could not envision this selfish version of Aunt Ginny. All she had ever known was this selfless woman consoling her now.

"When Caleb came back with food, all I remember was pouring out my heart to him, confessing my selfishness and anger, and begging him to forgive me. He told me that he had been blaming himself for not only not trying to save Bancroft but for not trying to ease my pain. He had chosen to let me be angry instead of loving and understanding what I was feeling, which had widened the gap between us. He said that on the way back with our dinner, he was praying about how to make things better, and He heard the quiet whisper of Yehovah saying to pursue me in love, just as He pursues His children. This reminded him that regardless of what happened, anger should not get a foothold in a marriage, so he actively pursued my heart to help it heal through his love for me. That was the moment we chose to continually pursue each other each and every day for the rest of our lives."

Marnie closed her eyes and pictured the hotel scene reconciliation.

"That was our first step in safeguarding our marriage. From then on, we have committed to open communication and making a quest to put each other's needs first.

They swayed in the ease of the evening.

"And it was exactly two hundred and eighty days later that Drew was born."

The pair laughed, and Aunt Ginny gave Marnie a squeeze.

"I want to try and live day by day, Aunt Ginny." Marnie felt the first hint of hope that things would be fine with Arodi, and she started living in that hope. She would plunged into those prayers daily and relentlessly pursued petitions until she garnered answers.

## *Fifteen*

Time ticked along. Marnie's days were filled with a frenzy of activity leading up to the Swan Ball and some stolen moments along wooded paths or behind high bushes with Arodi. He helped ease her stress by providing daily lunches outdoors so she wouldn't have to prepare them.

"So you're heading to the woods again to dine?" Fallon asked as she packed half of a warm strawberry shortcake for Arodi. "What is it you do out there with all this food, if you don't mind my asking?"

Arodi didn't mind despite his era's present understanding of how conversations between masters and servants were supposed to be. He viewed the employees on equal footing and, in so doing, endeared himself to them, and they felt at ease speaking freely around him.

"It's not what, Fallon, it's who," Ari teased, popping some strawberries in his mouth as the trio stood in the kitchen.

"You have a lady friend you meet out there?" Fallon questioned.

"Oh, no, Fallon, you can't see her. None of us can. She's invisible!" Ari laughed.

Fallon looked befuddled. "I don't understand."

Arodi gave Ari a look. "Don't confuse her. Yes, Fallon, it's for a lady friend."

"Nelly Taylor?" Fallon asked with a smile. "She's been a frequent visitor lately."

Ari chuckled. "Afraid not."

"It's a secret lady friend then? I've read stories like this." She seemed quite giddy with a grin and giggle.

"She's not a secret, she's just not available to meet everyone at this moment." Arodi looked at the basket Fallon packed. "Is this ready?"

"Yes, sir." Fallon nodded.

"Good, thank you."

"Give her my regards, young man," Ari said.

"That I shall." Arodi made his way to the woods, woods that Marnie said had been replaced by sculptures and hedges. He found the stone table that still existed in her time and began unpacking their lunch. He checked his pocket watch. If she were running behind, she could not send him word of her arrival, so he sat and waited.

*Arodi, what are you doing? Your father sent you here for business and you've ended up indulging in pleasure and leisure. And for what? No, not for what? For who? Her. Marnie. But how? How is it all going to come together?* Arodi sat pondering and decided the best course of action was prayer.

Half an hour ticked along before she appeared.

"I'm sorry I'm late."

"The braised turkey is cold." Her belatedness wounded Arodi. More and more, their time was cut short or interrupted. He had no real claim to her time and tried to appreciate what moments they did spend together, but it wasn't enough.

As she sat down next to him, Marnie explained, "Arodi, I couldn't get away. Simone had a thousand things to do, and I'm not even sure I could stay fifteen minutes long. I'm sorry."

She had been giving him a list of excuses and reasons for her frequent tardiness lately, and it was wearing on him. He felt as though he didn't expect much, but at the least, he wanted her to maintain her integrity by keeping her appointments. It was rude to be constantly delayed for engagements.

Arodi, clearly frustrated, opted for a more tender approach, "I've barely seen you these past few days. It seems that I get mere moments with you, and then you must return to this job you have. Is this what it's like for women in your world?"

"What exactly does that mean? Are you asking if I should just drop everything and be right where you want me when you want me? That is not how it works in my world, Arodi." Marnie sounded upset and defensive.

"That is not what I said." *How can she misconstrue what I was asking and not understand?*

"True, but that's what you meant." Marnie pushed the picnic basket away from her. "I'm not hungry now." She pulled out a technological device and began looking at it.

Arodi contemplated his word choice carefully. "In a way, yes, I did mean women should have more time for their men, but not like you're thinking. You make it sound selfish that I should want to spend time with you."

"I have a job. I have responsibilities and tasks that I have to accomplish in order to keep my job. I have bills to pay, and I'm trying to save money for a house. We're not all born into extravagant wealth, so some of us have to work for a living."

Arodi's eyes narrowed. It sounded like she resented his natural-born status. "You know nothing of my background and the work I've done. Do not comment on matters you do not possess familiarity with."

"Don't take that tone with me. You assume my life is filled with as much leisure as your own. It's not. A lot of women work hard for a living so they don't have to depend on men to provide for them."

Arodi was having a hard time following how rapidly their conversation was becoming combative. He wasn't trying to argue with Marnie, but he threw more cards on the table since they were headed into uncharted territory. "I suppose you also work, so can you afford that device you always carry? The one that causes constant interruptions, and you never stop staring at it."

Marnie looked up from her phone and into Arodi's eyes.

He could feel the heat behind his eyes. *Why are we arguing? I just wanted to spend some time together.* He thought Marnie's face softened some.

"Arodi, I'm sorry." She tucked the device away, moved toward him, and placed her hands on his face. "I forget how very different our worlds are. Please stay and have lunch with me."

Arodi complied. He felt like a child at times around her. She knew so much more about the world than he could ever know. "I do not want to feel belittled for not knowing the social mores of your time."

"I wasn't trying to belittle you. A lot has changed since your time, and I'm not always the best at remembering that. I appreciate all of the efforts you make and the lengths you go to so we can have these delicious lunches together. After the Swan Ball, it will settle somewhat, but my work keeps me very active and busy."

"I do not want to compete with your work." Arodi feared this was the predicament of the modern man. How could a man romance a woman and win her heart if she were constantly engaged with work? How would a woman ever allow herself to be wooed and pursued by a man if she were always chasing another dream? The quest to her heart didn't end in marriage, it was a perpetual journey. While he didn't envision Marnie ever staying home alone to wait on him, he did envision a life together where they had freedom to choose how to spend their days, beholden to none. It was idealistic, but Arodi held fast to what he believed was the right course. "Let me give you some money so you don't have to work."

"Excuse me? I like working."

Arodi could sense the tension reemerging. "What I mean is, let me give you some money so you don't have to work as much."

"It would take way too much money, and I couldn't accept it. I need you to understand that, for now, this is how things are."

It was the first time Arodi questioned a future with Marnie. He could get past the impossibilities of living in different eras, but he wasn't going to compete with this all-consuming work position. Forget that the position was what drew them together in the first place; he was now locked in on how it was driving them apart.

"I think I should like to dine alone and think about things," Arodi said. He needed to go through the past few moments with deeper analysis.

"Maybe you should." Marnie started packing up her belongings

"Good day." Arodi began unpacking his lunch.

"Bye," Marnie quietly offered and walked through the trees.

* * * * *

*What on earth just happened? Was that our first fight? So now what? I'm not supposed to have a job or a career or use my skills and talents to do anything? What does he want me to do? Sit by the phone? Well, not the phone since he clearly hates phones. Maybe sit by the window and wait for him to send a messenger my way telling me what to do with my day? He can't escape his 1840s expectations of what a woman is supposed to do. Should I be at his beck and call? No. That's never going to happen. I'm an independent, educated woman with aspirations and goals.*

Even as Marnie walked away, validating her reasons for leaving him sitting there alone, she knew she'd missed something. This wasn't Arodi's style at all. She had to have misunderstood something, and because of her pride, things had snowballed from there until he had basically asked her to leave.

Marnie stopped in her tracks. She had a choice to make, just like Aunt Ginny. She could continue running the errands Simone had for her, checking things off her list, jeopardizing her entire future by asking for some time off. As she looked up at the treetops, squinting as light filtered down to the ground, Marnie called Simone.

"Hey, Simone, it's Marnie."

"Marnie, excellent. I need you to change gears. I just received a picture from a party hosted the other night with the most luxurious centerpieces, and I have to have them. I don't care what it takes or how you do it; you just get them. I just sent a picture to your phone. That is the priority over everything else. Got it?"

"Absolutely." Marnie waited for the picture to come in. *No way.* It was the centerpiece that she had created for Briscney's party.

"We only have a few days before the Ball, so stop whatever you're doing and get this handled. If you can pull this off, I'd say you've earned the right to work on some of our next projects ."

Marnie tried not to blush at the flattery. "Thanks, Simone. I will get this accomplished."

"Great, bye." Simone ended the call.

Marnie stood dumbstruck. Her goal had been to gain enough experience so that she could compete with Jasmine Rose in a few years. She was talented and skilled enough to run her own business, but she needed these experiences under her belt. Just as she was in the middle of her self-congratulatory thoughts concerning her accomplishments and achievements, she peeked around the hedge where she'd left Arodi.

What did he mean by wanting to spend more time with her? What did he mean by not wanting to compete with her work? Not that she wanted to compete with his work, but he did seem to prioritize spending time with her. Wasn't this just like Aunt Ginny and Uncle Caleb? They made each other a priority, and what they did, they did together.

Marnie sighed. So what if she could compete with Jasmine Rose someday? So what if she could be at the top of her profession? If she didn't have anyone to share it with, was it really worth it? Marnie realized that calling Arodi selfish was just a way to avoid looking at her own selfishness.

Marnie walked back toward the place where she'd left Arodi.

"What are you doing back here?" He looked up from his meal.

"I came back to apologize."

"I believe you already did."

Marnie held up her phone, "Look, it's off."

Arodi took a bite of turkey, unmoved by her gesture.

"I called to tell Simone I wanted the rest of the day off. I want to spend it with you. Although she doesn't know it, she's just lightened my load considerably, and I have more free time than I've had in recent weeks, so I can spend it all with you."

Arodi picked up a carrot and bit into it. He didn't even look in her direction.

Marnie cleared her throat. "I think I misunderstood what you were really wanting when you said you wanted to spend time with me. I've been trying to work full-time and be with you full-time, which is taking its toll on me. I accused you of things that were out of line, things that are not true expressions of what I really know about you and your character."

"Where does that leave us?"

"Where it always does, in the present. Here and now. This moment. I will do whatever it is you want to do for the rest of the day." She had started off being pridefully committed to her own way and her own independence but somehow ended up setting it all aside for him. *Is this what Aunt Ginny did when she chose to die to self? She didn't pursue a path filled with pride and selfishness but chose to exhibit gratitude, trust, and love.*

Arodi looked into her eyes with firmness. "I am not the kind of man who would ask you to walk away from an endeavor you felt so strongly about. If this job is what you feel you should be doing today, I will not get in your way."

"Arodi, working is not what I want to be doing today. In the back of my mind, I always think about the way my aunt and uncle live their lives, and that's what I want in my life. They set their own hours, and they do what they want to do together."

"Living this way, in two different worlds, I don't know how I can help you with your career or you with mine. Maybe our worlds are too far apart for this work."

Marnie instantly felt a knot in her stomach as she waited for his next sentence to be the break-up phrasing. She could not fathom this. She reached over to take his hands in hers as she came to her knees before him.

"Arodi, you already helped me. Your white orchids were such a success that Simone tasked me with doing nothing else until I recreate the very same centerpieces for the Swan Ball."

Arodi gave a small smile, "I did help on that, didn't I?"

"Yes, and I will do the same for you. Whatever you need within reason. I just can't tell you about the future."

Arodi seemed to soften. "Are you still hungry?"

"Famished. What has Fallon cooked up this time?" She wanted to meet this Fallon who prepared such delicious food and thank her for her efforts. How had history treated Fallon? Recorded history had seemingly left her out of any stories about the Millers or Bellamys.

"Today, we have fresh vegetables and braised turkey with strawberry shortcake for dessert." Arodi fixed Marnie a plate and handed it to her.

"Just so you know, I don't know how to cook this well." *Why would I tell him that? Like we're going to be together in the future and I'm going to be in charge of meal planning? I don't know how to handle this. I can't seem to live in the moment and not think about the impossibilities. I just can't do it.*

"Why would you cook?" His question was as serious as they came.

Marnie chuckled, "Right, why would I? Well, this looks delightful." *He has no idea how different things are in my world. He probably thinks I have servants that cook for me.* Marnie nibbled on her carrots.

"Has Drew secured an escort for the ball?"

"Yes, Bella accepted, saying his invitation was sweet and original. I look forward to meeting her." Marnie took a bite of turkey. "Delicious."

"I would like for Drew to have this," Arodi handed her a brown parcel tied with string.

"I'll give it to him." Marnie finished off her lunch with Fallon's shortcake. "I'm stuffed. Thank you for bringing it. So, what is it you had in mind today?"

## Sixteen

Marnie followed Arodi behind large boulders into the thick of the woods at the modern-day Percy Warner Park. The pair entered a hidden cave—a cave she didn't know existed, and by the looks of it, no one else did either. While it certainly wasn't the most romantic place, she wanted to be supportive, so holding tightly to his hand, she let Arodi lead her into the dank, dark tunnel.

She thought she heard cars overhead, so maybe they were under a high-trafficked road, but as Arodi pulled her along, she saw hints of sunlight up ahead. They emerged from the dark tunnel, and she was blown away.

She found that they were behind the three-hundred-foot-high waterfall in the park. As far as she knew, there were no known entrances to the backside of the waterfall. As they stood there, holding hands, the water rushed down; it was powerful and loud. A mist coated everything behind it, including Marnie and Arodi.

"When I said I wanted you to be free to spend time with me, this is what I envisioned." Arodi leaned closer to her ear as he spoke over the sound of rushing water.

Marnie looked into his eyes and placed a hand upon his cheek. She drew him toward her and kissed him as the spray from the waterfall dotted their faces. It was the reconciliation kiss she wasn't sure they would get to have today. It was her apology for the distractions and interruptions, the unspoken communication of how much this relationship meant to her and how it deserved more attention than she had given it. It was further validation that her heart belonged to Arodi, and there it would remain.

He responded by pulling her closer, matching the motion of her lips.

She pulled back slowly, "Thank you, Arodi." *He wasn't being selfish. He wanted to share something with me but needed my full attention, which he hadn't really had. Modern societal demands have definitely placed a whole new strain on relationships.*

He put an arm around her as they admired the view of the cascade before them.

What a magical moment this was for Marnie. She wanted this kind of life with Arodi, one where she walked beside him while learning, sharing, and exploring with him. She closed her eyes and listened to the roaring water, allowing it to relax her. Drew had shared countless articles with her discussing the health benefits of waterfalls, and, in this moment, she had to agree. Every nagging thought washed away with the falling water.

"This was a Shawnee Indian sacred place at one point. Warriors would jump from here to prove their bravery. To keep them safe, they would bring an offering."

Marnie began exploring with Arodi and discovered a large cache of items: jewelry, weapons, clothes, dishes. The clothes were decayed, but the weapons were still intact. Some of the beadwork on the jewelry was broken in places, but it was recognizable. "I don't know if I should take it. It really belongs in a museum, but then I'd have to disclose where I found it."

"What good are these items doing here?" Arodi asked with a shrug of his shoulders.

Marnie bent down.

"Wait, let me." Arodi began collecting several of the items. Marnie watched as the age faded, and they looked fresher. "They probably look better in my time than yours, is that right?"

"Yes."

"I thought so." He finished collecting the items and tucked them into various pockets he had. "The Shawnee moved on about a hundred years ago from this area, so these things have already aged somewhat by my time."

"Thank you, Arodi. This was more fun than I ever imagined, and you're right; I didn't understand what you meant. If men would show women that they simply wanted to spend time with them, discover and explore places with them, and have adventures together, more women would be less committed to their work and career and more inclined to spend more time with their men. Thank you for this and what you have done for me. Today, you've shown me that these are my desires, too."

"I must confess, Marnie, that I am jealous for your time. While I have neglected my business matters to spend time with you, you have diligently performed your duties. There was some truth to what you said about my leisure."

"Arodi, I'm sorry. I was angry, and it was wrong of me to cast stones."

"I'm sorry for the amount of frustration I caused in our conversation earlier. I cannot expect you to spend every free moment with me."

"I hate to hear that."

"Why?"

"Because I basically have the next few days off until the ball, as long as you're able to get me some of those white orchids again."

"Anything you ask. How will that help you have time away from work?"

"Simone doesn't know how long it will take to get them."

"I will send for them tonight, and I can have them here by Thursday. Will that work?"

"Yes, and thank you. I'll pay you for them, too. I'll have to think of a creative way to invoice it." Marnie smiled. "That means we have two whole days to spend together."

"I wish that were true. I received correspondence this morning that two investors will be staying with us through the weekend and should arrive this evening. I must show them where I've scouted for the factory and see if they'd like to join this joint venture."

"So, while I'm able to take off work, you're headed to work." *Lovely irony.*

Arodi pulled her into his arms. "It makes my previous words sound somewhat hypocritical, doesn't it?"

Marnie laughed, "No, it doesn't. I understand." Marnie shivered slightly. She wasn't sure if it was from being near Arodi or the waterfall's chill.

"Shall I give you my shirt? I'm afraid it's all I have."

Marnie was speechless. A shirtless Arodi behind a magical waterfall completely hidden from everyone could lead them down a road they should not go. She knew that there would always be the temptation to forge ahead into places that were reserved for a husband and a wife, but a shirtless Arodi would put her one step closer to that temptation. How difficult would it be to resist him then? Marnie knew Arodi hadn't meant anything by offering her his shirt to keep her warm, but just the thought of him standing before her shirtless made her slightly unsteady on her feet. While she was never one to place herself in a position where she would be vulnerable to her desires, Marnie sensed the danger their mutual attraction could lead to if their desires for each other ever supplanted their desires for righteousness.

Marnie knew there were really only two solutions to this attraction between them: life without Arodi, which she could not imagine, or life with him. She dared not tell him the idea of marriage to him had even entered her mind. It was too much, too soon, to think of. Yet, she had never experienced this level of longing in a relationship. *Am I in a relationship? Does he think of me as his girl, his intended? What exactly are we?*

Arodi began untying the string around the neck of his shirt.

Marnie rested a hand on his chest. "No, I'm really OK."

He placed a hand atop her own.

She traced over the fabric of his shirt, feeling his heart beating against the muscular flesh it covered.

The swiftness of passion swooped them up for a furious ride with a sudden frenzy of kissing leading to Marnie finding her back against the smooth rocks and Arodi pressing in closer to her.

She could tell that Arodi was trying to keep his desires in check, and she was not helping that by keeping her hands tightly around his neck, tempting him to hold her even closer and kiss her more deeply. She tore away from him, realizing only then how saturated she had become against the rocks.

"I'm sorry, are you alright?" Arodi asked, taking a few deep breaths.

"I'm fine. I want to apologize, Arodi. I've never felt like this before and it alarms me how easily I find myself getting carried away with you."

"So, it's not just me, then? You are equally concerned about whether our boundaries are pleasing or not to Yehovah?"

"Yes, and it's becoming increasingly more difficult."

"I am sorry for my actions, Marnie. I do not want to behave in an unsavory manner."

"It's fine right now, Arodi. I just think we have to pray and be very careful so we do not fall into temptation."

Arodi smiled. "I agree, Marnie."

Marnie, no longer chilled, couldn't seem to shake images of Arodi's picture on the cover of a romance novel."We should head back to Cheekwood now so I can change."

"I'll lead us out then." Arodi reached for her hand and led the way through the cave and back toward the woods.

*Seventeen*

"What is this?" Drew asked, looking at the brown parcel Marnie handed him while they were in Aunt Ginny and Uncle Caleb's kitchen.

"I don't know. Open it up."

Drew pulled out a pocket knife from his jeans and cut the string. He unwrapped the contents, pulling out pants, a shirt, a waistcoat, shoes, and a pocket watch. "It's engraved." Drew held up the watch, "To my friend through time." Drew's face grew sullen. "I hate not knowing how long this will last. Of all the people on earth, why us?"

"We may not be the only people. We may just be the only ones to realize it."

"What's the point or the purpose? I pray and get no answer. You pray and still get no answer. Are we in this so you can walk away with a broken heart, and I can lose a new friend? It's almost cruel. I thought I was onto something, but I don't hear any responses to my pleas."

"Then I have to remind you that a longing fulfilled is a tree of life, and trees take time. So we'll wait." Marnie placed a hand on Drew's arm. She knew it was hollow comfort. She thought of the C. S. Lewis quote and how it applied to Drew and Arodi: "Friendship is born at that moment when one person says to another: 'What! You too? I thought I was the only one.'" No one could understand and connect to Drew like Arodi had. In a world where close male friendships were rare and misunderstood, Marnie hated to see the telling signs on Drew's face that he, too, was fond of Arodi's friendship and equally saddened that one day, all of the wonderful times together could abruptly end.

Drew studied his new watch.

"Oh, hey, look at these artifacts I acquired." Marnie offered it as a distraction.

"Whoa. Are these real? They look so well preserved." Drew took the bait and began poring over the new treasures.

"Yeah, it was really cool. I went to grab them, but Arodi did first, so I got the 1849 version, which is way more intact than our version would have been."

"Where? How? Did you encounter an Indian tribe and trade them a treaty for this?"

Marnie laughed. "No, there was a hidden passage behind the waterfall at

103

Percy Warner, and these items were left there."

"Why?"

"The way Arodi explained it, it seems that they were gifts to their god for protection."

"And you think we should bring these 'sacrifices' into our home?"

Marnie thought about it. Now that Drew mentioned it, did these items have any place in their set-apart homestead? "Well, they aren't fashioned like idols, so maybe they were just items left behind and not left for any false gods. Arodi was just sharing the legend he had been told. I don't know. What do you think?"

Drew pulled out his laptop. "I think we should do some historical research." He began typing. Drew and Marnie looked over the artifacts and tried to match the items to historical accounts. They decided that if they kept the items, it would be a private family collection. Turning the pieces over to the State or any private museum would certainly raise questions for which they would have no real answers.

* * * * *

How quickly time raced toward the first Swan Ball. Aunt Belinda retreated from pushing Nelly on Arodi, freeing him to spend more time with Marnie, while Ari spent more time with Nelly, taking daily walks between the estates, having tea with Nelly and her mother, and promising Nelly the world's best tour of New York should she and her parents visit the city.

"Nelly has certainly occupied a lot of your free time of late." Arodi started with Ari. They were under a large Maple tree playing a game Nelly said she played in France: pall-mall, which entailed hitting balls through hoops.

"Now, don't go thinking I have an attraction to her. I mean to travel more. I'd like to visit South America next." Ari knocked one of the balls with a stick and it missed the hoop. "Your turn."

Arodi obliged and tried to gauge strike force and distance. "I think it's grand that you've been most attentive to Nelly and smoothed things over with her family after my outburst."

"What of your mysterious friend? Are you planning to introduce her this summer? Perhaps at the upcoming ball?"

Arodi struck his ball, and it came close to the hoop. "Our worlds are vastly different, and if I can find a way to make a future with her, I will do my best to ensure a proper introduction."

"My only concern is a possible scandal. I shouldn't want anything to bring harm to our family name during our time here." Ari lined up his shot.

" I assure you that there won't be any scandal." *How can there be? She doesn't exist in this world. Besides, if I dared to explain myself, Aunt Belinda would have me carted off for spouting such a fantasy. Ari, I wish I could explain everything to you.*

Ari hit his ball through the hoop. "I know you will always put the family

104

interests first but don't miss out on something wonderful because of status or reputation. If you have feelings for this girl, then I know she's worthy of such affection regardless of her place in society. I look forward to meeting her should the occasion arise."

Arodi hoped such a time and place would occur.

* * * * *

Arodi spied Marnie early in the morning on the grounds the day before the ball. He stole away with her into the woods, tucked deep into the most lush and private of enclaves. Beyond the thick hedges surrounded by verdant grasses, bushes, and trees, he led her to a place she had never been to at Cheekwood. He was sure it still held the utmost privacy in her time as well.

Having an ever-ready blanket on the ground for them to sit and recline upon, Arodi patiently waited for Marnie to meet him. He was accustomed now to her presence without a chaperon and wondered how men with less morals than him behaved around an unaccompanied woman. To him, it seemed a license for lasciviousness, and yet the freedom to speak his heart and mind around her was welcoming.

On this particular day, Arodi's heart overflowed with joy when he saw her, and he wasted no time in lowering Marnie onto the blanket while simultaneously kissing her in a maneuver he had never contemplated nor tried on any woman since Marnie was the first and only woman he had ever pursued. The natural flow of the moment paralleled so many of the explorers' accounts of when they encountered a new wilderness for the first time: observe, discover, taste, memorize, touch, experience, chart the new terrain with copious notes and diagrams, then make a map of every curve, peak, bend, and every beautiful view afforded.

He felt no reservations about her movements, and he could not control the thoughts formulating in his mind. Her lips were soft, and she always applied what she called beeswax to them. Arodi thoughts flashed to the fourth chapter of Song of Solomon, "Milk and honey are under your tongue." He gently stroked the back of her head as he held it, keeping her at just the right angle for him to kiss. He inhaled deeply the lavender scent that he now associated with Marnie. What kind of beauty treatments caused this woman to smell so enticing and stir a longing in his soul? Arodi immediately chastised himself for letting his thoughts wander to how she bathed. King David watched a woman bathe once, and that led to a myriad of sins and entanglements. Arodi chastised himself again.

Marnie applied pressure to the back of his neck, signaling she wanted him to move in closer, deepening their passion. Arodi felt his heart race and his pulse quicken. He should just give in to this blissfulness and stop analyzing things so much. No sooner had that thought taken hold when he experienced an unfamiliar, internal nudge that made him give pause. He was headed in the wrong direction. He switched to kissing Marnie's cheeks and neck while he forced himself to take an emotional step back. This moment could lead them down a path that would cross the boundaries they had set.

This wasn't right. He would not go any further than the wonderfully delightful kisses they shared, even though he suspected he could. He refused to spoil the Gift of Marnie. She was a man's daughter, and more importantly, she belonged to Yehovah. They had not declared an intent to marry, nor had there been any witnesses to such a promised betrothal, and how could there be? No one could see both of them at the same time, so how could anyone bear witness to their union? What had started as a yearning for a friend had transformed into a heartfelt desire for a wife. Not just any wife, but this fascinating, beautiful woman for his wife.

"What are you thinking about?" Marnie asked, pulling away from Arodi's kiss.

"About how much I desire you, but also that I do not want to cross our boundaries." He sat back, and she sat up.

Marnie searched his face. " I want to be honest about my feelings. I've never had a serious relationship before, so I didn't realize how hard it would be to stop in the heat of the moment. I feel as though I can't even trust myself to know when to stop, but you're always so composed and in control of your emotions. I never thought I would be in a position where my judgment could be so clouded."

Arodi smiled as he gathered her into his arms and held her close. "My composure is not for lack of wanting you, Marnie. Believe me, my struggles are real, but we are not husband and wife. Marnie, I do not believe there is another for me, so I am earnestly praying and seeking for a future together. Why would I risk ruining the future plans that Yehovah has for us for short-lived pleasure now? Love is patient, lust is quick." He took her hands into his. "I know not how honor and reputation are viewed in your world, but in my time, they are to be preserved and safeguarded. If you find that even my kisses betray my desire to maintain purity toward you, you shall not encounter my lips again until we know it is the blessed path."

Marnie smiled, "Arodi, I totally agree that we should not go beyond kissing. Being caught up in that precise moment, I might not care, but I would never want to jeopardize our future."

Arodi wanted to drop to one knee and propose to Marnie right then, but he had to wait for guidance from Yehovah. Marrying Marnie would require a ceremony, witnesses, and housing, not to mention the most challenging obstacle: living in two different eras.

## *Eighteen*

The Swan Ball embodied elegance, pizazz, and glamor. It was a time when Nashville's finest stepped out in their best Victorian style for the evening, keeping with this year's theme: gowns, hats, gloves, and canes. Mimicking every aspect possible of a period long faded, carriages met the patrons at the front entrance of Cheekwood and took them to the mansion's front doors.

From food to music, décor, and style, everything looked as though the patrons had traveled back in time. Mulligatawny soup, roast goose with stuffing, Yorkshire pudding, and the aroma of savory sweet breads filled the air from the large outdoor kitchen constructed for the event. The dessert table featured sweets from every color of the spectrum, enticed all who walked by to slow down and take a closer look. Recognizable Beethoven melodies resounded flawlessly through the air, further enhancing the mood.

Marnie stood in the mansion's ballroom, directing people to the massive tent on the lawn, where perfectly decorated tables awaited them. The previous evening, Marnie had met Arodi to get the white orchids and finish the centerpieces. She had placed them on the tables early that morning. Simone was elated that the centerpieces had turned out so much better than she had thought, thanks to Marnie's handiwork and creativity.

For the past week, both Arodi and Marnie's work had encroached on any available personal time, but tonight would be different. Simone told Marnie that she was officially off the clock at 7:30 pm, even though the Ball did not start until eight. Why had Simone done that? Was it because she wanted to give Marnie the time off as a reward? Or maybe it was because she didn't want Marnie around when she accepted thanks on behalf of Jasmine Rose.

Marnie decided that it didn't really matter. She had done her due diligence and then some to help make this night perfect.

Drew walked up to Marnie wearing his authentic clothes from Arodi. "What's your job?"

"Oh well, if you're not sure what table you belong to or how they're numbered, I will show you that. I'm your basic greeter. Nice threads, by the way."

"Thanks, I was going for the snazzy look tonight." He spun in a quick circle.

"Where's your date?" Marnie looked around at the people in the ballroom carrying on conversations.

"She's just freshening up. And," Drew looked around surreptitiously, "where's your date?"

"We have plans to meet later."

"Well, here's a thank you note from me when you see him." Drew handed her stationery, which appeared to be from Arodi's time.

Marnie saw a young woman walking their way wearing an exquisite purple gown.

"She stitched it herself. What do you think?" Drew asked, following Marnie's gaze.

The woman approached with all of the grace and poise of true royalty.

"You must be Bella?" Marnie extended her hand.

"Yes, it's so nice to meet you." Bella clasped her hands to Marnie's. Her soft blond curls bounced lightly. She wore a black velvet teardrop hat and looked like she had walked out of the era.

"Bella, this is my cousin, Marnie." Drew suddenly remembered his manners.

"Your dress is absolutely stunning," Bella said. "It's very true to the mid-1840s."

"Bella has her Ph.D. in American History." Drew proudly added.

"Well, I had some help with my dress. And yours is superb." Marnie commented, thinking Bella could have stepped off the page of the earliest fashion magazines.

"Drew tells me you helped put this on, and I must say, it's wonderful. Where is your escort for the evening?"

"I am actually just here to work tonight, so no partying for me."

"What a shame. Cheekwood is the perfect date night."

Drew smiled big at Marnie with saucer-sized eyes when Bella used the word "date."

Marnie saw Simone watching them. She didn't want Simone to think she wasn't working, so she politely nudged them along. "You guys should go take your seats and enjoy the dinner. I hope to see you both later this evening," Marnie said.

"Of course." Bella curtsied, fitting right in with the theme of the night.

Drew and Bella moved to their table.

Simone approached Marnie wearing a red and white floral gown with long poet sleeves. "You look exquisite, Marnie. I should've used your seamstress. It's like you've walked off the page of a history book, and your hair is absolutely adorable." Simone sported a large hat filled with pink, white, and red feathers.

Marnie had forgone the hat and opted for a Victorian-inspired hairdo. Waves and twists were tucked and pinned, and streamers of curls touched her shoulders and back. She felt like a princess tonight and could hardly contain her excitement about seeing her prince soon.

"I received the dress as a gift from a family friend who's well acquainted with antiquity," Marnie explained.

"I'll bet all the available gentlemen will request your hand during the dancing later."

The London Symphony Orchestra supplied the music for the evening. They only accepted twenty-five offers a year to perform beyond their regularly scheduled events, and Jasmine Rose had been fortunate to retain them.

"I will be sure to enjoy the music," Marnie said.

"Great, well, go on now. You've earned an evening off. We can chat on Monday about your next project."

"Thank you, Simone."

They curtsied, and Marnie beelined to the wooded area just off the lawn. *Next project. I wonder what it will be. I wonder if she'll promote me. I could take the company in so many new and exciting directions.* Marnie was practically floating as she beamed from Simone's accolade.

Draped from the massive branches of an old oak tree, Marnie had made sure the decorators placed the fairy lights and papier-mâché lights in the branches to create the perfect ambiance. The aroma of night-blooming jasmines filled the tucked-away cove where Marnie waited for Arodi.

She knew the patrons would dine first, then dance, but the orchestra would be continuously playing. It was such an enchanting evening. The katydids, crickets, and possibly a lone cicada provided a beautiful accompaniment to the woodwind soloist currently playing. Moonlight wove its way between and through leafy boughs dotting the grass in splotches and speckles. She looked at her phone to check the time. Arodi had agreed to meet her at eight o'clock. She incessantly kept glancing at her phone, watching 7:42, 7:43, 7:46, 7:47, and 7:53 all pass by.

Right at eight, she heard the orchestra play the beginning chords of Chopin's Nocturne Op.9. No.2. *Thank you, Music Appreciation Class.* Marnie reflected on the steps she had taken to create a romantic atmosphere in the hideaway for the evening and felt the song fit perfectly. She looked around for Arodi, checking both possible ways he could enter. She looked from her right to the left and then back to the right.

Marnie wasn't sure whether Arodi appeared or manifested, but he was finally here, looking handsome in his navy frock coat, matching waistcoat, which hid most of his white shirt, and brown tweed pants. To finish off the ensemble, he wore a brown and gray ascot and black dress shoes. Time stood still, and Marnie held her breath as he slowly approached, grinning. His hair was swept back, held in place by whatever means they used in his time.

"You look absolutely ravishing this evening." He seemed to drink her in. "These are for you." He proceeded to hand Marnie a bouquet of lavender and white roses.

She accepted them and brought them to her face. "They are heavenly." She inhaled the richness of the floral arrangement, which was masterfully pieced together and tied with a deep purple ribbon. Everything he did was executed flawlessly.

"May I have this dance?" He bowed with an extended hand.

"You can hear the music?"

"Chopin, right? *The Sound of the Night*? I arranged it." He grinned.

Marnie placed the flowers on the stone bench behind her and accepted his hand. She moved close as they slowly swayed beneath the fairy lights, surrounded by the trees, bushes, and music. They were tucked away in their own private music box without a care in the world. *The Sound of the Night* never lost its appeal, whether it was played in 1849 or in Marnie's time.

"How did you do it?" Marnie asked, looking into his eyes, her fingers twisting and untwisting in his locks of hair.

"A man in 1849 is not without resources to affect an event in the far future." He smiled.

She knew that all too well. He had affected every part of her heart. Marnie looked at him with certainty, "It was Drew."

"How is my friend and his lady friend?"

"They look lovely together. And," she pulled out the thank you note Drew had given her, "he wanted you to have this."

Arodi accepted the paper, tucked it into his vest, and pulled her back in close.

Marnie imagined she and Arodi looked picturesque under the branches with the low lighting and dressed in their authentic attire. She wished that she had thought to have brought a camera with a timer, but it probably would've captured her and not him. It saddened her to think she would not have a photo to remember this night. She needed to commit every minute to memory. From the time she saw him enter their enclave, she'd remember every step they took as they danced. She'd remember the feel of his jacket and the way he held her hand as they danced. His twinkling eyes staring back at her, and his simple and sweet smile on his face would be etched on her heart forever.

She rested her head on Arodi's shoulder. "Is this how you dance in 1849?" As the music continued, she closed her eyes, wanting to capture everything about this night with him.

"It's a little more spacious than this."

"Shall I take a step or two back?"

"Only if you are prepared for me to step with you."

How long could the orchestra play this song? Could it go on forever? The notes were soft and flowed poetically. This was now Marnie's absolute favorite song. She knew she would download it later and listen to it on repeat...for at least two solid weeks.

Marnie breathed in the scent of Arodi as she swayed in tune with him. He smelled of bergamot and lemon. She pressed her cheek against his to feel its warmth and its smoothness. She was glad he had dispensed with the mustache she so often saw in many of the portraits hanging in the halls of the mansion.

She felt his hand move from her lower back up to where the tendrils of her hair hung. As the music continued, he traced his fingers along her shoulder blades with light strokes.

It was a precious moment in his or her time, and the year didn't matter because it was a moment of timelessness. It was just a boy and a girl enjoying a dance, oblivious to any distraction outside of their world, sharing the same space and heartbeat.

As the song ended and another began, their dancing remained the same. Neither was concerned with precisely performing the dance steps or matching the timing of the music. Tonight was simply about spending time together in close proximity and enjoying the evening.

Arodi led Marnie to the bench. "Did Simone like your artistic centerpieces? Did you tell her they were yours?"

"Yes, she liked them and no, I did not tell her they were mine. Thank you again for your help. I know it's been a sort of a whirlwind these past couple of days, and I'm sure you have much to tell me about the factory."

"We found the location and will draw up an offer next week. I've also received wonderful news. My family has arrived in Nashville and will come to Cheekwood soon."

"Everyone?"

"Well, all but Ari. He decided to head back to New York, but my father, mother, sisters, and brothers are all coming to visit."

"How old are your other siblings?"

"Noah is twenty-one, Tamar is seventeen, Yitzak is twelve, and Sarah is six."

"You must be so excited to see them."

"Indeed, I am. They will spend the rest of the summer here. We have so many fun things planned. I look forward to taking the older ones to the waterfall and hearing about their studies. I do enjoy my time with them."

"I'm happy for you."

"I wish they could meet you." Arodi held Marnie's hands as they sat. He turned toward her. "I want a life with you, Marnie. I want to introduce you to my parents and have you meet my entire family. They would adore you."

"I would love to meet your family, and my aunt and uncle would feel the same about you, but there's that question of how would we do that?"

"I wish sheer will could affect it, but I suspect this is much more supernatural in nature than anything. Perhaps it's a test of faith?"

"Anything is possible."

Arodi drew Marnie closer to him and sat seemingly lost in thought while the orchestra continued playing.

"I keep praying for a long-term solution." He shared.

"You know I want that more than anything, but Arodi, I try so hard not to get my hopes up. I know in my heart that there will only ever be you. I want a life with you and I want to meet your family, but how? It scares me more than I realize to think that at any minute, the bridge could close, and I'll never see you again. It would've been so much easier to walk away before now, but I didn't want to then, nor do I want to now. Do you think you can find a way to make it work?" She searched his eyes for answers.

"Not me, but I know the One Who can." He leaned his head against hers.

She could hear him praying in Hebrew, which brought her to tears. *Yehovah, he's so perfect for me. Please make a way for us to be together.* She held tightly to his hand while he prayed. It was ethereal and precious, and she believed his every request would be heard. Tears of mutual consent rolled down her cheeks.

He slipped his ascot off. "I'm sorry, I don't have a handkerchief tonight, so this will have to do." He dried her tears with his ascot, then tenderly kissed her.

"Thank you."

He folded up his ascot and placed it in his pocket.

They sat on the bench together while the melodious sounds from the mansion filled the air, and, at least in Marnie's time, the lights glowed from above. On the most magical night Marnie had ever experienced, it felt as though time stood still. She believed that there was nothing that could hinder their relationship.

*Nineteen*

Rain saturated the world around Marnie as she watched streams of water gush outside from her perch on the patio. The rain barrels were full, the fields saturated, and the Harpeth swelling with the runoff. Marnie snuggled under a soft gray and blue alpaca throw, warm and dry, hearing the gentle, comforting thunder rumble miles away. No birds, no bugs, nothing dared to take flight during the storm.

"What a monsoon!" A drenched Drew came in and slipped off his sturdy yellow rain slicker. He removed his rubber boots and hung the jacket on a peg above the tiled patio floor over a plastic tray meant to catch the rain dripping off the items hung there.

"Weather forecast says three days of rain." Marnie typed away on her computer.

Drew ran his hands over his hair and reclined on the patio couch. "Are you working on another event?"

"Yes. Presently, we're handling a party for a horse owner who is the favorite to win the Triple Crown next year."

"Local fella?"

"No, he's from Brazil. He bought two hundred acres out in Leipers Fork, and that's where we're hosting this event for him."

"Cool."

Marnie could feel Drew's eyes on her. "What did you come out here for?" She closed the laptop lid.

"I was just messin' with the horses in the barn, talkin' to Mom and Dad." He cleared his throat. "So, what'd you think of Bella?" He sat up.

"She's cute. Did you two have a good time? I didn't see you after dinner." *Mainly because I was so caught up in the most charming fairytale setting a girl could ever dream of.*

Marnie could not help it as she replayed that night in her mind. The dress, the music, the man, and the soft fairy lights perfectly placed in the tree branches, illuminating two hearts swaying slowly together. Marnie snapped back into the conversation where Drew was talking.

"She's a total history buff. We went on an insider's tour of Cheekwood. She showed me where the original herb garden was and some initials carved into the side of the house from family members. She is so knowledgeable and fun to be around."

Marnie smiled. It was the simple things that impressed Drew. "That sounds fascinating, and I'm happy for you." *I can't even imagine how pleasurable it would be to do that with Arodi, where we could interact in public with one another, and people could see us together. No sneaking around, no hiding.* Marnie didn't feel they were doing something bad, but keeping their relationship a secret weighed on her.

"What about Arodi? Is he coming by?"

"His family is in town, which I guess sounds kind of silly to speak like it's the present tense since it already happened."

Drew nodded. "When will you see him again?"

*Isn't it silly to think of seeing him in the future and speaking of it this way?* "We don't really have any plans. I am not able to get to Cheekwood daily since my work is in Franklin now, it's been harder to find time to meet. I imagine he'll come by on a ride, or I can always drive over there to see him on the weekends." Marnie tucked her laptop into its leather bag. "Have you figured out any more of the science behind it all?"

"I can't see that the hole in time is changing, but I've come across a ton of stories where folks swear they've experienced time travel. Stories that are similar to ours. I could forward you the blogs and websites devoted to their testimonies if you want to read some of them."

Marnie held a hand up, "No, that's OK." She ran her hand over her throw, smoothing out a wrinkle. "Did anyone believe them?"

"Not yet, and they had proof similar to the artifacts we have, but they were dismissed. I shared some of the articles with Bella."

"And what did she say?"

"She said that she couldn't rule out time travel as a possibility. I'm a hundred percent convinced I've found my soulmate."

Marnie tended to agree. Their interests were so similar, and from what Drew said about Bella, she seemed like an educated, polite young woman.

Drew's phone vibrated. "It's Bella. I'm gonna take this inside." Drew walked into the house and answered the phone.

Wasn't it nice to be able to pick up the phone and speak to someone you cared about? Marnie only had one mode of communication with Arodi: face-to-face. She would settle for letter-writing if that were possible. Cheekwood had provided a rhythm to their encounters, ensuring they would meet. What would it be like now that she wasn't there every day? What would it be like when they broke ground at the new textile factory, and he was there every day?

Marnie let out a sigh and watched the stormwater race through the fields.

*  *  *  *  *

The rain was loud that evening, but it lulled Marnie to sleep.

"Marnie! Marnie!"

She opened her eyes. What time was it? It was still dark, so what woke her? She had drifted off to the sounds of *The Sounds of the Night* playing on repeat on her phone.

"Marnie!" It was Arodi's voice, muffled, sounding like he was outside.

She grabbed her robe, hurriedly put it on, and zipped downstairs barefoot. When she opened the door, she saw Arodi standing nearby, calling her name.

"Over here!" She softly called. She turned on the front porch light and stepped outside, gently closing the door behind her.

Arodi ran to her. His attire was disheveled, his five o'clock shadow fully prominent. He was breathless and appeared distraught. He was dry, though, so it must not have been raining in 1849 that night.

"What is it?" Marnie placed her hands on his arms.

"Sarah, my youngest sister, is terribly sick. The doctor says it's diphtherite. My mother says people all over Nashville are dying, and they won't risk any of us getting ill, so they aren't coming to Cheekwood. I must go to them. I don't know how long I will be gone, but I must go to Sarah. I rode out here to tell you because it may be weeks before I see you again."

*Diphtherite? It must be diphtheria or close to it. How do you cure it?* "Arodi, is there a cure?"

"I don't know of any cure, but the doctor will do everything he can for her."

Marnie knew antibiotics had the ability to save Sarah, but not in 1849, and now she faced a dilemma she was sure no one she knew had ever had to face. Sarah could be saved by modern medicine, and Arodi would be the conduit for the delivery of life-saving antibiotics. All Marnie had to do was procure them and explain to him how to administer them to Sarah. Drew had warned her not to change the past, and though she couldn't save Lincoln or stop Hitler, she might be able to save a little girl from dying.

Arodi cupped her face with his hands. "Marnie, I know the risk I am taking by going to Sarah. I could end up infected. I'm healthy and strong, but I know this may be our goodbye. I debated whether to tell you, but I had to come to you and let you know I love you and would never put you in harm's way. I'll return if I can. It's just she's my sister. I must go to her. She's asking for me."

Marnie could see the tears welling up in his eyes. She pulled him against her and held him as he shook with sobs. There would be no goodbyes, not with Marnie around. She knew what had to be done. This man was a treasure. He was a man fully committed to his family. This was it. This was the kind of partnership she wanted. This man needed her help and viewed her as his equal. His respect for her was just like her uncle had for her aunt. They were better together than apart. This relationship had to be from Yehovah, and she would no longer question it.

She held him close, realizing how beautiful the embrace of a woman could be for a man. She could be a source of comfort and confidence. He trusted her with his tears. And in that moment, Marnie matured. She would be there for Arodi as his equal and a source of emotional and spiritual strength. She knew the risks and would rise to the task of this life-saving action.

He pulled back with a sniffle and wiped his eyes. "I must go. Pray for Sarah and our family."

Marnie took a deep breath, "Arodi, I can help."

"How?"

Marnie gently touched his cheek, "The future has its ways. Where are they staying?"

"Mary Claiborne's Boarding House in Nashville."

Marnie had not heard of it. She had some research to do. "I will find it. I can meet you there in the morning."

He sniffed again. "I am going to ride through the rest of the night so that I'm there by morning."

"I'll be there."

"Is there a cure in the future? Can you save her?"

His look was equally one of hope and desperation, and Marnie had no time to waste. "I'll do my best."

"Thank you." Arodi kissed her. "I must ride now. I will watch for you tomorrow." He disappeared into the darkness.

Marnie went inside, quickly dressed, grabbed her keys, purse, and a rain slicker, then headed out into the night.

*Twenty*

"How is she?" Marnie stood outside of the present-day Smith House as Arodi sat on the steps. The house, which was new in Arodi's time, hosted the wealthy, but in Marnie's time, it was a restaurant. In 1849, Italian architecture was wedded with antebellum touches, and it boasted six exquisitely decorated bedrooms with personal bathrooms for each. During Arodi's lifetime, the boarding house would host families visiting the area, men coming to Nashville for business, and Union soldiers planning the Battle of Nashville while an entire nation was in a crisis.

Arodi let out a sigh. "She's feverish and hallucinating. I've been praying." He looked like a man who had been awake all night. Dark circles under his eyes, hair a ruffled mess atop his head, and stubble on the bottom half of his face.

"Here," Marnie handed Arodi a glass jar. "I can't tell you what it is, but a teaspoon of this three times a day will save her. You can start now and then give it to her during mealtimes."

"Where did you get this?" He examined the jar.

"It doesn't matter; just trust me. You must give her the entire dosage until it runs out. She will feel better soon but do not stop until it's all gone. Do you understand?"

He nodded, still looking at the jar. "I understand." He kissed her cheek, "thank you."

"Go save your sister. I will come back here every couple of days to check on everyone, OK?"

Arodi nodded. He looked at the jar again, then at Marnie before turning and going up the stairs.

He vanished through the doorway, and Marnie wondered if that was the last time she would see him. Perhaps the whole purpose of her meeting Arodi was to save a little girl, and now that the deed was done, the bridge through time would be closed. Someday, these last few months would make for a lovely story to write or base a movie on.

Marnie suddenly felt saddened by the thought of this being the end. What if Yehovah had closed the bridge because He had meant to save a little girl the whole time and used His creation to do it? Life without Arodi in her timeline had once been reality, but it was now an impossibility for Marnie.

Marnie walked along the sidewalk in the direction of where she had parked. The rain had stopped. It was still overcast, but no showers for the moment. Downtown Nashville was abuzz with activity. Commuters parking in garages, suit-wearing executives briskly walking to their offices, and a few people asking for a handout. Marnie wondered what it was like for the homeless in 1849. Was someone helping them? Did they have a place to sleep at night? What were humanitarian efforts like in Arodi's time?

*I just changed history. What have I done?* Marnie imagined the good and bad that she may have done just then by giving Arodi a cure for his sister. Drew wasn't going to like what she'd done in the least. Was it right? Was it wrong?

Marnie tried to imagine if Sarah were her sister, a helpless child who had suddenly fallen ill. Wouldn't she do anything to ease the suffering and pain of her sister? How could she not use modern medicine to save her?

She weighed the pros and cons of her decision, and each time, it hinged on whether she could save a life. Sarah won out every time.

* * * * *

"I don't like it," Sarah cried.

Arodi gave her a teaspoon from the vial Marnie had provided.

Her once-soft curls were wet with sweat, making her hair look darker blonde than it really was. She looked so frail in her linen nightgown, lying against the pillows.

"Mamma!" Sarah called.

Alice came to the bedside wearing a bell-shaped skirt and a long-sleeved shirt tucked into it. Her hair was in a long braid, and she looked weathered.

"I'm cold, Mamma!" Sarah cried out and reached for her mother.

Against the doctor's orders, Alice played nurse to Sarah, even sitting with Sarah in bed, risking her own health. She brought the covers up to Sarah's chin.

Arodi pondered dividing the medicine between his mother and Sarah but tucked the vial in his pocket instead. He reasoned Marnie could get more if they needed it. He sat in a chair near the fireplace as his mother sat on the bed. He was pensive and pained. He had arrived at the house in the middle of the night to meet his father in tears in the parlor. Sarah wasn't just Hutchison's princess. She was special to the whole family. Arodi has finally gotten his father to agree to lie down for a few hours. The other children were packing to return to New York and were under strict orders not to encounter Sarah.

Sarah wriggled her arms out from under the covers and clung to their mother.

Alice kissed the top of her head. "Shh, shh, just rest, my love. It will be alright."

Sarah fought sleep as the fever caused chills. She went from cold to hot in a

118

flash, and Alice patiently attempted to relieve all the symptoms.

Arodi saw the newspaper headlines about the outbreak and knew that the death toll was climbing. He vowed to pray without ceasing. He reached into his pocket and made imaginary circles with his finger on the vial. *It's going to be fine. She's going to make it. She's a strong girl. Mother won't get sick. The other children are fine. Everyone is going to be well. Yehovah, I am frightened, but Your perfect love casts out all fear. I ask You to pour it upon me in heaping doses and save my sister. Spare my family any loss. Please heal Sarah.*

Arodi would keep watch with his mother over Sarah until she had finished the last dose and had recovered.

* * * * *

Marnie made it back to the car and drove home.

It was still early, so she quietly entered the house. To her surprise, Drew was sitting in the living room, apparently waiting for her. "Erythromycin," he said.

That was the drug Marnie had given to Arodi for Sarah. Marnie braced herself for the lecture from Drew as he steadied his aim with daggers in his eyes.

"Do you have any idea what you've just done? I had to cover for you. What were you thinking concocting that story about an undocumented friend's daughter who was facing a life-or-death situation? And to get that medicine, did you trade six months' worth of horse boarding? Do you know how surprised my parents were when the pharmacist showed up this morning with his daughter's horse to board? They asked me what I knew about it, and I covered for you. I said I knew all about it, and whatever it was you did, you felt like it was necessary. So don't you dare tell me you gave that to someone in the past. You'd better tell me it was for someone in the here and now because you are not going to do this to my parents." His tone and inflection were that of anger.

"I will pay them the rent money for the six months."

"Not the point, Marnie. Who did you give that medicine to?"

Marnie averted his glare.

"Let me guess." Drew held up his phone, "Three hundred eleven people died from a diphtheria outbreak in Nashville this time of year in 1849. I'll bet now that figure will be three hundred ten. What did you do?"

Marnie burned with indignation at Drew's callousness. "It was his sister, Drew. I won't make the case for her life."

"You don't know the future, and you changed it. Maybe she was meant to die, and now she doesn't. You don't know how this changed her life and her future."

"She's a little girl, and she could've died."

"So now what, Doctor Foster? Do you try to save all the others with modern medicine? I can show you a ton of articles from the 1840s filled with horrendous tragedies. When do you want to start?"

"What is your problem?"

"My problem? My problem is that I had to lie to my parents this morning to cover for you. You kept telling me not to go all mad scientist and mess up the past, but you have completely disregarded those boundaries and altered an entire family's course of history at the expense of mine!"

"Our family, Drew. I'm still a part of this family. It was one life. I did what I could to save the sister of the man I love."

"You're too emotionally involved. You're going to mess this up big time. What if your actions reverse the outcome of the Civil War? We never should've let things go this far. I made a huge mistake by trying to figure it out. I never should've opened that portal any wider."

She knew Drew was more than angry. He was also hurt.

"Where do you think your relationship with Arodi leads, Marnie? There's no future because you're emotionally involved; it's changing too much of the past. How are you not going to spill the beans about the war? How can you keep a lid on all of this? How are you going to stop yourself from saving the next child that is injured or sick?"

"I honestly don't know, Drew. I don't have answers." Marnie was awash with raw emotions. "I just acted without thinking because it was an emergency. And you're right. I would help any child that came to me regardless of the reason or the time period. If Yehovah doesn't want me helping sick kids, then He will have to close the door because I'm going to help those in need as long as I can. I can't believe you're being so uncaring and so heartless about this."

Drew looked away. "All I am saying is that you don't know the consequences." His tone was lower.

"I didn't ask you to lie for me, and I didn't lie either. Sarah's parents aren't documented in our time, and her life was in danger. There wasn't an opportunity to explain. I didn't know the pharmacist was going to show up here today. I will apologize to your parents. Maybe it's best if I move back to the cabin and give you some space."

"No arguments there."

Marnie shook her head.

Drew added, "I'm not opening that portal anymore, either. This has been going on for three months, and enough's enough." Drew went to the kitchen, leaving Marnie alone in the living room.

## *Twenty-One*

"But Arodi, I really am all better. Can't you make Mother take me to Cheekwood? I want to see everyone. Please." Sarah begged. She and Arodi sat outside at a table on the hotel grounds, having tea together while Alice wrote her correspondence letters from their room. Sarah's blonde curls were held atop her head with a salmon bow that matched the material of her salmon-colored dress. Long, white cotton pantalettes covered her legs. Her legs dangled from the chair since her black-booted feet could not reach the brick-paved ground. "You said I took all my medicine."

He and his mother initially disagreed about medicine. At the outset, Alice dismissed it as snake water until Arodi revealed his source was a trusted lady friend. Since then, she had been pressing him to invite Marnie for tea or dinner once Sarah recovered and before they departed for New York. Arodi made excuses that she was out of town, which was technically true. He wanted his mother to focus on caring for Sarah and not on his relationship with Marnie.

Now, he beheld the sight of his darling youngest sister, and emotions flooded his heart. How close would they have come to losing her without Marnie's intervention? He knew that she was a messenger from Yehovah, sent with the life-saving medicine that Sarah needed.

Sarah ate some honeydew and sipped her tea.

"I think it would be best for you to return home with Mother and plan a trip later in the year. Your cousins will be back then, and you can visit with everyone." Arodi offered.

Sarah hung her head. "But I haven't seen you at all this summer. You're not coming back to New York, are you?"

*Not returning to New York? Sarah, you're right. I belong here and am tied to this place now. I cannot see myself ever leaving. I came for a season, and it has altered my life.* "I will come back to New York. I just don't know the timing." Arodi downed the last bit of tea. "Now, let's find out from Mother if we can go for a carriage ride around the city before supper."

Sarah beamed and proceeded to gather a few grapes and a butter cracker for the walk upstairs.

* * * * *

For the next two weeks, Marnie divided her time between work projects and visiting Arodi downtown to check on Sarah. Alice sent the other children home to New York, cutting their trip to Nashville short. Arodi remained with his mother and Sarah downtown while his father visited Cheekwood.

"Is she outside with us?" Marnie asked as she and Arodi stood outside of the large house. He had shaved, fixed his hair, and looked every inch the successful businessman. Marnie wore a silk short-sleeved mango-colored shirt tucked into a high-waisted navy, pleated, below-the-knee skirt with a peacock print on it and low brown heels. Her hair was in a large braid, resting forward on her left shoulder.

She looked around to see if anyone was passing by them, careful not to appear as though she were talking to herself.

"She just now raced back indoors for lemonade."

"I wanted to give her something."

Arodi drew Marnie to him and kissed her cheek. "You already have."

She let him hold her, treasuring each moment in his embrace. She felt him relax with his arms around her, and she could only imagine how emotionally exhausting this had been for him.

"Here," she reached into her leather saddlebag purse and pulled out a necklace. It was a turquoise stone with wire on the front of it, twisted and shaped like the tree of life. "Drew gave me this the day that I left for summer camp many years ago. The day before, we were rock climbing. I got too close to the edge, and he had to grab me just as I was slipping. He wanted me to remember how precious life is, which reminded me that he saved mine." She handed it to Arodi, "I want Sarah to remember that you saved hers."

"I didn't."

"Yes, you did." Marnie kissed his cheek.

Arodi smiled.

Marnie's phone vibrated. She looked down at the screen. "Simone wants me to check out some light fixtures at a store, so I need to head over there. I hate to cut our time short; I hope you understand."

Arodi nodded. "My mother plans to leave next week as long as Sarah feels well. She's been astounded by her comeback."

"She seems like a fighter. I wish I could meet her."

"She's back outside now. Let me give her the necklace." Arodi turned and called, "Sarah, come here."

Marnie wished that she could see the small girl, but she couldn't see anyone but Arodi.

"A very special person wanted you to have this as a reminder of how brave you have been these past couple of weeks."

Marnie saw the necklace dangle from Arodi's finger and then watched it disappear. *Sarah must have taken it. I hope that she likes it.*

Arodi laughed. "Yes, you could say she's an angel, and I will say thank you to her when I see her. Can you go ask Mother what activities she has planned for today? Thank you."

Marnie watched Arodi as he watched Sarah go back inside.

"Her eyes lit up when I handed it to her," he smiled, "much like my eyes light up when I see you. And see you again soon, I must." He held her hands. "Can we spend the day together after my family leaves? I must spend the rest of the week with my father for business matters, and then I will need to see my mother and siblings off, but I feel as though we are overdue for some quality time together."

Marnie squeezed his hands in delight, "Yes, I agree, and I have some time next week."

"Meet me here in five days." He handed her a piece of paper with latitude and longitude degrees on it. "Around eleven in the morning."

"You've had this place in mind for a while, haven't you?"

Arodi grinned. "I have."

"I'll be there." Marnie wondered where she was supposed to meet him. She would look it up later.

"'Til then, my sweet." He bowed, kissed her hand, then turned and went towards the house.

Marnie waited until he went inside before pulling out her phone and tracking down the location of their next encounter.

* * * * *

Life in the once-lonely cabin did not feel that way any longer.

Marnie worked remotely for Simone, providing suggestions for the next event and handling all matters from her quaint spot on the picnic table or inside upon the modest beige settee. The quiet was a welcome break from listening to Drew talk about his latest self-proclaimed scientific breakthroughs. Their last exchange replayed in her mind, but she didn't reach out. She would extend no olive branch. Sarah was better, so Marnie felt justified.

A couple of days before her promised meeting with Arodi, Marnie attended dinner at Briscney's.

"Did you get a new vehicle? That slate is gorgeous." Marnie asked as she entered Briscney's living room.

"Hi, Marnie," Jeremy said. "It's good to see you again." On a rare occasion, Jeremy was home instead of at work and would be joining them for dinner tonight, along with the stranger seated in the chair across from the couch where Marnie looked at Briscney, who smiled nervously.

Briscney stood and hugged her. "Marnie, that's Talmidge's Benz. Talmidge Turner, this is Marnie Foster. Talmidge and Jeremy work together."

Talmidge, who seemed to be all ears and teeth, stood and extended his hand to Marnie. His hair was light brown, and he wore navy khakis and a white polo shirt.

She hoped she was able to conceal her befuddled look as she shook his clammy hand.

123

Talmidge started, "I had hoped to chat with you the night of the party here but wasn't able to find you. Briscney said you're working hard as an event planner, is that right?"

"Yes, Jasmine Rose has taken up a lot of my time recently." *Half truth.*

"Marnie, can I get you something to drink?" Jeremy offered.

"I'm assuming Briscney's homemade limeade is an option?"

"Yes." Jeremy went to the kitchen.

"Dinner won't be ready for another twenty minutes, so have a seat," Briscney instructed while also not making eye contact with Marnie.

Marnie knew that was totally on purpose. Briscney did not want to catch the flashes of ire in Marnie's eyes.

Marnie sat in the matching chair opposite from where Talmidge positioned himself back, glad for the long, rectangular, wooden coffee table between them.

"Talmidge was just telling us about his passion for sailing."

Jeremy returned with a glass of cold limeade for Marnie.

"Thanks." She accepted it.

Jeremy sat next to Briscney on the couch.

"I've done my fair share of sailing around the United States. My favorite place is Rhode Island because of its history and culture. When the opportunity came up to buy a second home there, how could I turn it down?"

Realizing she was surrounded by some of the big leagues of wealth and affluence, Marnie let her thoughts turn to Arodi. Arodi was in the same league, but he was so different from them. He never boasted about his wealth or bragged about his acquisitions. He knew the importance of embracing life's simplicities. Joy could be found lounging by the river banks, discussing nature. Bliss was walking through the forest, hands locked together. Marnie tried to focus on what Talmidge had been saying about the architectural details of his second home while name-dropping from the various owners, neighbors, and elitist guests he had entertained. She strained to stay engaged in the present conversation, but her heart and thoughts were in 1849. *Is this what Arodi felt like when his aunt was trying to force a relationship with Nelly? How had he remained focused on the conversation during dinner? Poor, pitiful, single people are at the mercy of our friends and family.*

Briscney attempted conversational bait. "Marnie's family runs a horse farm not far from here. How's that been doing lately?"

Marnie bit. "Splendid. We've branched out with boarding and continue to get offers from producers for movies. I think we're looking at some TV shows, too."

"I'll tell you what, some of the best horseback riding I ever did..." Talmidge's personal tangent took over, and Marnie exercised politeness and patience while he shared about his adventures and cowboy tales.

*The Wild West. Arodi could be a part of that if he went westward. He would make a handsome cowboy.* Marnie amused herself by relating everything back to 1849. It helped get her through dinner, dessert, and the herbal tea served after dessert. Thoughts of Arodi carried her home and only paused when

Brisceny's apology text came in, vowing never to let Jeremy suggest a suitor again.

Marnie noticed, however, that she didn't vow to never attempt a setup again.

## Twenty-Two

Five days had never seemed so long. She hadn't been able to distract herself with enough work to avoid thinking about Arodi, wondering what he was up to, and wishing she could call him just to check-in. He was but minutes from her, and yet he wasn't. Marnie parked along the side of the road on the Old Natchez Trace at the spot Arodi told her to meet him. She wore a blue and white belted jumpsuit with white sandals. She had left her hair down, partly hoping Arodi would be enticed into running his fingers through it as they picnicked or lounged. She did not immediately see him, so she walked along the road.

"Marnie!" He called to her from a field with a picnic already set out. "Over here!" He wore his riding breeches, but she noticed his shirt was looser, seemingly more casual than his normal attire.

She walked towards him, "I don't know what this looks like in your time, but in my time, it's trespassing." She had to climb over a wooden post and rail fence to get to him. The caretakers had mowed the field, so sandals were not a problem for the walk to Arodi.

"We will be here but a moment. No one will know. Come, eat." He had raspberries, figs, cheese, and bread spread out for them. "Just a little something before we take a walk."

Marnie joined him, giving him a quick kiss on the cheek. *How did he keep his skin so smooth without a modern razor?*

He handed her some cheese.

"This is wonderful," she said, taking a bite of cheese from 1849. She decided not to concern herself with the implications of that. She'd already eaten plenty of meals from that time, and it hadn't yet caused any issues. Tell me about the meeting with your father."

Arodi swallowed a large piece of bread. "We've solidified the contracts and will have our factory in place before winter. I'm drawing up the housing plans for our workers and procuring a relationship with a local doctor to service our workers. That means I'll be moving to Nashville full time." He looked intently at Marnie.

"Congratulations, that's excellent news."

"I'll need some land of my own."

"Right." She nodded.

"A house, too."

She nodded, not sure where this conversation was going.

Arodi reached over, taking hold of her hands. He gently raised her hands to his lips.

"And I've decided that I will need a wife to share it all with."

Marnie looked at Arodi. Her heart seemed to jump at least three feet high, and she knew she had stopped breathing. She didn't want the tears to well up, but they did. *Yehovah, tell me you've shown him a way to make it work— something that I haven't thought of because I can't do this much longer. I love him, but how do we make this work with this time distance between us?*

"There, there. This isn't supposed to be a sad occasion." He used his thumb to tenderly wipe under her eyes.

Marnie glanced down, unable to find the words her heart wanted to say. Her tears seemed to flow with a life of their own.

"Hey," he tilted her chin up, "I think I'm onto something. I can set up a corporate trust that will own the land and house I build. I can put substantial funds into the corporation, which would pay for any upkeep. That way, you can live in our house during your time."

He hadn't really found a way; he'd found what he thought was a loophole. "What about a wedding? Witnesses? Children? What if they lived for a little bit in both worlds, but then the bridge between us stopped? How could one of us live with that separation from each other or our children? How would you know the corporate officers would do what you wanted with the money anyway? They could embezzle it, steal it, and re-purpose it. The law is more complicated in my time. I think it's too risky."

"What in life isn't risky?"

"It's unnecessarily risky."

"So you won't even entertain it?" His brow furrowed.

"Arodi, you are just starting out in the world. How are you going to afford to pay property taxes? We have those in my time."

"I've been following along with what's happening in our country." He pulled out what looked like a newspaper. He looked it over and handed it to Marnie. "There's gold in California. A man could gain sufficient wealth by prospecting. I could leave and be back by the middle of fall."

Marnie read over what he handed her:

Californian (San Francisco), 15 March 1848

In the newly made raceway of the Saw Mill recently erected by Captain Sutter, on the American Fork, gold had been found in considerable quantities. One person brought thirty dollars worth to New Helvetia, gathered there in a short time. California, no doubt, is rich in mineral wealth, great chances here for scientific capitalists. Gold has been found in almost every part of the country.

She had watched enough documentaries to know that this was a terrible idea. Violence, murder, banditry, disease, and accidents are all unnecessary risks. "No, it's too dangerous. You might get hurt or sick. I wouldn't have any way of knowing how you were." Marnie wanted to immediately Google "Arodi Bellamy gold rush" just to see what happened, but she stopped herself.

Arodi sat with a flummoxed look on his face. "So you care what happens to me, but not enough to marry me?"

She could almost see his thought process, which Marnie had to admit made sense. How could she refuse his advances in one breath, then, in the next breath, demand she had a say in how he lived his life?

"Marnie, I expressed my intentions from the start. Friendship, and then, as I got to know you, my intentions were courtship for the purpose of marriage. Do people still marry in your time?"

"They do, and just as many divorce. It's truly a sad state of affairs."

He was quiet.

Marnie looked at the raspberries.

"Where did you see our relationship going?" He asked.

She detected the sorrow in his voice. "I don't know. I didn't know any of this was possible."

"I desire to marry you, Marnie, but you need to decide if you want to marry me."

"Arodi, I do want to marry you. I just don't see how it'll work."

"Would you take some time to decide if you can commit to marriage to me, even if we don't have everything figured out?"

She looked deeply into his eyes and saw only hope, honesty, truth, and tremendous love for her.

"Yes, I can do that." *Yehovah, please reveal more of Yourself and Your plan so that I can see the path You would have us take. I want to follow and trust Your plan for our relationship.*

"Marnie, while you decide, would you do me the honor of wearing this?" He produced a ring with a large, blue sapphire stone in between two not-so-insignificantly-sized diamonds.

Marnie was mesmerized. "That looks like it cost a fortune. I could never accept it." She said, but she could not take her eyes off of it.

"I saved a man's life, and he insisted on gifting me this ring in his appreciation so it did not cost me anything."

"Who would do such a thing?"

"He was British royalty, and suddenly, all of his jewels didn't mean so much to him, so he gifted it to me. I would like this ring to represent my current intentions." Arodi slipped it on her finger. "I pledge my love to you, Marnie, and will find a way to take care of you. I will find a way to make a living for us. For as long as we have this bridge through time, I have faith that Yehovah will show us the way and make our paths straight. Think about all of these things when you look at this ring."

The simplicity of his faith should have bolstered her own instead of the injustice of their situation that she felt simmering beneath the façade of trust. She wanted to blame it on the difference in time periods. Arodi couldn't understand how her world worked. Yehovah had to be more present in Arodi's time because of the lack of scientific breakthroughs. Even as Marnie thought it, she knew that she was wrong. Yehovah was the same yesterday, today, and tomorrow. She realized that Arodi exhibited more trust and faith than she did when faced with the conundrum of sharing life in modern times with a man from 1849.

"Could we take a walk?" Arodi stood and offered his hands to help Marnie up.

As they strolled through the woods, so many thoughts ran through her mind, and Arodi knowingly gave her the space to process everything. She moved along on autopilot, pondering the nature of his request. *Can I accommodate his 1849 proposal in my time?* Rational thought being what it is, the answer was a firm no. *And what about this beautiful ring?* She wanted to grab her phone and do all the research she could on it.

"Is the river still here?" He asked, finally breaking the silence.

Marnie looked at Arodi as they made their way to the banks of the Harpeth. "Yes, it is." How she envied the river right now, too. Its entire course was mapped out. There might be bends and twists, but there were no unknowns. Everything flowed the way it should. There weren't any missing pieces of the river yanked from their proper places and put into another river. Nothing was segmented or improper. It just was what it was: a free-flowing channel of water, providing life to the plants and animals along its route. How Marnie wanted her life to be the Harpeth. No mysteries in its course, curving in unbroken fashion through fields and forests, rising and lowering with the rainfall; Marnie appreciated the rhythm and pattern to the Harpeth and wanted peace like the river to attendeth her way. She could hear the lyrics to *It Is Well* playing in her mind as they watched the water flow smoothly around the bend.

Arodi placed an arm around her and pulled her close to him. There was steadfast comfort in his embrace, and Marnie leaned into him. It would be well; she wasn't sure how, but she felt the whispers of peace encircle her.

* * * * *

Scratching his head, the jeweler looked at Marnie's ring with his monocular. "Where did you say you got this?"

She stopped at a jeweler's business in the Grassland Community, minutes from her home, to have the ring appraised so she could insure it. "That's an invasive question."

None of the jewelry twinkling and sparkling through the see-through countertop compared to the item held between the thumb and forefinger of the jeweler.

"It's just very unique. I am sure that these are Israeli diamonds, and the sapphire is from Burma. It's one of the most impressive pieces I've ever handled. The value is at least four hundred thousand."

Marnie was in shock. "Four hundred thousand dollars?"

"Yes." The jeweler filled out a piece of paper. "I would be very cautious and careful with this ring."

Suddenly, Marnie felt like she was in a Tolkien novel and wasn't sure if she should protect the ring or take it to Mount Doom and cast it away. She slipped the ring back onto her finger and pulled out her wallet to pay for the appraisal.

"No, no. There is no charge; It's on the house." The jeweler handed her the documentation stating she was wearing nearly half a million dollars on her left hand. It was a dizzying reality.

"Thank you." She gathered herself and walked outside.

She got into her car and sat lost in thought. *Who was she marrying? Was she marrying him? How could it work? Could it work? Did it matter? Didn't it?*

## *Twenty-Three*

Arodi had said that he would wait patiently while she made her decision. *Why was this so hard?* Though several days and nights had passed since his proposal, she still wrestled with her final response. She had even made "yes" and "no" columns on notebook paper that were filled with reasons supporting both sides. It helped being back in the cabin. The silence gave her the space she needed to fully analyze the situation without distractions.

She practiced signing her name with different-colored gel pens: Marnie Bellamy. She introduced herself to imaginary people in the room: "Hello, I'm Mrs. Bellamy." *Who would believe I was married? Should I care?*

Marnie placed a pillow under her cotton pajama shirt to see what a protruding belly would be like as she stood in front of a long mirror. Of course, she wanted children with Arodi. In his world and his time, there was never a discussion about "if" there would be children; in Marnie's immediate world, it was the same. Today, the world at large is not kid-friendly, but families like hers are the beacons and bastions of hope. Marnie pulled her shirt tighter and pushed her abdomen forward, emulating a full-term pregnancy as best she could.

How on earth would she ever explain a baby? She took out the pillow and slumped on the twin bed she had upstairs. Maybe with Drew's help, her family and friends would understand. Maybe he could show them by enlarging the portal.

Drew. She and Drew hadn't spoken or seen each other in a week. What if he staunchly refused to clear her good name based on principle? How would her family take the news of her relationship with Arodi? Would they be able to grasp the un-graspable? What was Yehovah's will in this? She was tired of indecision. Figuring out parallel universes seemed too complicated for her present circumstances. Besides, she would never know how the "yes" and the "no" played out simultaneously.

She reread the list of qualities she had made about Arodi. He was gentle, kind, honest, dedicated, intelligent, hard-working, compassionate, inquisitive, positive, faithful—was there a trait she didn't admire? Didn't he embody all of the traits she has always wanted in her spouse? Paralytic thoughts threatened to freeze her from what she knew when she spent time with Arodi; he was her choice regardless of the obstacles and uncertainties. She wanted a life with him. Marnie's phone made a noise. Aunt Ginny invited her to dinner.

*The future Mrs. Arodi Bellamy graciously accepts.* Marnie text a quick "yes," then made plans on how to tell Arodi the good news.

* * * * *

"There's my girl. We haven't seen you in a good week." Aunt Ginny hugged Marnie.

"I've been so swept up with this new event and its crazy hours. I thought it would be less disturbing for everyone if I was back in the cabin." She fibbed.

"Yes, Drew said you were swamped." Uncle Caleb said.

"Oh, is he here?"

"He'll be along shortly." Uncle Caleb poured some lemonade into a glass and handed it to her.

Marnie fiddled with the ring on her finger.

"What a lovely piece of costume jewelry!" Aunt Ginny admired. She took Marnie's hand to inspect it.

"Oh yes, I got it after the Swan Ball." The half-truths came easier now.

"You'd never tell it wasn't real." Aunt Ginny pulled out a large glass bowl from the fridge. "Let's start with a good salad. The meatloaf needs about another twenty minutes."

Chit-chat, surface-level conversations are where they spend most of their time while waiting. Marnie had missed their company.

"Did you save me some of that mouth-watering meatloaf?" Drew entered and raised his eyebrows when he saw Marnie. He placed his messenger bag on a hook by the built-in desk in the kitchen before grabbing a plate.

"Hurry up, Drew. Marnie was just sharing that she's been seeing someone. I want to know all about him, and I want to meet him." Aunt Ginny said.

Marnie and Drew shared a look. She'd done it. She'd opened up that there was a suitor in her life but had not let on at the level of commitment. She knew her engagement and wedding could not be kept a secret for long, and she was ready for her aunt and uncle to believe in the impossible. Drew would have to come around now and share that he, too, knew about it.

Marnie opened her mouth to share more details.

"Before we hear more about that, Mom, I want to share an interesting letter that I found today," Drew interjected.

"Oh, Drew." Aunt Ginny moved her hand in a shooing motion, but Drew didn't stop.

"Yep, it was a letter from an inventor to his grandpa."

"Drew, we can discuss this after Marnie fills us in." Aunt Ginny said.

Drew continued, undeterred, "He was the inventor of the modern-day incubator."

Marnie's eyes cut straight to Drew's. She was born prematurely and spent

132

two months in an incubator. Why would Drew blurt out such a random detail?

"Drew, that is enough." Uncle Caleb warned.

"No, I want to hear what he has to say." Marnie put her fork down and looked hard at Drew.

Drew swallowed. "This inventor saved the life of his own daughter by placing her in the incubator. He wrote this letter to his grandfather thanking him for all the encouragement and support that he had given him along the way."

Marnie could not ignore the waves of nausea beginning to churn in the pit of her stomach. Drew wouldn't share this kind of information if it was meaningless. "Who was the grandfather?" She asked.

She swore she saw tears in Drew's eyes.

"Arodi Bellamy." At the quizzical look on Aunt Ginny's face, Drew explained the connection between Arodi Bellamy and the Swan Ball and thought that Marnie would find it interesting.

Marnie was quiet as she connected the dots Drew wanted her to see.

### *Twenty-Four*

"How could you tell me like that?" Marnie cried as she and Drew sat on the wooden picnic table outside of the cabin later that night. The climbing roses and clematis were full of mauve-blue and scarlet colors, perfumy in fragrance. Still, Marnie's eyes locked on the bleeding heart planted below, fixated on the irony of the plant's name and her current situation.

The frogs croaked loudly, yards from where they sat.

She had made it through dinner and then quickly excused herself, claiming she had work to do.

Drew followed her to the cabin. "You were about to tell them about Arodi and that you were engaged. Yeah, I see that ring, which is worth a fortune, by the way."

"You have the wrong Arodi. It's not the same man. He loves me. He proposed, and we are going to get married." She would go through with marrying Arodi just to prove Drew wrong. He was not going to stop her.

"Arodi married Nelly Taylor." Drew handed her the envelope, which was protected by a plastic sleeve.

Marnie was aghast. "Nelly? No, that's impossible." She looked at the faded ink in disbelief.

"I tried to tell you we can't change the past. And if you marry him, you might just marry yourself to death. Besides, who knows who else you'll affect." He looked down at the brick patio.

Drew was right. Even if Marnie was willing to risk her own life by marrying Arodi, she could not risk the lives of others. She had promised to save any life she encountered when it was within her means; to pretend like she hadn't made those vows lessened the devotion she had professed to save Sarah's life.

Her world was spinning. Her heart was sickened by this news. There was no greater pain than what she felt at that moment. Cascades, torrents of all of her worst fears from giving her heart away, came in a horrendous downpour.

*I understand now. This is how my friends felt when they broke up with their boyfriends. It really is the end of the world. This is why people don't get involved so deeply in a relationship. I think I'm gonna be sick. Why can't my life be a story? In a book, there'd be a way! There'd be a sign, something. But*

134

*there's no way to make this work*. Marnie hated all the times she had read fairytales as a little girl. She hated that she'd believed her life would match Snow White's or Sleeping Beauty's when it came to finding love. She despised the songs and imaginary games she played that always had a happy ending. Her life just wasn't to be so. This was way more complicated than any bedtime fairytale.

It wasn't just that they couldn't be together, but he was destined to marry another. Was he lying to Marnie about his feelings for Nelly? Was he courting her in 1849 while he courted Marnie at the same time? It's not like she'd ever know the difference. She couldn't see Nelly. It was the perfect setup for Arodi to have two love interests.

*Could he really love Nelly?* Marnie realized she barely knew anything about this woman because, up until this moment, Nelly hadn't mattered. Well, maybe she wasn't sure in the beginning, but when Arodi promised her that Nelly was of no interest to him, she trusted him. Marnie couldn't stand the idea of him treating Nelly like he had treated her. Those lunches were hers; the spot next to him on the picnic blanket was hers, his embrace, his kiss. Everything belonged to her, not Nelly.

Irrational, frightful thoughts plagued her as she sat in tears, helpless as could be against the onslaught of this verifiable evidence and its meaning.

Marnie wasn't sure how to face this revelation. How many blankets could she hide under? How long could she remain locked inside the cabin? Facing the present reality was impossible. Her stomach was twisted in knots, her head pounded, and she had a hard time breathing. She was certain she would remain frozen at the picnic table for days.

It barely registered when Drew helped her to the couch, made her some chamomile tea, got her a blanket and a pillow, and promised to check on her in the morning. She was convinced she would never sleep again; she was too exhausted to sleep. Everything good in her life was suddenly an object of taunt and misery.

She drank her tears mingled with tea. She cried into her pillow all night and into the morning.

She knew what had to be done, but did she have the strength, courage, and resolve to do it?

* * * * *

Marnie didn't perceive that three days had passed. Three days of permanently swollen eyes, a bathroom trash can overflowing with mountains of tissues, and a voice that could only crack, cry, and sob. Three days of doing all the research she could, then verifying what she already knew over and over. All she knew was her bed and pillow were drenched in salty expressions of raw, unbridled heartache.

It took her every bit of those three full days before she could open the blinds, shower, and begin the process of doing what must be done. Or was it

135

what must be undone? A minty green t-shirt, pair of jeans, taupe slip-on shoes, no makeup, damp hair tossed into a bun; she barely noticed what she wore or how she looked. None of it mattered to her. She had one objective. One mission.

She drove below the speed limit to Cheekwood, creeping along the road, searching desperately for ways to avoid the inevitable.

When she parked and got out, she took a full breath. Normally, the sweet smell of the flowers in full bloom would welcome her senses, but today, the aroma was too sweet, too assaulting. How dare the world sing, celebrate, and flourish while she suffered! She interpreted the insects' and birds' songs as mockery, and unbeknownst to her, the seed of bitterness took root.

Marnie walked slowly toward the mansion, knowing at any moment Arodi would detect her, and life as she knew it would be forever altered. She paused at the terrace and took a look over the grounds. Spring had been filled with all things new, bright, and wonderful, but just as the blossoms of the spring flowers were fading into the summer, so were Marnie's hopes. She closed her eyes and desperately wanted to return to that moment when she pulled that first letter from the rocks. She envisioned a world without doing so and tried to see herself happy without knowing Arodi even existed.

She would've had a carefree summer of fun with friends and work, and maybe a beau from her own timeline, if Arodi and 1849 hadn't swept her up.

That's how her life was supposed to be. She was once like the Harpeth River, free-flowing and doing exactly what she was supposed to do, but because of this rift in time, Marnie's heart was left awash on the banks of despair in its destructive wake.

"Marnie!"

She needn't turn around to see his smiling face. She could tell he was happy to see her just by the sound of his voice, piercing her heart and spilling forth sorrow.

Standing before her, fresh and clean and beaming in a long-sleeved white shirt tucked into canvas trousers, he kissed her cheek and encircled her with his arms, "How are you?"

*Yehovah, make the moment freeze. Take this scene and tuck it into a snow globe so I can always look upon his handsome face, those brilliant, loving eyes, and his warm smile. I cannot do what I must do. I cannot break his heart or mine. Please, spare us from this sorrow.*

Marnie squeezed him back. "Let's take a walk." She knew she couldn't hold it together and refused to break down in front of Cheekwood's patrons.

Arodi looked questioningly at her but released his hold on her. Marnie guided them to the path through the woods, purposely going in the opposite direction of where they shared their night during the Swan Ball. Once they entered the thick shade provided by leafy green trees, she turned to him, "I've been debating on how much of the future to tell you."

Arodi waited silently for her to continue.

"What if I said 'no' to your proposal?"

"I would wait until you said 'yes.'" He held her hand.

She fought back tears. "For how long?"

"As long as it took."

"Arodi, what if I told you I was going to die, and you could cure me?" The tears welled in her eyes as the conversation turned solemn.

"Are you ill?" Arodi cupped her face, seemingly ready for action.

She could see the panic in his eyes. "Not exactly." Marnie looked around where they had stopped. "Do you see a place to sit here?" Marnie asked.

"Yes, there's a bench," Arodi said.

"Good, let's sit down." They did.

Arodi held her hand, waiting for her to reveal information she had never wanted to convey.

"I'm not ill, Arodi, but if we marry, I might die."

"Isn't everyone set to die at some point?"

The birds dared to chirp louder.

"Yes, Arodi, but that's not exactly what I mean. I fear that I might disappear as soon as we marry."

Arodi smiled. "I'm sorry, but I don't understand. Do you mean you might come into my timeline?"

*If only it were that simple! Yes, Arodi, I would give up my time and all its luxuries for a life with you in 1849. I would do it if it meant we could be together.*

Marnie sighed. "Sometimes babies are born too early, and no matter what you do, they don't live. But in the late 1800s, an inventor found a way to help those babies. He created a way to keep them warm and comfortable so they could develop into stronger, healthier babies."

Arodi studied her eyes. "I don't see how this affects our marriage. My family has always produced strong, healthy babies."

Marriage. Babies. *Arodi, I want to marry you. I want to be with you all the days of my life. I can't do this. I can't say no to you. Please stop looking at me. Stop making this so hard.* Marnie rubbed her fingers over Arodi's hands. "Arodi, your grandson is the inventor of that life-saving device."

"Our grandson?" He sounded excited and proud.

She was being robbed of life. She couldn't face it. *Our. He said our.* Tears swan-dived from her eyes. There would be no son or no daughter with Arodi to have the inventor grandson that would eventually save Marnie's life. She felt a tremendous darkness sweep over her as lives that never were to be between her and Arodi vanished. "No, your grandson, not mine. His grandmother was Nelly Bellamy."

Arodi jumped up. "Impossible! I would never!"

Marnie sniffed. "If you don't, I might die along with thousands of other children. I was one of those babies, and his invention saved my life. The course is already set. It's already happened."

"No, I refuse to believe it."

"Do you think I would make this up?" Marnie pulled out the plastic-covered letter and handed it to him. "Drew found this in the archives and brought it to me."

Arodi studied it, seemingly bewildered by what his eyes saw.

"I've done the research. It's true. You marry her."

"This is unacceptable. Don't you see, Marnie? We're being shown this information so we can change it. I was never meant to marry her. I was meant to marry you. Give me the invention. I'll create it, and history will be fine," he pleaded with tears in his eyes.

"No, I can't do that. It wouldn't be right."

Arodi sat back down and rested his elbows on his knees, shaking his head. Tears slipped down his cheeks. "I won't do it. I can't do it. I don't love her; I love you, Marnie."

"Would you want to risk my life?"

"No."

Marnie grasped his hand, desperate for him to understand. "Then you see why we can't be together, right?"

"No."

She knew the thoughts that were going through his mind. She'd been there. She knew he was confused right now. She also knew that the heartbreak that would soon surface for him, as well. "I've had more time to process this than you, but I think we shouldn't see each other any longer."

Arodi hung his head. "I cannot say goodbye to you. You mean everything to me. I'm going to find a way for us to be together."

His determination in his voice matched what she saw in his eyes. As she looked into his eyes, she saw a revelatory awareness spark.

"You had decided to say yes to me, didn't you?"

She thought she had exhausted her tears, but she felt them begin to pool in her eyes, and she shook her head.

"You cannot deny that you love me and want to marry, Marnie. This information from Drew does not change anything; it only means we have one more obstacle to overcome, and then we will be together."

Those tears pooling in her eyes began to fall freely, seemingly with a life of their own; she could not stop them. "Arodi, I love you and want to marry you, but I can't risk the lives of thousands of people. I can't go on seeing you because it's too hard."

"I would never risk your life or the lives of others for my own happiness, but you must see this for the interference that it is. There is no way I would ever marry Nelly Taylor."

They sat in silence, but not total silence. The bees still buzzed, the mockingbird overhead sang, and the world continued to move forward.

As much as she wanted and had spent the past few days praying for a different outcome, she needed him to move on without her in his life. "I have finished the job at Cheekwood, so I won't be coming back here anymore." She wiped at the tears in her eyes. *I'm trying to hold it, but it is so hard. I love you more than even I realized, Arodi. It is breaking my heart to know that we cannot be together.*

"Marnie, please don't," he shook his head and pulled her close to him.

"I have done a lot of thinking since Drew showed me this, and I think the purpose of our meeting and experiencing love like this has been to teach us a little about Yeshua's walk and what He experienced."

"In what way?"

"It's all about the sacrifice, Arodi. Yeshua's life is the example we are to follow. He loved us so much that He willingly sacrificed His life to save ours, just as we are to sacrifice our love and future together to save others." *Yehovah, he has no idea about the thousands of children who would go on living because he and Nelly's grandson invents the incubator. I really thought we could find a way to be together, but now, I do not see how that is possible. I can't do this on my own. Give me strength!*

"You really believe that this is the proper course?"

Marnie slowly nodded her head. She knew that Arodi would always be her one and only true love; her fairytale was ending with him. She would never love another like this. *The pain is almost unbearable!*

She would lock her heart away to keep it safe and spend the rest of her life limping along, isolating her emotions from true human connection. She would die a single woman, an accomplished businesswoman, but would never again love, which is exactly what she wanted right now.

"This would not be fair to Nelly," Arodi stated. "A loveless marriage. A husband who will spend every day of his life wishing for you, Marnie; your embrace, your smile, your kiss, an entire life with you." Arodi looked intently at her.

Marnie glanced away from him. She could not stay strong with him looking at her like that. "I never said that it would be easy."

They sat without speaking. She watched him wrestle with himself, trying to absorb the far-reaching impacts of this news. His brow would furrow, then shift to his right, then back to the left. His brow would soften as if he had discovered another loophole, but then he'd frown again. She watched him heartbreakingly war with himself as she did her best to remain resilient, strong, and unmoved from her position.

He finally turned toward her. "The only reason I would do this is for you and only because you believe you may die if I don't marry Nelly."

His reluctant acceptance shattered her heart. "I know."

"Can we continue to meet occasionally?" He took her hand, turned it over, and gently rubbed his thumb over the spot where her pulse was betraying her resolve to end their relationship.

"No, Arodi. I cannot continue to see you in any capacity, especially after your marriage. It would be too much of a temptation for both of us; how would we be able to resist one another?" Tears began to flow again. "I can barely control myself from crossing the line right now, knowing that this is it and that I will never see you again." She knew Arodi was fighting with his desire, too.

She could see it in his eyes and feel it in his touch. It was for the best this way. He would go on to wed Nelly and have children and grandchildren. Marnie had no clue about her own future, but she knew that the only man she ever wanted to share her life with would wed another.

That realization, along with Arodi's nearness as he continued to caress her pulse point, was causing her thoughts to go down a path they should not go. *Did he know what she was feeling? Thinking? Did he realize that she wanted to be with him intimately? She would never be Marnie Bellamy, so why not partake in what was never going to be lawfully hers? She could have Arodi before Nelly and have him right now.* "The thought of you being married to another woman is enough to cripple me; I could never handle seeing you after you two are wed. I wrongfully thought you belonged to me. Knowing that she will be the one you share your life with, your bed with, a home with, children with; it is just too much for me to handle." *All of his evenings. All of his mornings. All of his kindness. All of his kisses. Every affectionate word now belonged to another.*

Tears spilled down Arodi's cheeks again as he embraced her.

Marnie allowed herself to focus on the feel of his arms around her, the way his heart beat in unison with hers, the scent that was so uniquely him.

Marnie wanted a future with Arodi. She couldn't stop herself from imagining the day she and Arodi's first child arrived. Arodi would be smiling and crying as his son, their son, took his first breath. She could see Arodi horsing around with their passel of children, racing around, scooping up little ones, heartily laughing, hugging them close to him. She continued to play out the scene in her mind: two exhausted parents crashing into their bed only to see a little girl standing in silhouette at their door, teddy bear in hand, wanting to sleep in their bed for the night.

Marnie nearly sobbed out loud. She was now robbed of it all. Penniless and destitute in the ways of a home and a family. She'd never realized how much she wanted those things until faced with the reality she would never have them with Arodi. In that instant, she knew she would not feel this way for another man as long as she lived.

"Marnie, I cannot marry her; she means nothing to me," Arodi said, loosing his embrace a little.

She tilted her head so that he was looking at her.

*Do not cry again. Hold it together for a little longer.* "But she means everything to me. This marriage between you and Nelly ensures I don't die as an infant, nor do any other innocent children whose lives we cannot risk."

Arodi was silent again for another minute. "I would only be doing it to save you."

She couldn't tell if he was saying it to convince himself or if it was a reassurance to himself.

"I know. My heart can't comprehend any of this. I'm broken, Arodi. I need to try and salvage what I can of myself so that I can make the best of this, which is why we can't continue seeing one another." *Lies, lies, lies.*

"I have one request, one condition." He searchingly looked at her. "Give me today to say goodbye. This is almost too much for me to bear, but I won't let you go until you spend the day with me."

Marnie knew that she would not deny either of them this last opportunity to be together. She secretly hoped he meant that he would hold onto her forever, kissing away her fears and doubts and that she would wake from this nightmare safe in his arms.

"Today, Arodi. That's all I can give you."

## *Twenty-Five*

It was a day of slow walks and talks, laughter and tears, a day that was ending too quickly for both of them. Wading in the creek, hiking through the forest, holding hands, stealing kisses along the way. Arodi must've created a hundred different plans for them to be together, but Marnie was the voice of reason each time. Anything that could alter the timeline and lead to the demise of innocent lives would never work. She could not live with herself if she messed that up for others.

Marnie was angry at their situation. In her anger, she cried out, pleading and begging for Yehovah to fix things, but no dove descended, no voice from Heaven erupted, and no guidance was given. Marnie knew that this summer of impossibilities was drawing to a bitter close.

She memorized everything she could about him: his elegant fingers, lips, thick hair, the way he smiled at her, kissed her, and held her. It was a lovely afternoon that both fulfilled longings in her heart and broke it. She wished for an impenetrable door to seal off her heart, but at the same time, she wanted nothing more than to give her heart to Arodi. The pendulum of emotions she felt swung back and forth and back and forth until the light around them began to fade.

As the day came to a close, the sunset glowed fiery orange, with a pink blanket resting on a cloudless horizon.

As they stood outside Cheekwood at Percy Warner Park, Arodi took Marnie's hands and yearningly looked into her eyes. His look alone caused her to cry because she knew this was the beginning of the final goodbye.

"Marnie, I will not pretend that I like this, but if it is what you desire, I will not come to you again. However, know that this is my pledge to you to continually pray for you each and every day. I pray that Yehovah sends you reminders of me. When you see the bluebird resting on your windowsill and the butterflies that encircle you, that will be me saying hello; when you feel the warmth of the sun, that will be me embracing you; when you feel the raindrops on your skin, those will be my kisses. At night, my love song will be from the whippoorwill. I will leave you alone, but you will see me each day in your time."

"You're making this so hard for me." At that moment, Marnie knew that If he asked her to marry him again, she would say yes. She would do anything he wanted. His love rendered her powerless, but she knew that he would honor her wishes. *Could they find someone in his time to perform their marriage ceremony?*

Marnie glanced down at their joined hands and allowed her imagination to take her to a future with him; after the ceremony, he would take her to the cabin he spoke of, the one he must've slept in alone, but she would be with him this time. They would never leave the cabin. They would make a life hidden away from both of their timelines. She envisioned waking up next to him in a cozy bed, spending her days decorating their home while he was outside chopping wood or fixing up the cabin in other ways. She would learn how to cook his favorite meals and pictured the two of them reading together, snuggled by a fire. And just as she dared to imagine what their sons and daughters would look like, she stopped. They would have no children together; Arodi would have a different family.

Arodi tilted her chin up to look at him, "Marnie, you will always be the only woman for me. I will never love Nelly. I will be looking for you in my children. Know this truth, Marnie; the moment my grandson tells me about the invention, I'm coming to find you."

Could she wait that long? She could do it. She could handle forty years or so. No, she couldn't. She wanted to be with him now, not some far-off date in the future. Marnie felt as if her heart would never recover from the injustice of their situation.

"Today, I will say yes to that hope because waiting for you is worth my lifetime, but I don't want you to withhold your love from your children, Arodi, and I don't want you to be cold to Nelly. That's not right."

"What do I tell my sons when it's time for them to choose a bride? How can I teach my children to do something I'm incapable of?" Arodi's face was tear-streaked. There were no right responses. His questions met with stillness and silence except for the lone katydid in the tree above them.

Marnie openly wept. This wasn't right. He shouldn't have married Nelly; he was supposed to marry Marnie. But what of his children and grandchildren? Based on the letter, he was obviously close to his grandson, so he had to have shown love to the child who would grow up and beget the inventor. Because of that amazing love, his grandson was going to save her life.

Arodi wrapped his arms around her while she sobbed.

Marnie wiped her eyes as the tears slowly subsided. "If we are ever going to survive this, you must forget about us. Tonight, in the same place we began, we must say goodbye. Don't look for me, don't come find me. I am not coming back to Cheekwood again." And she meant it. Cheekwood would become taboo in her life, a place never to mention, visit, recall, or suggest.

"Through the years, if I see you, what do I do?"

"Pretend you don't." If it were possible, Marnie's heart broke a little more.

"I will never recover from this heartache."

"I won't either." They stood there suspended in time, reading the love in each others' eyes. There was no concept of seconds or minutes. This was an eternal encounter, an ethereal embrace yet edging them toward an end.

Arodi was the first to break their contact. He took a step back and pulled out a box from his pocket.

Marnie had no idea he had been carrying anything. "What's that?"

"It's a music box that plays our song from the Swan Ball, Chopin's Nocturne Op.9. No.2." He began winding it. "For our last dance."

Immediately, the song took Marnie back to the Swan Ball. She could picture them as the beautifully clad, innocent, starry-eyed couple living in that moment, which had been full of possibilities. They had no foresight into the oncoming tempest that would shatter any promise of a future for them being together.

Placing the music box on the ground near them, she let Arodi pull her in close as they barely swayed while the music played. How long they stood there after the music ended, she didn't know. Her tears saturated Arodi's shirt where she'd rested her head. "I will hate this song after tonight."

He cupped her face and kissed the tears from each eye, leaving a trail of feathery kisses down each of her cheeks. His lips were a mere whisper-breath from hers, "No when you hear it, you must remember my love for you and be thankful for the time that we have been blessed with." He claimed her lips in a kiss that spoke of the passion and love he felt for her, a kiss that said she belonged to him now and forever.

There was no way Marnie could remove herself from Arodi's embrace. She prayed their transcendental night would last forever.

Internally, Marnie begged Arodi to map it out one more time, telling her how they could make it work. It had made sense to him earlier in the day. Now, she wanted it to make sense to her. *What if we could be married just for tonight?*

It took everything she had to remain standing as he kissed her. She desperately wanted him to pull her down to the bed of pine needles beneath their feet and get lost in a sea of embraces and kisses. There was but a thin T-shirt separating her skin from his, which Marnie was ready to remove should his hands suddenly find themselves beneath the fabric. He kissed her like she imagined a man would kiss a woman if it were the final time they would ever see one another. She knew he was trying to give her enough kisses to last a lifetime. They were passionate yet tender, holding the fullness of his promise to love her beyond this night. Marnie could not envision life beyond these final moments without Arodi. *Would risking her death be worth it?* .

An owl called out from above in the trees, bringing them back to reality.

Marnie reluctantly pulled back from Arodi. It was well after the sun had set. She saw streetlights turn on in the distance. "I have to go. If I don't leave now, then I don't think that I can."

He nodded and bent down to hand her the music box.

"Oh, your ring." She started to remove it.

"No," he closed his hands over hers, "it's your ring."

"I cannot accept such generosity."

He looked deeply into her eyes. "You will." Then he handed her the music box.

There was no denying those chocolate eyes anything they wanted.

"Goodbye, my love."

"Goodbye, Arodi."

She slowly pulled away from his hands, which covered hers, and walked to her car. Each step intensified the heartache that she felt. *How would she survive without him?* She refused to look back. She wanted her final memories of him to be those of him looking into her eyes, not standing alone under a tree.

*Twenty-Six*

"It's been too long!" A noticeably round Briscney hugged Marnie as they met on Briscney's back patio.

"Yeah, that last event had me so busy. I needed every bit of that trip to the Mediterranean." Marnie had spent two weeks trying to fool herself into believing that she was fine, healing, and Arodi was just a summer fling.

She thought of him every moment on that trip and yearned to see him, hear his voice, and feel his touch. From the breathtaking sunrises to the radiant sunsets, from the deliciously indulgent food to the friendly people and the music that lasted into the night, Marnie had prayed to see Arodi. She craved for a sign that no matter where she was on the planet or her timeline, he would always be there, and though he wasn't, she knew that he was. He had been right. She found reminders of him everywhere, even halfway around the world.

Marnie could not wait for fall to be here. She wanted each green leaf that had witnessed her exchanges with Arodi to drop. She needed them to shrivel and wither so there would be no more testament to all that once was.

"Did you meet anyone?" Briscney stabbed at some spinach.

"No." *Oh, Briscney, if you only knew, but those days have long passed now.*

"Speaking of dating," Briscney began.

"We weren't speaking of dating. You asked if I met anyone," Marnie corrected.

"Anyway, one of Jeremy's associates came over the other night, and I vetted him. You may have recalled seeing him at the retirement party, but he was dating someone then, so I didn't even consider him an option. He's single now and brought you up because he noticed you."

The retirement party. Marnie found her thoughts returning to that night when she and Arodi shared their first of many wonderful kisses, a night she would give anything to relive. What she wouldn't do to go back and do things differently, but she couldn't keep thinking of what could have been. She should be talking with Briscney.

"Well?" Briscney said. Clearly, she had been speaking while Marnie had been daydreaming.

"I'm just not sure I want to date anybody right now."

146

"So, is this baby going to have any playmates his or her own age?" Briscney teased.

"There's time for that."

"OK, we'll table that conversation for now. So, what about Drew and his girlfriend?"

"I wouldn't call Bella his girlfriend yet. They spend a lot of time together, but both are so committed to research that I'm not sure they even have time for romance. She's very driven and dedicated to preserving and examining Nashville's early history. She and Drew were thrilled to find some old paperwork at a house in Franklin right before I left, which I think will provide some insight on early city planning."

"And what about Jasmine Rose? Did you get the promotion?"

"I would have, but Simone basically told me that taking the vacation hurt my chances."

"What'd you say?"

"I'd enjoyed my tenure with her but needed a break. So, I decided to start my own business. I have my first event booked with a country music artist in a few weeks."

"You quit?"

"Yeah, I did."

Briscney stared disbelievingly at Marnie. "You didn't have anything lined up, and you just quit?"

Marnie nodded. She had faith that a job would come, and it did. She silently berated herself for not having that kind of faith when Arodi first told her he wanted to marry her. Clearly, she wasn't letting go of him that easily. "How's Jeremy liking the firm?"

"He agreed to take some time off when the baby comes, but he said it would only be for a week, so we're trying to get his mom to come stay with me and hire a nanny."

"Oh, how do you feel about that?" Marnie poked around at her salad. She had to make it appear she was somewhat interested in food, though nothing intrigued her taste buds.

"Like I'd rather have my husband home with me. Every time I bring that up, he reminds me that our mortgage is over three thousand dollars a month, and the partners are already not pleased with him being home on the weekends. I suggested downsizing and hanging a shingle on our front porch, but he said that we couldn't afford for me to stay home if he was practicing solo."

"Briscney, I am so sorry. I can't imagine the tension you feel."

"Sometimes, I think back to those days when I was nannying, and we were struggling to find creative ways to pay the rent. You know, we used to have date nights at the grocery store. We'd eat to our heart's content with the free samples, then go to the pedestrian bridge. We spent hours looking at all those shining lights in the city and imagining what it would be like to live in one of those beautiful houses. It was just a game to me. I had my man next to me; wherever he was, that was my home. Now we have this gargantuan house where I spend most of my time alone and a child on the way. Marnie, there are days when I want to be the one driving by this house and imagine who lives here while I go home to a husband who is home by six every night."

Marnie cried with and for her friend. She had missed the opportunity to support and encourage Briscney because she had been caught up in her own whirlwind relationship with Arodi. She felt like a horrible friend. Although she and Arodi had parted, she still spent all of her time missing him and reflecting on the what-ifs that could have been. She had been so wrapped up in her own pain that she had missed the broken heart right in front of her.

Marnie went to Briscney and held her. "I am so sorry, Briscney. I haven't been here for you, and I have no excuse. That's all going to change. I'm here now, and I'm my own boss. We're going to pray for Jeremy, for your marriage, and for those mountains to move."

Briscney nodded. "I didn't want to unload all of this on you while you were working so hard. I'm so lonely here and don't want a nanny for my baby. I just want Jeremy back."

Marnie could empathize more than Briscney would ever know.

* * * * *

Later that evening, Marnie pored over a letter written by Emily Dickson. *"When the Best is gone -I know that other things are not of consequence - The Heart wants what it wants - or else it does not care. Not to see what we love is terrible - and talking doesn't ease it - and nothing does - but just itself."*

As Marnie reflected on what she had read, the words resonated deeply in her heart. Briscney wanted her old life with Jeremy and a present husband. Marnie wanted Arodi and no one else; he was her best. *Oh, Emily, if you only knew how true your words were still.*

Marnie had stopped caring about anything else, but for Briscney, there was hope. Realization hit Marnie full force; Yehovah was using her pain to increase her empathy for others. He is always there, active, and present in her life. Her best friend had been vulnerable with her and confided in her. Marnie would not take that lightly. *Yehovah, thank You for using my pain for Your good. Continue to heal my broken heart and strengthen me so I can support and encourage Briscney. I lift Briscney and Jeremy up to You and trust that You will work things out for Your good.*

## Twenty-Seven

The purple flowers were peeking from the lilyturf around the paperbark maple with its reddish leaves, detailing those observing that fall was upon Middle Tennessee. Outside of the cabin, Marnie sat at the picnic table, taking advantage of the fall weather, as she responded to an email requesting a bid from a local non-profit for an event. She had finished an early morning workout and had not changed from her black running shorts and teal top. She had forsaken exercise when she started working for Simone and again when Arodi had occupied all of her free time. It felt good to hit the park trails again for a jog or brisk walk. Dawn air has a powerful, healing, magical aspect to it, holding the promise of a new day.

She heard a car approach and looked up to see a silver Subaru Outback pull up to the cabin. Marnie watched as a woman dressed in a black pantsuit, carrying a leather-bound folder, got out. Her shoulder-length, dandelion-colored hair barely shifted as she closed the door and walked toward Marnie.

"Marnie Foster?" The woman asked.

"Yes, that's me." Marnie stood up from the table to greet the woman.

"Hi, I'm Karen Reynolds," she extended her hand, which Marnie shook. "I'm an attorney with Reynolds, Morgan, and Gordan. I'm glad to catch you. I actually wasn't sure you'd be here today for me to deliver this news."

"What news?"

Karen smiled, "Miss Foster, we've been holding your estate in trust for well over a hundred years, and it's time for the asset distribution."

* * * * *

"How big is this house again, Karen?" Drew asked while he and Marnie stood in the foyer of the very house on the Old Natchez Trace that Marnie had always fantasized about owning. She had always assumed it had been a working plantation with slaves, but it was not. The house had been fashioned after the plantation style that was common in the late 1800s, with an expansive porch, a welcoming balcony above, and stately ionic Greek columns. The arched windows on the east side of the house would let in all the beauty and majesty of the sunrise, while the ones on the west side would perfectly capture the river and glorious sunsets. There were French doors accessing the outdoor living spaces, and Marnie counted four sets of them downstairs.

"It's almost seven thousand square feet," Karen replied as she looked over some papers.

"And the acreage again?" Drew asked.

"Fifty."

Drew laughed. "Fifty acres of riverfront property in Franklin, Tennessee, and your firm has just been holding this in trust for Marnie for over one hundred years? Arodi, you are one crazy guy." Drew looked up toward the dual-sided grand staircase beyond the foyer, simply taking it all in.

"I'm sorry, I don't mean to pry, but was he a relative of yours? Our firm has been wondering for years about the connection between you and the trust and whether you would be here when it was time to hand it over. Your trust is a legendary one in my office."

"He was a friend of the family," Drew said.

Marnie was silent as she felt his eyes on her. She knew Drew was worried that she would break down and cry like she did so often. He had eventually stopped talking about Arodi for the most part. Every time Arodi was mentioned, Marnie's heart was broken again. Would she ever stop loving him?

"The trust is well funded, so it is able to make the property tax payments and cover any other bills you incur for the upkeep of the place. Of course, you would be entitled to those funds once it's all settled."

"How'd he do it again?" Drew asked.

Karen glanced at her paperwork. "One percent of the annual Bellamy textile factory profit was always reserved for the trust. When Levi's Corporation made the acquisition, one percent of five hundred million is no small sum. Thanks to Mr. Bellamy's foresight, twenty-five percent of the one percent was invested, so now the trust has about twenty million dollars in it."

Drew began laughing again. "Wow, Arodi. You really did something amazing."

"Excuse me, I'll be back in just a minute." Marnie quickly disappeared, walking beyond the powder room, around a corner into what must have been a library. She could no longer hold it together as she leaned against one of the blank walls. *I can't do this, Arodi, I can't.* She started to sob as her legs seemed to collapse beneath her, and she slid down the wall, landing on the floor with a soft thud. She didn't want any of this, not the house, the land, the trust. She wanted Arodi. He had kept his promise to take care of her even though it was not his responsibility. She imagined him rounding the corner with open arms. She would run to him, cling to him, and never let him out of her sight again. Her sobs turned to soft hiccup sounds, and she knew that he would not round the corner; she knew he would never hold her again. *Yehovah, it is too much to bear. Please give me strength and wisdom; I cannot do this alone.* Marnie felt a tender peace descend and enfold her like a warm embrace. She thanked her heavenly Father for reminding her He was still with her.

Her mind reeled while she sat on the floor. She had been drawn to this place for years, not knowing that it was already hers. How many times had she wanted to be in this very front yard overlooking the Harpeth? How many times had she gone out of her way when she was driving home just to gaze upon the majestic home tucked in the woods overlooking the river. It was hers and always had been. The firm, acting within their legal capacity in accordance with the terms of the trust, had used it as a high-end rental until the date on which it was to be turned over to Marnie.

"Why, Arodi? Why did you do this?" Nothing but silence answered her.

She wiped her face as best she could, took a few deep breaths, and then rejoined Karen and Drew outside.

"There are current contracts for the pasture rentals, which we can end, or you can continue them. I know you are surprised and have much to think about, but we'd like you to come to the office tomorrow and sign the deed." Karen looked down at the paperwork again. "Just so you know, everything has been paid for already. I think this would make a good story for the press, too, if you were interested."

"No! No press." Marnie said. "This needs to remain private and discreet. I'll be there tomorrow to sign anything you need to be signed."

"OK, and we have a lot of paperwork to get through, so I will be there at about eight in the morning. Here's the property survey," Karen handed Marnie a piece of paper with a map of the parcel. "I'll leave you both to explore and take it all in. Just lock up when you're finished." Karen held out the keys.

"Thank you," Marnie accepted them.

"You're welcome. See you tomorrow." Karen walked along the brick path that led back to the driveway and her vehicle.

"This is absolutely wild," Drew said with a grin. "You're a millionaire."

"You're a millionaire, Drew."

"My parents are millionaires," he said matter-of-factly.

"Drew." She used her stop-it-Drew tone.

"Is he here?" Drew looked around.

"No, and he won't ever be here. We will never see him again."

* * * * *

"When are you gonna let me tell Bella about this? It's killing me. She would totally believe it. Just the other day, we were talking about some archived reports on Area 51..."

Marnie raised her eyebrows and walked back inside.

Drew followed behind. "Never mind. So, can I tell her?"

"No. I don't even know what to tell your parents. It's not believable; this guy from the 1800s lavished me with gifts through time, and now I'm wealthy. Any sane person would question that and ask what I had to do to get these gifts. So, no, we can't tell anyone."

Drew sighed.

"Drew, if I tell the truth, your parents are going to think I'm crazy."

"Look, they know something is wrong and that you want your space, but Mom's really concerned about you, and so am I. You've been so sad since Arodi left, and I get that, but becoming a recluse isn't going to help. My parents think you went through a bad breakup, and it's had a negative impact on all aspects of your life. They know that you quit your job and never come over anymore."

"What do you want me to say? Drew, I'm not OK, OK? I didn't ask for this house, this land, the trust. I didn't ask to meet and fall in love with Arodi, but it happened. I can't change that fact. And you know what? You're right; there are days when I am barely hanging on, and I think about all that I've lost. Then, there are mornings where I start out great and then I see or hear something that reminds me of him, and I don't think I will make it through the day. Drew, what do you want me to say? What do you want me to do?" Her voice cracked as the tears threatened to break free.

Drew was quiet for a moment as Marnie's raw emotions dispersed throughout the cavernous house. "I don't know."

"Me either." Marnie sighed, wiping the tears from her eyes.

Drew shifted his weight from his right to his left foot. "Can we at least explore a little more? I wouldn't be surprised if there are secret passageways. C'mon."

They explored every nook and cranny around the house but did not find any hidden rooms.      Marnie admired the view from the room she planned to use as a library or office while Drew continued his inspections. Looking down at the ring she wore on her finger, she knew that denying Arodi's provisions was pointless, so she allowed her imagination to release creative juices and splatter the room with shelves, colors, books, and a large desk.

Drew entered the room where Marnie was, knocking on the walls and tapping the floor. "I think this fireplace is imported. It's marble. Nice." He rubbed over the mantle and then returned to investigate the room. "Hmm."

"What?" Marnie dabbed the corners of her eyes and turned around from her gazing.

Drew was on the floor near the fireplace. "This wood plank," he kneeled before the fireplace. "It's not like the others." He leaned in closer. "Whoa! There are initials here! A.B. Are these Arodi's initials?"

Marnie walked over to where he was as Drew pointed to the letters etched into the wood plank. *They could be anyone's initials*, Marnie rationalized.

Drew pulled out a pocket knife.

"What are you doing?" Marnie asked.

"What? You own the house." Drew traced the outline of the hardwood plank with his knife and stuck the blade beneath its edge. With a gentle pop, he raised it up. Using his cell phone's flashlight, he looked inside. "Interesting." Drew reached in and lifted out a bundle of letters tied with a purple ribbon. He brushed off the dust and dirt, looking at the top envelope,

"They're addressed to you, Marnie."

## Twenty-Eight

For hours, she had been sitting outside on the front porch in one of the white wicker rocking chairs.

Drew had politely left, saying that he would give her the time alone.

The letters were from Arodi and began just after their last moment together. Some letters were pages full of his heartache, pain, and longing for her, wondering if she felt the same. Some letters were accounts of his day and all the things he wished he could experience with her. What was apparent throughout the letters was his sorrow and misery. Marnie knew the hurt all too well; his words pierced her heart and opened fresh wounds.

A chilly wind whipped across the porch, causing Marnie to pull her fleece jacket tighter around her. She looked around for Arodi, but he was nowhere to be seen.

Her eyes fell on the last letter.

*Marnie, my love, I find myself pouring everything I have into work. I helped the builders break ground on the factory and have worked with the men to start this house for you because I can't let you go. The prayers I've prayed, the tears I've shed. Time isn't releasing my heart from this torture. I fear I am trapped and won't be much of a husband or father now, but I know that I have to be for you. Knowing you will still be on this earth gets me through my days of toil and, oftentimes, drudgery. I pray for joy, but it eludes me. I pray for peace, but I'm restless. Yet somehow, I have to find a way to strike up relations with Nelly. Ari has written that she is visiting New York. I am to leave in two days' time and, not knowing what is coming and yet what must happen, I must stop writing these letters to you, which I know you may never see. I shall bury them beneath the floor of the house as a symbol of burying my emotions, knowing until the Resurrection, my heart shall remain hidden in a casket of grief and a frozen tundra of sorrow. Until we meet in the next world, my love, Arodi.*

Marnie knew she had to release his hold on her heart. She couldn't live under the tortuous what-if thoughts any longer. She wanted to appreciate Arodi's love and kindness in all that he had done for her and, somehow, move forward. She didn't want to remain stagnant and stunted. She had to view all Arodi had done for her as his farewell gift to her.

The time would come to share Arodi's gift with her aunt and uncle, but the time for healing and moving forward was upon her. Arodi had blessed her more than he could have foreseen, and his timing was perfect as she entered the field of entrepreneurship.

Her new focus would be on building her clientèle and finding ways to give back to the community. Drew would help her brainstorm on scholarship possibilities, community events, and more.

Marnie smiled as she gathered up the letters and took them back inside, tucking them beneath the floorboard where they had lain all these years. "Goodbye, Arodi."

* * * * *

Late September in Franklin still felt like summer, with a cooler morning or evening sprinkled in every now and then as a foretaste of the coming winter. Over the course of the remaining summer, after she signed the deed to the property, Marnie hired a crew to build a large, raised roof barn made of cedar wood and a pavilion where she had been hosting multiple weddings, birthday bashes, and concerts. By offering steep discounts for use of the newly-launched venue, every weekend in August had been booked, and she now had events planned through the end of November.

Presently, she walked through the barn with an up-and-coming country music artist, Kennedy Perkins. Marnie embraced the conservative business attire: pink flats, black dress pants, a pink button-down blouse tucked nicely into the pants, and a giraffe-print skinny belt. She carried a tablet as they walked, typing notes and discussing her ideas for Kennedy's concert. Kennedy, who had streaks of pink, blue, and purple strategically placed in her almost-white blonde hair, wore a denim skirt with brown moccasin fringed boots that matched her leather fringe vest that went over her yellow, sleeveless blouse.

"So, Kennedy, you'll be on this stage, and then we'll have the seating out here." The pair stood on the stage Marnie had built in the pavilion, looking out toward the imaginary audience. Kennedy, hoping to break into the music business, was going to host a special series of concerts followed by a Q & A session with musicians. Her manager thought it would be great marketing for her, and for a modest fifty dollars, aspiring musicians could see this rising star and learn some inside tips.

"Yeah, it all looks fabulous. I think my band is supposed to swing by, and we'll talk about where we want everyone." Kennedy's southern Georgia accent only enhanced her image. She looked at her phone and rapidly touched the screen with her thumbs, smiling, presumably sending a text. She returned to the conversation. "They should be here in like five minutes. Do you mind if I go take some pictures with the horses?"

"Not at all. I'll wait here for the band."

"Awesome. Thanks." Kennedy moved away from the pavilion to the paddocks about two hundred feet away.

Marnie continued the horse boarding business, undercutting the market in that arena as well. Her business decisions were part of her charitable desire to assist those drawn to the opportunities in Franklin but not yet able to afford the high price tags that accompanied most things. Presently, she had seven horses of various breeds boarded on her homestead.

She watched Kennedy take selfies with a black horse that came up to be nuzzled, and Marnie sighed heavily. She and Kennedy were close in age, but they were light years away from maturity. The space between Kennedy's carefree naiveté and Marnie's experiences of the summer allowed the bitterness and cynicism she felt to rear its ugly head once again. *Would she ever be free of these two seemingly constant companions?*

She watched Kennedy, youthful and vibrant, strike multiple poses and thought back to the day at Cheekwood when she found Arodi's first note. She now understood every Greek tragedy, every ounce of Shakespearian angst, every chart-topping love song that spoke of sorrow. She had lived it all in the course of but a few months, and it had altered her.

She felt as though she had aged twenty years inside, suddenly becoming a sage in the trepidations of romantic entanglements. She thought that she had steeled herself against cynicism and bitterness, but apparently not. Marnie touched the high collar of her blouse. There were times she felt herself slipping into the abyss of hopelessness, forgoing all semblances of youth to avoid attracting suitors. The wound was too fresh and raw despite the dressings she applied.

She heard Kennedy laugh as the horse nudged her. It wasn't her place to warn Kennedy of the dangers lurking one heartbeat away, one long gaze, one seemingly innocent, gentle kiss. No, Kennedy must not become like Marnie, swearing off all human connections that could lead to imbroglios. Kennedy must discover how to traverse the trails of relationships without hearing the equivalent of an ancient mariner woefully explain how a shift in the timeline acted as an albatross around her neck.

Kennedy posed again with the horse for what must have been the twentieth time, drawing a weary sigh from Marnie. She felt her phone vibrate. It was a text from Drew.

"Where r u? At main house, some band is here looking for u and some singer I've never heard of."

She text back.

"At pavilion, can u walk them over?"

*Drew responded,* "Yeah, c u in a few."

Moments later, the band reunited with Kennedy, and they all flashed their phones and started posing with the friendly mare. *Oh, to be young and innocent again,* Marnie thought. The men in the group had various lengths of hair and appeared to all use hairspray. They all wore blue jeans and t-shirts, making them look like all the other bands in Nashville.

"So, what's up?" She asked Drew.

Drew had some paperwork and eyed her reluctantly. "Could we go somewhere private? I have something to share with you."

*Private. He has another ball to drop about Arodi. I just know it. But what? The worst has already happened. Please don't let it be a wedding or birth announcement.*

"Let me go and touch base with them." Marnie approached the group by one of the paddocks. "Hi, and welcome. I just wanted to let you discuss your setup and everything. If you all need me, I'll be out in front of the main house where you parked."

They nodded heads. "Cool. Thanks." One of the guys said.

Marnie went back to Drew. "Let's walk and talk." They took a path that wound around the paddocks through the field toward the main house.

"My mom asked if you're still managing the household and estate over here."

"What did you tell her?"

"I said the present estate holder is still away, and since Yehovah owns it all, I didn't feel like it was a lie."

"I'm not ready to tell them, Drew. Just keep details to a minimum. Besides, aren't they away on a movie set with the horses for a little bit longer?"

"Yeah, another month at least."

The pair paused at the parked BMW SUV the band members had rolled up in.

"Business is booming for them and you, I can see," Drew said, "I looked this band up on the Internet. Kennedy is supposed to open for some big names this fall."

"Yeah, her career is about to soar. She has a decent voice and a good manager who's marketing her right, which elevates her to a whole new level. I think we're private enough for you to tell me what's up," she said.

They passed by the New England aster in full pink violet bloom growing next to red penstemons as they walked along the lush backyard pathway toward the front. "I was having lunch with an archaeologist friend of mine who's recently begun conducting research on the Carnton Plantation, including an inventory of all of the soldiers, family members, and friends of the family buried there."

Marnie knew in her heart where this was headed, but she kept silent.

"In the cemetery, under that willow tree, they found two headstones that were not previously recorded. The headstones were so far off the beaten path that no one really paid attention. Anyway," Drew handed her the yellowed paper, protected by a plastic sleeve. "My friend found this."

Her eyes studied it.

Arodi Bellamy, interred 1901

Nelly Bellamy, interred 1914

Every time Marnie thought that she was healing, something happened, and she realized that her heart may never be whole again. Walking away from Arodi had been the hardest decision she had ever made. After the discovery of his letters to her, she had made the conscious decision to return them back to their hidden compartment in the floor by the fireplace and said goodbye to him once more, but she always returned to the memories; memories of him holding her close, praying with him, sharing lunch with him, talking to him, kissing him. *Will my heart ever heal?* Tears threatened to fall at any moment, so Marnie took a deep breath and faced reality. "How about that? It looks like they had a good, long life, doesn't it?"

"Are you OK?"

"Yeah, for the most part. There are days that I feel like I am going to be fine, but then something happens and I realize I may never heal. Two weeks ago, I dropped the music box that he gave me and broke it; that was a really rough day."

She thought back to that day; she'd been in a hurry and accidentally knocked the music box on the dresser while grabbing the silk scarf she'd laid on the dresser. She had watched in what seemed like slow motion as the music box hit the floor, shattering into several pieces. She felt frozen in time as she recalled their first dance when Arodi had enlisted Drew to help him play The Sound of the Night at just the right moment. He looked so dashing as he materialized out of the darkness underneath the soft, golden lights with a big smile. How she adored his smile. Music transcended time and transported them to their own mystical place as they swayed to the tender tones of the waltz. Each time she had opened the music box, Marnie was carried back to that evening. As she stared down at the broken box, she thought of her shattered dreams of a life with Arodi, the children they would never have, the home they would never build, the talks they would never share, and felt the rush of futility rain down.

"Marnie, I'm sorry." Drew brought her back to the present.

They stepped up onto the brick-paved front porch, where there were various selections of newly added outdoor furniture. Drew chose the white resin wicker couch and Marnie the matching chair.

"I see that you still wear the ring he gave you." Drew nodded to the ring that was just a drop in the bucket compared to the vast wealth Arodi had bestowed on her.

"It's my reminder of him. I see people in love walking hand-in-hand, sharing a smile and a laugh, whispering sweet accolades in a language that is known to only them, and realize that is something I will never experience with him, so I look at this ring and remember the times I spent with Arodi."

"I didn't mean to make you sad; I just wanted you to know that he lived a long life."

"Thank you, Drew."

She let the thoughts come as they sat there. *Nineteen O one. Did he have a cane? Did his hair turn snowy white? What about his teeth? What became of that smile? Did Nelly see the same smile I did? Did his children ever photograph him?* She wanted to know. It felt wrong on one level to try to peer into his life because, for him, it hadn't happened yet. But in Marnie's time, it was old, forgotten news. She was also curious about Nelly. How many children did they have? What became of all of those children? What was their married life like? Did she know Arodi didn't love her? Did Arodi ever come to love her? Did he ever tell her a science fiction story about time travel and two lovers who desperately sought a way to be together but couldn't find a solution, so they returned to their respective lives?

Marnie shook her head as they sat.

"I know, it's a lot to take in," Drew said. "I miss him, too."

Shared sorrow over the loss of the same dear friend. Marnie was thankful that Drew knew him and could remain a bastion of sanity if she ever doubted that Arodi had been real. The Arodi-shaped hole in her heart had found no solace. She would always love him and was not sure she was even capable of loving another. Though she doubted that Nelly had replaced her, she envied their marriage. It would not have been a perfect love, but it had been a sound marriage. She'd told him to give his love to his children, to be kind to Nelly, and to support his children and grandchildren so that the babies, including herself, could be saved through the invention. So, didn't she want Arodi to do that? Yes, but why did it have to come at the expense of her own happiness?

## Twenty-Nine

October's cool raindrops dotted Marnie's large navy umbrella as she walked through the cemetery at Carnton. She had to see for herself. She had to know. It wasn't that she didn't believe the document Drew had shown her, but she had to go see for herself. She didn't analyze her motives—she just felt compelled to go, so she went.

It was a Sunday morning, and very few patrons were outdoors at this time. She made her way through the cemetery toward the large willow tree. Vibrant yellow, orange, and red leaves came down with the shower only to land on top of the earth, eventually browning and decaying, which is symbolic of what happens in a cemetery. *Maybe this is a mistake. Maybe it's not really him there but someone with a similar name who married a woman named Nelly.* Marnie tried to convince herself as the rain gently and rhythmically beat on her umbrella.

She walked up a slight incline on the path and looked ahead. Tucked on the east side, there were two markers. Marnie slowly approached. She felt the air escape her lungs as she stood there staring. *Arodi and Nelly Bellamy.* She kept reading and rereading their names, the years they were born, and the years they died.

Marnie walked over and squatted inches from Arodi's headstone.

She knew he wasn't there. He was gone. And yet, he could still be somewhere watching her from his timeline. She glanced around, hoping to catch a glimpse of him.

No one ventured through the cemetery; she was all alone. She turned her attention back to the headstones and looked at Nelly's.

*That should be my name. I should've been buried next to him.* She shook her head. *No, Marnie. It had to be this way. There was no other way.* She chastised herself for making it all about her and her happiness. Their lives had been long and, hopefully, wonderful together. But did she really hope they were wonderful?

She argued back and forth with herself until her thighs ached from her position. Then she stood and stretched her back, gently twisting to give her muscles some much-needed relief. What did she expect to get out of this visit? Closure? A surprise visit from Arodi? None of it came.

The falling rain matched Marnie's tears drop for drop as she reached out to the One Who could ease her pain. *I just thought that maybe if it wasn't him, there might still be a chance for us. Yehovah, my heart is so broken. I know this is but a glimpse of the pain we have caused You, but it's too much to bear. I can't move forward no matter what I try. You created my innermost being and know what I am feeling. Arodi never leaves me. He's in everything I do: my thoughts, my dreams, my desires. I don't know how to let go and move on. I just don't know how to do it.*

Marnie's tears slowly began to subside. She closed her eyes and took a deep breath, hoping that when she opened her eyes, the name on Arodi's gravestone would be changed, but it wasn't. His name was right in front of her.

With a heavy heart, she turned away from the graves.

She walked back to the car, got inside, and checked her phone.

Drew had text.

*Vietnamese for lunch? U, me, Bella? Charlotte Pike.*

Marnie nodded to herself. She needed to try to put to death the feelings for the dead and celebrate the life she had with her family and friends.

She text back. *Yes, c u there. Be there in 30 min.*

She started the car and left the cemetery.

* * * * *

Marnie, Drew, and Bella chose an open, red-upholstered booth that would seat four in the small Vietnamese restaurant. Bella and Drew sat on one side, Marnie on the other.

A young woman brought them menus.

"What would you like to drink?" She asked.

The trio ordered water with lemons and looked over the menu.

Marnie watched as Bella fiddled with her necklace as her eyes perused the menu. Marnie smiled to herself. Drew must've purchased Bella the same necklace he had once given Marnie. That was so Drew. He was the guy who bought the same shirt in every color at the store or brown and black shoes in the same style. She almost mentioned it but didn't want to embarrass Drew, so she kept it to herself.

"I'm glad you could come for lunch," Bella said. Bella flashed a look at Drew.

"I told Bella things didn't work out with your long-distance relationship."

"Thanks, it's not been easy," Marnie said as images of Arodi crossed her mind.

*Why would I ever think that I could go a few hours without thinking about him? And Drew should not have told Bella about my personal saga; it's really none of her business.*

"I know it's none of my concern, but I've been through some painful long-distance things myself, so if you ever wanted to talk, I'm here," Bella smiled.

Marnie sensed such genuineness she couldn't hold a grudge against Drew for sharing such personal information. Besides, he had lost a friend, too.

As they ordered, Marnie decided that she would try to make the best of the lunch.

Her phone vibrated for the seventh time while they were eating, and she finally looked at it.

"Sorry, guys, I've got to take a call about an event for Thanksgiving," she fished out a fifty-dollar bill. "It's on me. I have to scoot and make a few calls. Thank you both for a fun lunch, and we need to do this again real soon."

"Sure, and thanks!" Bella said.

Marnie smiled and exited.

She spent the afternoon working up an estimate for the use of her home over the Thanksgiving holiday and the cost of hosting an intimate concert one of the evenings. Once negotiations were settled, she relaxed on the front porch, sipping some warm apple cider out of a mug.

Drew pulled up and walked to the porch. "Is there more of that?" He nodded toward her mug.

"Help yourself."

He returned with a matching blue ceramic mug and leaned against the rails, facing Marnie.

"Nice touch with the jewelry," Marnie said with a smile.

"What are you talking about?"

"Bella's necklace."

Drew furrowed his brow. "I didn't give her a necklace. We aren't even going out. We are just friends. I mean, I like her and would like to be more, but she keeps me pretty much in the friend zone, so why would I give her jewelry?" Drew seemed to be lost in thought. "Unless you think that would show her how much game I have?"

"By using that phraseology, you just demonstrated how much game you don't have," Marnie laughed. "I wonder where she got it. It was exactly like the one that you gave me when we were kids." Marnie sipped her cider. "I gave it away."

"That was a gift for you."

"No, Drew, listen. I gave it to Sarah, Arodi's sister after she nearly died. I thought it was a good idea because you had given it to me after I had a close call."

"Marnie, I told you not to play around with the timeline like that. Do you even know what you could've done?"

"Drew, do you think Sarah passed it down to her children, and somehow it wound up in Bella's possession? I mean, she seems to know an awful lot about the Bellamy family, so maybe she's a distant relative, and her necklace is simply a family heirloom. Besides, turquoise existed in 1849, so it's probably not even the same necklace. I just found it interesting that she had it."

Drew was suddenly silent, lost in thought.

His silence alarmed Marnie.

"Drew?"

He didn't respond.

"Drew!"

He looked at Marnie.

"What if it's not an heirloom?"

"What?"

"Get in the car, c'mon!"

Marnie scrambled after Drew and jumped into the passenger seat of his SUV. They raced away, relocating some loose gravel in Marnie's driveway as he pressed the gas pedal.

"What is going on? You're not making any sense," Marnie said.

"Just let me think."

Marnie was silent as they drove along the road at a fairly fast speed, heading north toward Nashville.

* * * * *

Drew knocked on a front door.

Marnie stood to the side.

"Bella, it's Drew and Marnie. Can we talk?"

The door opened with Bella behind it. "Is everything OK? Come on in."

They entered a small but lovely apartment filled with antique furniture. It was like walking into a tastefully decorated museum that conveyed a sense of warmth and hominess.

"Please have a seat." Bella led them to her sitting area, which included a stunning leather slope-backed sofa, matching chair, and glass coffee table with intricately carved wooden legs connected by a turned leg.

Marnie thought she had amazing taste.

"I'm not sure where to begin, and I'm not sure it will even make sense," Drew said.

"What is it?" Bella asked.

"May I ask where you got that necklace?" He asked, pointing to the turquoise gem hanging around her neck.

She touched it. "It was a gift." She seemed a little uncomfortable.

"From who?"

"A friend."

"Who?" Drew pressed.

"I never met her."

"Oh my goodness," Marnie gasped. She finally caught Drew's train of thought. "Sarah?"

Panic flashed in Bella's eyes as she looked at Marnie.

Marnie looked closer at Bella and knew she had seen those same eyes and that same smile before; they were Arodi's. Marnie's heart nearly burst with excitement and anticipation.

She covered Bella's hands with her own. "It's OK. Your brother, Arodi, gave you the necklace after you got very sick, didn't he?"

Tears fell from Bella's eyes. "How do you know the story? I never told anyone about my family when I came."

Marnie wrapped her arms around her.

"When you came?" Drew asked before Marnie could answer.

Bella wiped under her eyes and sniffed. "My given name is Sarah Isabel Bellamy, Bella now, and I arrived eight years ago when I was sixteen. I was looking for Arodi. I figured I could find where he was in history, which was why I wanted to work in the archives."

Drew stood there shocked, trying to process what he had just heard. Sarah had crossed through the bridge of time and stayed.

Marnie was the first to respond, reaching to pull Sarah into a tight hug. "I'm so sorry I didn't see the resemblance sooner."

Sarah eventually pulled back. "You were the one who saved me. Thank you."

Marnie looked at Drew, knowing exactly when the implications dawned on him. He was the one who had gotten angry at Marnie for giving Arodi the antibiotics that saved Sarah. She could only imagine what he must be feeling now.

Marnie gently ran her hands over Sarah's hair and face in a motherly fashion.

"Since I have worked in the archives, no one has ever asked about the Bellamys, so when Drew began to ask questions about my family, I thought that maybe this was finally it; maybe Arodi had come through this year, and I would finally find him. When I met you, Marnie, at the Swan Ball, I was pretty sure that you had at least crossed paths with Arodi. You were wearing a gown from the 1840s that Fallon had stitched; no one does stitch work like her. I realized that he wasn't there since I never saw him with you.

"Oh, Sarah, he didn't pass through time like you. He was always in 1849, but I was the only one who could see him."

"Was he at the Swan Ball?"

"Yes."

Tears reformed in her eyes. "I was so close. I just wanted to see him and talk to him." She inhaled and closed her eyes. "You see, everyone but me thought he was dead."

Marnie was confused. "Dead? What do you mean, sweetheart? He married Nelly Taylor, don't you remember? They had six children together and they are buried at Carnton. I've seen the headstones."

"No," Sarah shook her head. "That's not Arodi."

Marnie exchanged bewildered looks with Drew.

"After Arodi disappeared, Ari took over the family business and used Arodi's name since he was already established."

The blow to Marnie's heart sent shockwaves through her being. She felt physically ill. The ramifications of Sarah's words avalanched in wide-scale disaster.

"That detail wasn't recorded in history, though," Sarah offered.

"Ari married Nelly?" Marnie incredulously asked with a whisper.

"Yes, they finally realized that they liked one another."

Marnie felt the room spinning. *Ari and Nelly's grandson invented the incubator. It never was Arodi's grandson.*

Finally, Drew found his voice and reached out to hold Sarah's hand. "What happened to Arodi?"

"He went to California in the summer of 1849 on a gold expedition. On the night he returned, there was a terrible carriage house fire, and my family told me that he died trying to save his horse, but I didn't believe it. I always believed the angel that had saved me had saved him." Sarah touched her necklace and bowed her head, "but since he isn't here, so he must've died in the fire."

Marnie couldn't keep up with the thoughts racing through her head. "Sarah, when did he come back?"

"I don't know. I think that it was in the fall, but I was so young, I just don't remember. I could never pinpoint the date even after I did lots of research when I arrived here ."

"Drew?"

Drew was busily typing and scrolling on his phone. "I'm working on it."

"Can you think of any other details about that night?"

Sarah closed her eyes, absently twirling her fingers around the necklace. "It was before Thanksgiving."

Drew typed and scrolled, typed and scrolled. "OK, I think I've got something. Here's an old journal entry published by the granddaughter of the stable boy. It was just published. She references the full moon, which was October." Drew looked up at Marnie and then Sarah. "Oh no."

"What?"

"Tonight there's a full moon just like it was in October 1849 when the carriage house caught fire. Tonight's the same night here and back then!" He yelled.

Marnie did not hesitate. She jumped up. "We can save him."

"How?" Drew asked.

"We're going to Cheekwood, and we'll find him before he goes to the carriage house. Drew, can you open the portal through your phone?"

"I don't know. But I can try."

"Great, I'll drive. Let's go save Arodi."

*Thirty*

During the summer and fall, family nights at Cheekwood often draw a crowd, and Sunday night was no exception. A blown-glass exhibit had been showing all season, and the colors and designs attracted hundreds of patrons that evening.

Marnie parked outside of the Cheekwood gates to avoid the trickling stream of traffic, and the three of them quickly exited the car.

"Sarah, you go with Drew." Marnie noticed the sorrowful look on Sarah's face. "I'm the only one able to see Arodi, and we need Drew to open the portal so you can see him."

Sarah looked like a little girl, touching her necklace, obviously afraid of what might happen to her brother.

"Hey, we're not going to be late, OK? It's going to be alright. I promise." Marnie turned to Drew. "Try the perimeter, the woods, and the trails. He could be on his way right now. I'll start at the carriage house, then go to the balcony to get a bird's eye view. I'll stay pretty close by there, so I don't miss him."

"How long do we have before closing?"

"Until ten, but I'm sure they'll let us stay as long as we need." Marnie tucked her phone in her pocket. "Let's stay in touch every fifteen minutes."

"Got it." Drew nodded and gave Marnie a quick hug. "It'll work."

"It has to, Drew; it just has to work."

Drew and Sarah quickly took to the exterior path, snaking through the traffic, while Marnie flashed her membership card at the people directing traffic and beelined toward the carriage house. She dodged and bobbed, weaved, and twisted through the sea of people who were clamoring to see the blown glass in the lights at night.

She scanned the crowds of people as she moved but saw no sign of Arodi. She arrived at the carriage house, where a speaker was explaining to a small crowd how to use the antique tools typically stored there. She walked from the front to the back, calling for Arodi, softly at first but increasing her volume the further she stepped from the group.

Nothing.

She dashed to the top of the balcony, straining her eyes at the ground

166

below for a glimpse, a sign, something to let her know Arodi was there. Children were racing on the grassy areas with glowing sticks and flashlights, but she did not see him.

*Could he be in the mansion?* She moved back inside through several groups of people. As she searched for him, each room in Cheekwood held a memory of him.

*Yehovah, please tell me we've come down to the 11th hour for this reason. Tell me that You are going to spare him because You spared him. Somehow, You already did it. He's alive. He will stay alive.*

Drew text. *Nothing here. U?*

Marnie sighed.

She text back: *No. Inside mansion. Will keep searching. U do the same.*

Upstairs, downstairs, outside the mansion, around the gardens, Arodi wasn't to be found. She retraced her steps and called out his name, not caring who gave her funny looks.

"Miss, are you looking for your son?" A Cheekwood staff member asked. "We can help."

"No, but thank you," Marnie said and kept moving.

Her eyes caught sight of a man from behind with hair the same length and color as Arodi's. He was twenty feet ahead of her on the path heading toward the pond. She tried to push her way through the people to get to him. "Arodi!"

A small child ran right into her and fell down, instantly bursting into tears. Marnie watched the man keep walking, but she stopped to help the little boy. Another man raced up and knelt beside the boy.

"Daddy!" The little boy raised his arms to the man.

"I'm sorry, miss."

"No, I'm fine. Is he alright?"

"Yeah, he will be just fine." A woman pushing a stroller arrived on the scene and took the crying boy into her arms.

Marnie moved quickly toward the pond where she thought the man had gone. He turned toward her, and she smiled, ready to meet his eyes. As he did, she stopped.

It was not Arodi; it was just a man who looked like him. Abysmal didn't fully encompass what her heart felt. Sinking, sinking, darker, darker, the embers of hope quickly fading, being replaced by dissipating smoke.

Her phone rang. It was Drew.

Marnie prayed he had found Arodi before she answered.

"Is he with you?" asking as she blinked back the tears.

"No," Drew solemnly said.

*Yehovah, guide me and my steps. Guide me to find Arodi in time.* Marnie tried to think about what they should do next. "Maybe you and Sarah should go to the entrance of Belle Meade. He may come in that way."

"OK, we'll go. Stay strong and don't give up. We're going to find him, OK?"

"Yeah. I'm going to go back to the carriage house."

Marnie rested on a stone wall just outside the carriage house, listening to the speaker with a new group of people. She wanted to be in the perfect place to catch Arodi when he arrived before he entered the barn. *Would he see her waiting? Would he even be looking for her, especially since she had told him she would never come back to Cheekwood again? What if he didn't want to see her? What if he had forgotten her? No, Marnie, you know Arodi, and he has not forgotten you.*

Marnie realized that the speaker was talking about the fire at the carriage house.

"I've done a lot of research about the fire that destroyed most of the original carriage house, and it would've taken about twenty minutes for anyone to notice a fire of that size. Even the fastest person coming from the lake house, where they were all staying, would have only been able to run it in about ten minutes. We know they were not in the main house. The entry recorded in Mr. Bellamy's journal said he was here at nine-thirty that night, so we can surmise that the fire probably started close to nine."

*Close to nine?* Marnie's heart sank even further if that were possible. It was almost 9:45 pm. Was the carriage house already burning down in 1849?

She called Drew.

"Yeah! What's up?"

"There's a speaker here at the carriage house, and he said the barn fire started at nine Drew, I think we're too late." Her voice trembled as the words lanced her heart.

"No, Marnie. Do not give up. He could be wrong about the time. Arodi is on his way. We'll head back your way. It's crazy crowded right now, but we'll keep looking as we head back that way to you."

"OK." Marnie couldn't help it. The tears flowed as she sat and watched the crowd of tourists slowly begin to dwindle as they proceeded to their cars, and red taillights dotted the road. Shock held a firm grip on her as she sat immobilized. She felt as though her heart had stopped beating while her mind spun out of control. She felt helpless as hopelessness began to take over her thoughts.

"Hey, Marnie." Marnie recognized the familiar face of Augustine, one of the employees, as he walked up.

Marnie snapped out of it. "Hello, Augustine."

"Are you alright? They told me to make my rounds and encourage folks to start heading out, but I'm here until ten thirty, so you can stay for a bit longer if you want. "

Marnie couldn't hide the tears. "I lost someone very close to me, and this was a special place for us. I'd like a little more time to say goodbye if it's not too much trouble."

"I'm sorry for your loss. You stay as long as you like, and I'll make sure you get to your car safely in a bit." Augustine moved on.

Marnie dried under her eyes. Forlorn and defeated, she stared into the darkness of the forest that hugged the mansion. *Would the darkness fully consume her now? Would it sweep her away in a wave, a violent torrent of lost hope, lost love, lost chances of a life she'd been hesitant to embrace?* She could almost see the future Marnie emerging from the thicket of black. Sunken face, removed of all positive emotion, hair long and stripped of its color. *Oh, Arodi, if I could only turn back time and make a different decision, that would be the right decision!*

She tortured herself with these thoughts until that cruel-sounding ringtone played. Someone's cell phone ringer was Chopin's *The Sound of the Night*.

Marnie signed heavily and wondered who would have that song as their ringtone. As she stood and turned to head toward where Drew would be coming in, she was greeted by a music box being held by a smiling Arodi.

She swayed, nearly fainting.

She took the music box from his hands and placed it on the stone wall. "Is it you?" she ran her hands along his arms, up his chest to his shoulders, through his hair, and finally cupped his face.

"Of course, it's me," Arodi said as he took hold of her hands, cradling his face.

Marnie, so overcome with emotion, couldn't say anything and let her tears speak for her. He was here, really here, standing right before her.

"I can't believe you're here." His smile took up the entire bottom half of his face. "You told me you weren't ever coming here again, and when I came back tonight and saw you sitting here, I was not sure if I should approach you or not. I've been down by the pond praying about you tonight, and while there is so much to tell you, I have to believe our meeting tonight is by design." He tenderly kissed each of her hands, "Marnie, I betrayed my word to you and went to California. I have just arrived back and decided to take a walk along the pond with my horse, Clemson." Arodi nodded toward his horse. "I don't know if you can forgive me..."

Marnie's heart was so overcome with joy that she leaned in and kissed him, letting her lips against his say all of the things she couldn't find the words to say right now. She felt two arms enfold her, and one hand began to stroke the back of her neck while the other brushed her shoulder blade. She had never tasted anything sweeter than the two precious lips passionately kissing her back. Their long-awaited reunion teetered on the boundaries of not being entirely family-friendly, but Marnie couldn't think and didn't care. She was holding onto all that she held dear.

She slowly pulled back, looking at him, and couldn't believe it; Arodi was really here. They assumed he went to the carriage house, but he had taken a walk to pray. He didn't go to the carriage house at nine because he saw her and wasn't sure if he should approach her or not. *Yehovah, Your plan is always perfect; never early and never late, but always on time, in Your time.*

"Arodi, it's me. I'm the one that needs forgiveness. You were right all the whole time. I was wrong. I was the one keeping us apart, not time, not the past, or the future. It's been me that has kept us apart."

"I am not sure that I fully understand," his eyes twinkled, "so does this mean we can be together now?"

"There's so much to tell you, but we will find a way to make it work." She did not care if anyone from her timeline believed in his existence. She was going to make a life with him no matter what.

"That makes me so happy, Marnie. I have to confess that I delayed in approaching you because after Clemson and I returned from our walk, the only familiar sight I saw was you. I was afraid I was a bit lost."

Marnie looked at him quizzically. "Lost?"

"Hey, Marnie, my boss says we need to try to leave a bit earlier." Augustine returned, interrupting their conversation.

"Sure, Augustine, I'll be just a minute longer." Marnie nodded, not taking her eyes off Arodi.

"You, too, sir. I believe the exhibition finished hours ago, so I don't know how you're going to get that horse home."

Marnie looked at Augustine. "Wait. Augustine, can you see him?"

"It's not that dark out. Yeah, I can see you both."

"And his horse?"

"Yeah, the horse, too. They had the demonstrations earlier tonight, so I'll need you both to move on in the next few minutes."

"OK, we will. Thank you." Marnie said.

Augustine walked back towards the main gates.

"Arodi, what do you see? Is there a fire in the carriage house?"

"No, it doesn't even look like the same carriage house. What is going on?"

Marnie mulled it over until there was only one possible conclusion. "Arodi, you're here! You actually crossed over into my time. Augustine can see you, and you could see him, right?"

"Yes..." Arodi hesitantly looked around. "Clemson passed through, too, then, as well as everything I brought with me from California."

"Did you strike it rich?" Marnie offered as a joke as she nudged him gently with her elbow. Arodi had no idea how much wealth his investments had produced for her.

"I already did the day I first saw you." Arodi smiled as he settled his lips firmly against hers in a kiss that spoke of the truth in what he said.

Marnie shared the sentiment. The overwhelming emotions of gratitude and disbelief were enough to make her breathless. "Oh, Arodi. There's so much more. Come on." Marnie exclaimed excitedly as she pulled him by the hand toward the entrance while Arodi held tightly to Clemson.

Marnie saw Drew and Sarah approaching. "Look," she pointed their way.

Arodi stopped, and the reins fell from his hand. He moved in disbelief toward Drew and Sarah, stopping in front of her.

"Do you know who I am?" She could barely get the words out.

He looked her up and down. "Sarah? But how?" He embraced his sister. They sobbed together, sharing a moment in modern times since they last saw one another in 1849.

* * * * *

The four of them had gone back to Marnie's flooded with emotions, words, stories, and utter disbelief. Arodi saw to it that Clemson was stabled for the night in the barn and then joined the others in the living room. The conversation flowed freely until Sarah's eyes were barely open, so Arodi followed her upstairs to say goodnight. Now, he sat beside Sarah on the bed in the guest room at Marnie's house. Sarah had slipped under the cotton sheets and wanted to share with him about what had happened after he left before she went to sleep. Everything about this night was surreal to him.

She explained, "Arodi, I was the only one who never believed that you had died in the fire. Yes, I grieved, but only because I didn't know where you were. Everyone thought I was trying to bury my grief in my books, but that wasn't fully true; I was reading all the time because I missed you, and it got into my head that if I just read enough or studied enough, I'd discover what happened to you. While I was reading through our library collections, I came across some dusty books on one of the back shelves and was intrigued. I found books that I had not read, such as *Rip Van Winkle, The Galoshes of Fortune,* and even some Edgar Allen Poe. These writings fascinated me, so I buried myself in their time travel plots, becoming obsessed with the idea that is what happened to you. Mother continued to become more worried about me, so in 1859, she sent me to stay with Ari and Nelly for the summer in Franklin, hoping that would help me realize you had died in that fire."

Arodi, reeled from the fact that he was not in his time, but sitting next to his baby sister in this time. He needed help getting the confusion settled and dissipated. "Sarah, I am happy that you never gave up on me, but I still do not understand how you came to live in this time."

"I'm getting to that part," Sarah said, giving him a quick pat on the leg. " One evening that summer, I was walking near the pond and saw some strange lights, like dancing flames, in the sky. I kept walking as I stared at the sky, mesmerized by the lights. They seemed to move and glow in a synchronous pattern. I don't know how much time passed, but I finally realized that I was walking on a path made of concrete, not dirt. As I looked around, I didn't recognize anything; all I saw were rows of houses filled with lights and boxes with wheels and lights moving along the road. My initial moment of initial panic was quickly replaced with curiosity. As I wandered around in awe, I realized that I was no longer in 1859."

Dawning and understanding were evident on Arodi's face as he fully grasped what Sarah was saying. He pulled her close for a quick hug. "I'm sorry that you were alone to experience this. You must have been so scared."

"Arodi, don't you see? It was all by His design. As I wandered around, I found myself outside of a coffee shop where I met this woman. We started talking, and she offered to buy me breakfast and a cup of coffee. As we ate, I asked her about lodging, and she offered me a job at the bed and breakfast she had just purchased in exchange for boarding. I agreed and went to work for her. As time passed, she realized I was very knowledgeable about the mid-1800s, so I helped her furnish the home with authentic furniture and conversation pieces. Soon, I began hosting tours of the home, explaining the history behind each piece. It was a time of growth and tremendous learning for me." Sarah paused. "You'll soon understand." She winked.

Arodi shared her smile.

"A little while later, she helped me enroll in the university where I majored in history, then continued my studies to the masters level, focusing on the mid-1800s time period. I viewed this as an opportunity to find out what had happened. I wasn't sure if you had died at some point in time or had been able to travel to a new time like I had done, but I was not giving up until I found out. Since I have been here, there have been moments of monumental loneliness, sadness, frustration, excitement, happiness, and contentment. I continually look for the hand of Yehovah in every encounter and every discovery."

"I just cannot believe you are here. I'm so thankful." Arodi ran a hand over her head, flashbacking to the last time he had seen her near death in a bed in 1849 before Marnie had saved her. Gone were her blonde curls replaced by straight blonde hair, or was that something women altered in modern times?

"I knew my angel would save you," Sarah said with a smile.

"She couldn't have done it without you." Arodi reminded her. He heard Sarah softly sigh as she relaxed against the pillows. "I'm proud of all you've accomplished, and I do not think it's speaking out of turn to say that this shall be your home from now on. You are my responsibility now in the absence of our parents."

"Arodi," Sarah laughed, "I'm almost the same age as you. We're not twenty years apart anymore, and while I appreciate the sentiment, there's a lot about this time period that I've grown accustomed to, with independence being just one thing. Now that I know you're here and you're safe, I am free to live my own life. There's still so much I want to do."

"I understand, but since I am here now, you must let me do my best to keep you safe in your endeavors."

"I think Drew would be more than happy to do that for me." Sarah's face blushed, with a slight smile showing.

Arodi laughed and gave her a quick tickle. "You should get some rest, Sarah. It's very late, and we can pick back up tomorrow. You can tell me more stories of the others."

Sarah yawned. "All right. Tomorrow then." She slid down and rested on the pillow.

Arodi stood and walked to the doorway, turning to gaze back at her once more. He was overwhelmed with many revelations and realizations, not to mention the whole time travel aspect. His littlest sister was here with him in what had been the future but what was now the present. *It is unbelievable, and I don't fully understand it all, but I will trust You, Yehovah. You have performed miracles since the beginning of time, so I trust this is a series of miracles from You. Yehovah, thank You for sending Sarah to this time and for finding a way for me to be with Marnie.*

Arodi knew that Drew would be working on the science portion of everything, and he looked forward to discussing the theories that Drew would espouse in the weeks to come. Arodi quietly closed the door and walked along the hall to the top of the staircase, not believing the grandeur of all his eyes beheld.

* * * * *

Marnie, still sitting on the couch waiting for Arodi to come back downstairs, jerked her head backward.

"Did you fall asleep for a second there?" Drew asked, his eyes not leaving the computer screen from where he sat with her in the living room.

"What time is it?" Marnie asked from the couch.

"Close to three."

"I was just waiting on Arodi."

Drew looked at her. "It's pretty wild, isn't it? All along, Bella was Sarah looking for Arodi, and we were concealing what we knew about him because we didn't want anyone to think we were crazy." Drew gave a hearty laugh and kept typing. "OK, I think I've got it." He stood, brought his computer over, and sat down next to Marnie. "So, Bella, er, Sarah, came through in the late summer of 1859 when she was sixteen. Look," he showed Marnie an article.

She adjusted her tired eyes to skim through it. "A solar storm?"

"Yeah, it knocked out the telegraph lines over the span of a couple of days, and the whole globe was talking about it. Lights in the sky, like a celestial fire up there."

"So what does that mean, Drew?"

"So what if there's more than one way to disturb the timeline? What if Sarah came through a portal that had nothing to do with frequencies?"

Marnie yawned. "It seems like a very heady conversation for this time of night."

Drew stretched his arms and gave a yawn. "Fair enough. I think I've had enough for the night, well morning. I'll head to my room, but it's pretty cool, yeah?" He stood.

"Yes, Drew and I will happily listen to all of your theories as they come. Marnie said.

Arodi entered the living room. "Sarah's asleep."

"Exactly where I'm headed, old man." Drew patted Arodi's arm as he walked by. "I'm really glad you're here."

"Likewise."

Marnie heard Drew climb the stairs.

"I don't want to keep you awake, " Arodi said as he approached the couch where Marnie sat, "but I should like to stay and sit with you for a while." He flashed her that smile she so loved, and he knew she would do anything he wanted.

*Thank you, Yehovah, for Arodi and for making a way for me to be with him.* "You may sit next to me." She patted the seat next to her and smiled as he sat.

He pulled her close to him. He looked around the room as he rubbed her upper arm. "I still cannot believe the fruit this place has yielded. The large windows, the fireplace, it's beautiful."

Marnie had furnished as much of the house as possible with antiques featuring Western European countries for each room. The formal living room, where they now sat snuggled together on the couch, held only pieces from Germany. Baroque chairs, the Biedermeier sofa they sat upon, candelabras, and artwork, all designed to portray the feel of a foreign country.

"Wait until you see the grounds. It's even more amazing." Marnie shifted and sat upright, facing Arodi. "Why'd you do this after I told you our relationship was finished?"

Arodi sighed as he thought of the best way to answer her question. "After you left that day, I tried to convince myself that I could spend the rest of my life without you in order to save you. After much prayer, I knew that I could not marry another, not when I had pledged my heart to yours. You were so adamant that I had to marry Nelly and were so willing to sacrifice your love for me that I knew I needed to do something for you. Marnie, I was so conflicted. I feared you would close your heart to another suitor, but at the same time, I flattered myself that I knew you loved me and that there would be no other man for you. The more time I spent in prayer, the more I couldn't shake the feeling that I was supposed to be the one who cared to care for your well-being to the best of my abilities. I knew it was wrong for me to not want happiness for you when you wanted it for me at the very expense of your own."

Arodi moved closer toward her and held her hands, lovingly kissing each one. "But, Marnie, my love, I could no sooner stop the ache in my heart than I could stop the sun. I thought time away in California on a wanderlust journey would cure that ache, but it did not. You were there, always there; your shape in every cloud as I rode out West, and your image emerging from the campfire flames at night. I'll show you in my sketchbook where I drew your face many times. Yehovah would not let me forget you, and my love for you grew more each day. When I reached California, I wrote Ari to have everything set up to provide for you, and he did that for me. Even though he never saw you, he trusted me and believed me enough to set everything up for you." Arodi shook his head. "And to think, he married Nelly Taylor. I knew he liked her more than he cared to admit." Arodi gave a heartfelt laugh. "I must say I am most relieved at that. I had never been able to resign myself to marry her. Good ol' Ari. You know, you have him to thank for all of this. He is the one who followed all of my wishes."

"We."

"We?"

"Arodi, this is ours. I don't want all of this without you. If you told me tomorrow that we were going to give it all away to go live in that tiny cabin you had tucked in the woods, I'd do it without a second thought. Arodi, don't you understand? None of this means anything to me without you. I tried to stop loving you, but I couldn't. My love for you transcended time, and I could never stop my heart from wanting only you."

"What about now?"

"I'll never let you go." Marnie, if it were possible, scooted in even closer. She softly ran her fingers along the side of his face, still astonished that he was here with her.

Arodi's eyes held a depth of love she had not seen in a long time, and she basked in his gaze. She knew that truth; she would never let him go.

His eyes left hers and roamed longingly to her lips for a brief moment before leaning down to possess them, testifying to the love he felt for her.

It seemed as if time stood still, and for that brief moment, nothing existed, but them, their lips moving together in an unspoken language only two lovers would understand while their hearts were beating as one.

Arodi reluctantly put some space between them and smiled at her. "These modern courtship customs will take some getting used to." He opened his arm, inviting Marnie to snuggle against him once again.

"Well," Marnie teased, "unless you want my reputation tarnished tomorrow, you're going to have to do something about it."

"It has been a long engagement, hasn't it? Over a hundred years for me. I suppose I need to stop procrastinating and get on with it. What do you think?"

"I'd say it's definitely about time." She rested her head on his chest while his fingers ran over her head. She let her eyes close, breathing in the last traces of the scent of 1849 on Arodi's clothes. She felt Arodi's lips leaving a trail of kisses along her head, more gentle strokes along her arms, and a peace wash over her.

The formerly known restrictions of time held no place for Arodi and Marnie. They both realized that whatever supernatural catalyst had happened that brought about the occasion for them to meet was far greater than coincidence.

In trying to understand and deconstruct the purpose behind this seemingly scientific impossibility, human logic had operated on missing information, nearly costing them their lives together.

Yehovah doesn't change. He is the same yesterday, today, and forever. He invented and exists outside of time. Marnie and Arodi proved that nothing was impossible for Him. It is so sweet to trust in Yeshua and how these two proved Him o'er and o'er during the course of their encounters and experiences. The measureless riches of His grace flourished as they asked for and submitted to His will for their lives so that they received His bountiful blessings and the joys He desired for them, which could be fulfilled in their time.

## *About the Author*

Born and raised in the Midwest, Brandi Hudson completed her undergraduate and graduate studies in Tennessee and Virginia before being admitted to the Tennessee State Bar. She teaches law at the collegiate level, maintains an active law practice, and currently resides on a hobby farm in the Nashville, Tennessee, area. In her leisure time, when she's not milking goats or collecting eggs, you'll find her reading, studying Scripture, thrifting, or planning to travel to the next destination, always welcoming the seeds those journeys plant for the next story.

www.ingramcontent.com/pod-product-compliance
Lightning Source LLC
Chambersburg PA
CBHW040823010826

48978CB00012BB/597